Jacqueline Dundas
2842 Parkhill Drive
Billings, Montana 59102
406-656-0316

≋ the multicultiboho sideshow ≋

Other Books by Alexs D. Pate

Losing Absalom
Finding Makeba
Amistad: The Novel

To Jacqueline

the multicultiboho sideshow

ALEXS D. PATE

To the struggle!
+ the laughter
Al Pate
4-13-00

BARD

AN AVON BOOK

This is a work of fiction. Names, characters, places and incidents
either are the product of the author's imagination or are used fictitiously.
Any resemblance to actual events, locales, organizations, or persons,
living or dead, is entirely coincidental and beyond the intent of either
the author or the publisher.

An excerpt of this book appeared in *City Pages* in 1998.

avon books, inc.
1350 Avenue of the Americas
New York, New York 10019

Copyright © 1999 by Alexs D. Pate
Interior design by Kellan Peck
ISBN: 0-380-97678-1

Library of Congress Cataloging in Publication Data:
Pate, Alexs D., 1950–
The multicultiboho sideshow / Alexs D. Pate. —1st ed.
p.   cm.
"An Avon book."
1. Afro-Americans—Minnesota—Minneapolis Fiction. I. Title.
PS3566.A777M85   1999   99-29476
813'.54—dc21   CIP

First Bard Printing: October 1999

BARD TRADEMARK REG. U.S. PAT. OFF. AND IN OTHER COUNTRIES, MARCA REGISTRADA,
HECHO EN U.S.A.

Printed in the U.S.A.

FIRST EDITION

QPM   10   9   8   7   6   5   4   3   2   1

www.avonbooks.com/bard

For the new days and you: Gyanni, Alexs, and Chekesha

acknowledgments

It's amazing how many people it takes to tell a story. People who were there at just the right moment with an idea or support. And this book, in particular, was helped by so many. I'm especially grateful to my friend, Ralph Remington, for all his support and encouragement. And thanks also to: J. Otis Powell!, David Mura, Duchess Harris, Rohan Preston, Mary Rockcastle, John Wright, Eungie Joo, Charlotte Abbott, Wanda Pate, Elizabeth Mckay, Jon Helfgot, Katie Leo, Cristina de la Cruz, Kimlar Satterthwaite, Napoleon Andrews, Omari Shakir, Bernardine Watson, Sarah Schultz, Carole Meshbesher, Serena Wright, Archie Givens, Marcela Lorca, Scott Malcolmson, the original Multiculti crew, and the Walker Art Center.

To one and all: No harm no foul.

It was my good fortune that Hamilton Cain became my editor. His deft hand was matched by a perfect understanding of what this story was about. And thanks also to Lou Aronica who has made a space for my voice.

To my agent, Faith Childs, I can only say what I've said so many times before: thanks. In a world where relationships are tenuous and temporary, we keep keepin on.

Finally, I owe so much to the fierce power that flows from Me-K. Ahn. You make this journey worthwhile.

I can pray all day and God won't come
but if I dial 911 the devil will be here in a minute.

—AMIRI BARAKA

It all depends
It all depends
It all depends
On the skin you live in

—SEKOU SUNDIATA

If I hadn't learned how to live without a culture and a society, acculturation would have broken my heart a thousand times.

—Kilgore Trout (An American Family Marooned on Planet Pluto)
   as written by KURT VONNEGUT, JR. in Timequake

I had not intended to write about absurdity because the book was about me and I had not known at the time that I was absurd.

CHESTER HIMES, My Life of Absurdity

≋ the multicultiboho sideshow ≋

although distressed, Ichabod Word answered his front doorbell with the sweetest smile. He hadn't had time to shower or to change his clothes in more than twenty-four hours. He wore a stained black sweat shirt and a pair of black jeans that were so stretched and beaten from multiple washings that they were in danger of losing their blackness. His apartment reflected his own internal disarray. There were stacks of brightly colored plastic plates and cups scattered about the living room. There was overturned and broken furniture. There was a dead body which Ichabod had carefully wrapped in two plastic garbage bags, tied firmly, and pushed into a corner of the dining room. The place was an absolute mess.

For the past two hours, before the doorbell interrupted, he had been sitting quietly, contemplating his situation. To be perfectly accurate, at about an hour and forty-five minutes prior to the ringing of the doorbell, he'd decided to call the police. It had obviously taken them fifteen minutes to arrive. And in that time Ichabod had slipped back into deep thought.

He'd planned it very carefully. By the time he appeared at the front door, he was completely prepared, steely, and fundamentally disconnected from his body. Not really the Ichabod Word that was the youngest child of the West Philadelphia Words. But a man who was simply using that name. He knew all about Ichabod. He had lived that life consciously. He just didn't feel like himself anymore. He felt new, expectant. Or . . .

Maybe he'd been gone too long.

Maybe he was too long gone from the hood. Too far away. Both intellectually and emotionally to still be that skinny little kid that everybody called Icky.

But now, as he stood opposite a chunky white man dressed in a tired charcoal gray JCPenney suit, he hoped his plan would work. The man held a badge and identification card up to Ichabod's face.

Ichabod nodded and pressed the lever that unlatched the storm door and opened it about a foot. The man leaned back a little to let the door pass and then stuck his thick head into the open space.

"Did you call the police?" he asked.

"Yes." Ichabod stepped back but held the door open with his outstretched arm.

"I'm Lt. Bill Bloom, Minneapolis Police Department." The detective grabbed the edge of the door with his pudgy calloused fingers. Ichabod noticed that his fingernails were chewed to frayed edges.

Ichabod opened the door wider and stood aside. He felt the cop's eyes focused on his. But Ichabod refused to look in his direction. Instead, he withdrew farther into the house. He tried his best to disconnect his actions from his intentions. He smiled as strongly as he could.

"You called about the Ron Abbott case?" The lieutenant breathed his words heavy, a slight hint of moisture sparkled in the space just below his ear. Ichabod struggled to keep his smile but he knew he couldn't remain silent much longer. He felt his intentions begin their embrace of the moment. He reached behind him to the small table that stood just inside the doorway, and grabbed his gun. With no hesitation he brought it around and planted it quickly in the policeman's temple. Lieutenant Bloom realized just a little too late that he'd been duped. He instantly reached for his gun, but felt Ichabod's hand yanking it from his waistband before he could get there to stop it from happening.

"I would advise you, sir, to cooperate." Ichabod brought all of his unspecified anger into his voice. If ever there was a time when being a black man might prove useful, it was this situation.

The city of Minneapolis had been caught up in the throes of a search for a missing young man by the name of Ron Abbott. He'd been missing for about a week and had last been seen at a bar in the Mall of America. It had occurred to Ichabod that if he called and said that he had seen the man on the day of his disappearance, a detective, preferably one working alone, would be dispatched to take his statement. After all, it was nine-thirty in the morning. He hoped that would increase the chances of them sending the type of officer they had.

Lieutenant Bloom felt the dull coldness of the nine-millimeter pistol at his head. He'd completely blown it. No partner. No backup. He'd already made so many mistakes he couldn't believe it. He let himself be guided to a chair.

"Do you know what you're doing? You heard me when I introduced myself, didn't you? You know I'm a police officer." Ichabod shoved the detective down into an armed cherry wood dining room chair. "I'm Lieutenant Bill Bloom, Minneapolis Police Department. Do you understand that?"

Ichabod was also sweating now. Lieutenant Bloom was

a big man. About 260 pounds of decaying muscle and gut. Luckily, though, the officer was in his midfifties and had already begun anticipating his retirement to Florida. He was only heavy, not necessarily much in the way of real resistance.

Ichabod slammed him down into the chair; there was a dull thud as his body came to rest there. His eyes opened wide and anger blazed.

There were strips of duct tape already lined along the table's edge. Ichabod plucked one and slapped it across Bloom's mouth, ending the cop's freedom of speech. "Shut up a minute. I know who you are. I was the one who called you."

He bound the officer's hands to the arms of the chair. His ankles to the legs. The cop expressed no further resistance. The duct tape and the gun that had bruised his head had their own calming effect.

Ichabod put the detective's gun on the middle shelf of his mahogany bookcase. He then picked up a pack of cigarettes from the floor and after a brief search for a match, which he found under the sofa, he lit one and began pacing in front of the bound man.

"I realize that I am standing here, in an apartment in Uptown Minneapolis, two blocks away from one of the finest urban lake systems in the entire world, and at my feet is a dead man." He blew a lungful of smoke into the air. At the mention of *dead man*, Bloom's eyes widened. He swiveled his head to the right and stopped as he spied the bundle of black plastic in a corner. He froze for a full second as the image and its meaning settled in his mind and then—with a snap—he quickly turned back to Ichabod.

"I know that we are already at some moment of crisis. And that I must comport myself in such a way that we might eventually be able to arrive at some sort of arrangement about what to do next." Ichabod flicked an ash from the cigarette in the air. He now stood in front of the detective and held his gaze.

Ichabod had to admit to himself that he was surprised at how suddenly awash he was in a surging inner strength. He'd never before exerted himself like this. He was always the quiet one. The one in the back of the room. He was smart. Everyone knew how smart he was. But he rarely stepped out of his inner world. He was always a follower. Immersed in books and ideas. The self-inflated writer.

He filled his lungs with smoke. This endeavor would test the very soul of his self-confidence. He had not deluded himself, he thought. He knew the danger he had placed himself in. He'd unplugged all the telephones, turned off the radio and television. He would communicate with the outside world when he was ready and not before. He knew that within a matter of hours, his face would be plastered on the pages of every paper. Dance on every television screen. No matter how successful he was, he was bound to die soon.

Ichabod looked around his apartment, the most dominant thing being a ceiling-to-floor, wall-to-wall mahogany bookcase. There were hundreds of books there. About all manner of things. About books even. Books had dominated his life though he'd not yet, in his thirty-eight years, managed to publish one himself. The room was a brilliant clash of dark and light. The oppressive bookcase. The windows that opened on Groveland Terrace and beyond to the gorgeous southern sun. His beige ultrasoft leather sofa sitting delicately on blond hardwood floors that held the sunlight upon its shoulders with joy. Dark and light.

Lieutenant Bloom's eyes flamed as he realized how explosive this situation was. He'd just that morning convinced his wife that they should move to Pompano when he retired in three years. The Minnesota winters had worn a hole in his hide, not to mention the job itself. He'd survived his whole career without once experiencing this kind of jeopardy. No self-respecting cop would have let this happen. He sighed. What was this about?

Ichabod finished the cigarette in silence, walked to the overturned marble coffee table and righted it. He picked up the clear glass ashtray from the floor and set it on the table. He stubbed the cigarette. He turned to Bloom and spoke in a modulated, but commanding voice.

"I beseech you to pay close attention as I recount the events that have led us to this. There is so much you must remember. And I'm well aware of how preoccupied you already are with your life. All the things going on. I know that even before you ever came into this room, you already had a lot on *your* mind. So many small and insignificant things that required your full attention, no? So many threats to our existence hovering just outside the door. Which is why I often keep mine closed, if you understand me."

Ichabod stared at Bloom. "Do you understand me?" The detective hunched his shoulders ever so slightly. "Well, not to worry. There is time for understanding later."

Ichabod wished he'd worn an ascot and smoking jacket. Suddenly he wanted to be Alistair Cooke. He wanted this story to be the weekly episode of *Masterpiece Theatre*. "I will come to the point as quickly as I can. But these are mysterious times, confusing times, and I am like a leaf swooshing down the gutter in a torrent of rainwater and other debris, both organic and not. I am a part of that confluence. The way things actually came to be. I was here."

Bloom watched him pick up the gun again. A nine-millimeter Glock, the gun of the moment. The officer could see the smooth, lustrous chocolate skin of Ichabod catch the sunlight that washed the room. His cleanshaven head was like a lightning rod. Everything seemed to flow from or into Ichabod.

"First, let me assure you that this has nothing whatsoever to do with the Ron Abbott case. I used that as a ruse. I don't know anything about that case. But I do know something about a murder. A murder that happened right here in this room."

Bloom watched Ichabod pace in front of him. His eyes occasionally shifted to the plastic-covered heap. He wondered what exactly was happening to him. Ichabod barely paused between sentences. His thoughts were percolating. Dividing like single-celled amoebas. He'd been training for most of his life for this performance.

"But what will happen when you have heard the full story? I have no idea how you'll react. That scares me. And worst of all, particularly if I fail to tell it perfectly, I know that we will be facing a rather dicey moment. Eh?

"And I appreciate the opportunity to get this out. You could have taken a totally different approach. I wasn't sure I could get the advantage over you. My limited experience with people who carry guns and badges speaks mostly of your intransigence and of your righteous certainty. But then my experience with those of your 'gang' in blue has come primarily from television. Oh, I've been stopped now and again by your fellow peace officers. But it has mostly been the Charles Bronson, Clint Eastwood, Mark Fuhrman images of blue blurs whaling on black skin which flicker from the running eye of television that influences me. Even plungers made for industrial toilets have been the tools of your torture. So my lack of experience is a badge of wonder to me. I've never felt that stick on my head. And I thank you for that. Truly. I have always been able to expect to be treated equally. Free to be disappointed, so to speak. But free nonetheless of bruises and bumps."

Ichabod lit another cigarette. His mind was alive with the construction of his defense. Yes. That's precisely what it was. A defense. He was speaking as clearly, as specifically, as he possibly could. You can't explain a murder with a simple accounting of "who struck John," as his mother would say. In an action as final as murder the contributing factors are complex and convoluted.

"I trust the story you are about to hear will relieve you somewhat of the anxiousness you must be feeling with my gun winking its eye at you." Ichabod blew smoke into Bloom's face. The policeman immediately recoiled, humiliated. If he survived this ordeal, Bloom knew he'd never live it down. He'd carry this disgrace into retirement.

Ichabod now slid one of the cherry wood chairs across from the detective. "If I could fully describe the warmth and passion that swirled in this very same room not more than five hours earlier you would never believe that such *community*—yes, let's call it that, even though you will probably hold me in disdain for doing so—such powerful love could result in this." He walked over to the garbage bags.

"I'm shocked and loathe to admit it, but even in this multicultiboho sideshow there is still a need for murder. It's not as though murder is unknown to us. Murders are committed every day. Hell, I'm not telling you anything you haven't heard. You are preoccupied with murder, aren't you? That's why you're here in the first place. You have a curiosity about the way certain people come to meet their untimely demise."

This speech was slowly unnerving the detective. Bloom felt the perspiration under his clothes. Frightened now, he studied the sweetly contorted face, the rise and fall of emotion in Ichabod's running oration. What, in fact, was he talking about? He was obviously very intelligent. But Bloom was finding it hard to follow his line of discussion. Besides, the main thing Bloom wanted to know straightaway was whether there really was a body lying across the room.

But Ichabod was not in a generous mood. He would not abbreviate his introduction to the story. He knew that the policeman would probably think he was crazy. But he could think of no other way to set the stage. Besides, he was already so angry that he couldn't stop himself. He found himself once again speaking and pacing before the detective. Occasionally he would halt and talk directly at the bound man. But most times he talked into the air as he walked, brandishing the gun for the drama and the point.

"I am an innocent civilian. True, there is death before us, but it is a new situation for me. I'm not as comfortable with this as you might think. I know I seem so confident and in control. But believe me, I'm quite out of sorts. Fighting trembles.

"Still I stand before you with a loaded gun. Me. And I'm a pacifist. I don't believe in violence. I really don't. I just want to be able to stop all the crazy motherfuckas who are running up and down the street from killing me."

Bloom closed his eyes.

Ichabod softened his voice to a chuckle. "Now, *there's* something. Carrying a gun to keep someone from killing you. The big question is would I ever use it. And I'm smart enough not to tell you that. You know what I mean? And don't think that this man who lies dead before us died as a result of a bullet from my gun. It simply isn't true, as you will see."

Bloom opened his eyes and tried to convey to Ichabod his readiness to be set free.

"But I must tell you a short story here to frame the larger picture." Ichabod was pacing again. His voice modulating from calm to agitated. He realized he wasn't as in control as he thought he'd be. Indeed it was quite stunning the way he had developed this elaborate plan to explain what had happened—explain it in such a way that the good lieutenant would smile fatherly at him and, perhaps even pat him lovingly on the back, perhaps even say something like, "Say no more. I understand." The way Ichabod had it planned, he would carefully explain who he was, what had happened, and why, and Bloom would let him go.

But now he spiraled into a stream of stories and feelings that he knew would confuse his captive yet were absolutely critical to tell. He wondered if the lieutenant had ever felt that way. The need to just talk. To say shit, which really did have a point—but when you actually heard it the first time you might not think it made sense at all. How many people began talking, not knowing what the hell they were going to say? Was that a good thing? Did Bloom ever have the desire to express his full measure of power, he being a white man in America; namely, the power to say whatever the hell he wanted to?

He heard himself speaking again. "You don't know this, but I'm the kind of guy who is cursed with a fiery temper. Otherwise known, particularly when found in black men, as an Ingrained Unconscious Tendency to Self-Destruction (IUTSD)."

Ichabod smiled again. "Now, although my anger can be furious, most times, if I may say so myself, I am as sweet as a purple plum. As gentle as your own sweet breath. Soft, actually. Like the inside of your own thigh. Can you imagine an African man born in America, called colored and nigger and afro and Negro and every other fucking thing under the cosmos, who is both sweet and quick to sour? This is more common than you'd think. If I know you as well as I think I do.

"And I do think I know you. It stems from something I learned in school. Perhaps Fanon, not sure. But it goes like

this: The oppressed know the oppressor better than the oppressor knows the oppressed. Which makes sense when you
think about it. It's just real sad.

"Anyway, last week I drove my car to the local bohe-
mian retreat. You know, the place over by the lake. On the
edge of the water. Where people do the art thing. And in
Minneapolis, where hipness is as fast-footed as anywhere in
the world, there be's some big-time frontin going on in this
place. It's one of those bars where you think about what
kind of clothes you have on before you go through the door.
Even if you only want a beer or a domestic glass of cheap
wine. Red, of course. White's kind of out. It's the sort of
place where they wear those black turtles and leotards. Leg-
gings, they call them now. The white boys wear big black
shoes and I swear I think the ones that the women wear are
even bigger. Big brogan, mud-crushing shoes. With white
socks and fucked-up jeans. Yeah, there are styles afoot there.
Pretty styles stylin buck wilin, frontin the artz scene: 'bein
in this play and that film' (in Minnifuckinsota people be
seriously frontin the film thang)."

Ichabod stopped, consciously finding the dramatic
pause. Bloom tried to say something, his mumbled and
muted words barely breaking the air. Ichabod stared at him,
feigned concern. As if to say, please do not interrupt this
important explanation.

"Anyway," he continued, "I pull my Jetta up to the steps
of this loring place and as usual there was nowhere to leave
it. No legal place. No spot. Near the park but not a parking
spot. So I double. Lights flash like in New York where they
don't give two shits. 'Go the fuck around, motherfucka,'
they say without opening their mouths. Even if the street is
skinnier than Whitney Houston before Bobby. You couldn't
go around even if you fucking wanted to. So you have to
back out before anybody traps you there. Stuck. You just

be stuck there until things change. And things do change. Eventually. 'You just wait your ass there. Okay? I'll be right back. Deliver this motherfuckin package. Okay? Be cool.'

"So, with my car double-parked I commence to hanging out on the outside. See, at this bar you can drink outside. Just across from the park. That's the spot. You know. Max and relax. Watch the peoples. Talk about them. Make fun of them. You know, like this weak-ass brother who claims he isn't black. Talks some shit about how he's really Swedish. Yeah, no shit. I heard him myself. Some blond woman standing next to him, totally transfixed. I mean looking at his toast-brown ass wondering (I'm guessing here): "What the fuck is wrong with you, nigger? You is a nigger, ain't you? That's why I'm talking to you in the first place. I mean, like if you're Swedish I'm wasting my fucking time. I could talk to thousands of Swedish motherfuckas. They're all over the goddamn place. The place is filthy with Swedes.

"But he thinks she down with it. He's made her feel comfortable. He's black but he's Swedish. That works. I heard him say his last name was Anderson. Or, was that Andersen?

"So I talk about the motherfucka. Every time I see him. Him and a whole bunch of other weirdos, too. That's the fun in going. This bar is the prime spot for frontin. Anyway, after awhile I finally saw a car pulling out from a parking space. So, I put my beer down and ran to my car. I turn my flashers off and pulled ahead to begin the parallel. Bam. White boys in a rusty boat pull in. They take the spot. Damn. I couldn't believe that shit. Would you? Could you? Somebody just taking what was yours by divine right. If you are the first one to see it it's yours. Isn't that correct? I thought so. But do white boys understand that? Nooo. Don't matter who saw it first. Just who's entitled to it. Privilege, they call it. I watched them pull in. I imagined there was a conversation, something like. 'There's a parking space.' 'Yeah, we got lucky' 'Hey, that nigger's gonna try and take your space.' 'Not today he's not.' Something like that.

"I couldn't help it. I jumped out of my car. 'Fuck this shit,' I said as he opened his door. 'No you ain't. I beg you. I beg you, I really do. Your pardon, I mean. That's my spot. I was gonna park there.'

"But this was a Saturday night and sometimes it seems that white boys choose that one night to drink a shit load of beer and smoke a whole quarter-pound of fancy weed and drink red wine and do poppers and all kinds of other crazy shit and when they do they rise to the heights of their privilege. Then a black man is a nigger and nobody can focus on the fact that any one of them, black or white, might be one step away from murder or being murdered. So the driver says to me, 'Well, you're not parking here now.'

"So I killed the motherfucka. No discussion, no arguing, no nothing. I just pointed my finger at the white boy and pulled the trigger. White boy dead. Another one bites the dust. *dent dent dent dddadent ddadent dadent dent dent dent dddadent ddadent dadent dent . . .*" Would you have arrested me for that? Deadly fingers. Nine-millimeter index finger of death.

"Still, I drove away in tears. Another day, another scar. Another tick, a flick, a smooth slick movement toward the end." Ichabod collapsed into the chair opposite Bloom. He was close to tears, exhausted. He had to hold it together.

"And because of that moment of crazy, mad, made-up violence, I know you're thinking that I might have killed this man, Dewitt McMichael, who lies between us here on the floor. And to be honest, as I've intimated, murder *is* all around us. And if it were that simple I would have surrendered myself to the sweet justice of the Minneapolis police, of which I know you have been entrusted with some responsibilities. But, alas, we are in this situation because it is so much more complex than that."

When Ichabod turned his head to Lieutenant Bloom he wondered if the chubby white man had fallen asleep. His eyes were definitely closed. His skin was relaxed, his breathing barely audible. For a moment, Ichabod thought the man looked cherubic, innocent, sweet. Like a child lost in a purely empty moment.

But as he leaned forward to touch him, Bill Bloom opened his eyes wide, indicating that he had not been asleep. How much of this was he supposed to listen to? He had also been thinking that right about now someone would be trying to get him on the radio. In a minute or two his cell phone would ring. He wondered what his captor would do then.

"My name is Ichabod. That's right, Ichabod. I know you've never heard of a black man named Ichabod. But my name is important here for that very reason. I mean, if my name was Leroy you'd have a pretty good idea of what was going on, wouldn't you? What about if I said my name was Half-Dead, Cudjoe, or Tupac. Right. I know. Dead man lying here beside me, I'm black, I'm holding a gun, my name is Willie or some shit like that, and I might as well go looking for a strong rope. Am I right or what? I could flash you that steely eyed killer's look and you'd have all the evidence you needed. But I ain't going out like that. The fact that my name is one which makes it difficult to automatically stereotype me is something I'm hoping will buy me enough time to tell you this story before all hell breaks loose."

When he was very young, no kid could have hated his own name more than Ichabod. He was teased incessantly. He'd had so many fights about it that he'd lost count.

The name had resulted in an elemental rift between him and his parents. From his earliest moments as a child, he had wanted to change his name. He'd pursued it with great energy throughout his childhood. But his parents had always insisted that he wait until he was out of high school before he did it. He never got to the point where he could just relax about it and let people call him that if they wanted to.

Still when he *could* change it, he didn't. Everyone was prepared for it. Everyone expected it to happen. The only mystery was what name would he take. But in a move that would come to define him, he never brought it up again.

When he was sixteen he had a girlfriend named Margo who lived on Christian Street in South Philly. She had said his name with such sexual breathlessness that it had completely changed his mind about it. He loved to hear her call his name. No matter where they were. On the telephone. At the movies. When Margo whispered "Icky" in his ear his whole body stiffened.

He knew he'd made the right decision when on his first day at college, one of his professors, glancing at the class list, asked what country Ichabod was from.

"What country?" Ichabod asked, his voice then not much more than a squeak.

"Are you American?" the man asked incredulously.

Ichabod nodded and realized for the first time that his parents had given him a small gift. If the professor, or anyone for that matter, could be even slightly dissuaded from treating him like a stereotype he would accept it as an advantage. A gift.

So he kept it.

Bloom couldn't help but think—at that precise moment—that Ichabod had no idea how much hell was likely to break loose. The detective was having a very difficult time tracking the line of Ichabod's story. He wasn't even sure whether it had started or not. Maybe Ichabod was still warming up. High off of his own power trip.

Ichabod pointed at the body. "I saw the whole thing. I saw how it began, how it escalated, and finally I saw this man fall. And I can tell it in literary fashion so you shan't be bored. I've bet my freedom on this. Otherwise you will condemn me, I'm sure.

"So, okay, we were having this party. I guess you would call it a party. This is Minneapolis, isn't it? You've got to be unemployed to find a real house party around here. You know what I mean? A real house. A real party. It's definitely a mini apple if you get my point. And artists don't know how to party anymore, anyway. It's all become such a big show. Chests puffed like grouse. Designer music with deadly cheese. Politeness so glaring you have to wear your shades but if you do you become a part of the glare. Such small exchanges between people. Almost nothing of meaning. No anger. No lust."

The lieutenant couldn't help thinking that he was being held by a madman. The type who imagined a world waiting for him to tell a story that in all actuality, nobody really cared about. Bloom certainly didn't want to hear it. He wanted to go back to his desk at the precinct. But he watched Ichabod strut around in front of him, pontificating. Waxing eloquent as if both of their lives weren't hanging in the balance.

"Perhaps it has something to do with me." Ichabod was actually slipping into self-reflection. He wanted to be more straightforward for the detective. But he honestly didn't think that was the best way to make his point. He had to understand. "Maybe I'm not being invited to the right parties. Suddenly I'm finding myself more and more in the company of doddering, frail, English Department professors and the young women who love them. And here I could go into excruciating detail if I so desired. Instead I will simply say that my part-time involvement as an adjunct professor in the English Department at Mupster University has revealed a cornucopia of loathsome employment practices and the vibrant existence of little fiefdoms. Little skinny incomplete and incompetent poets toss out teaching assignments to loyal followers and those who might have sex with them. Of which I am neither." He paused for just a second. "You might tell from this minor digression that my experiences at Mupster have not been entirely joyful. And you would be right."

He looked into Lieutenant Bloom's eyes and saw a man who was at war within himself. He could see the anger roiling beneath the surface. The officer's body glowed with rageful luminescence. But it was held in check, muffled and muted by an opposing desire to remain calm.

Ichabod read him correctly. The lieutenant knew that he had to try to control himself, try to be patient. But it was difficult. At the moment, all he could do was sit there, taped to the furniture, and listen.

And, Ichabod was committed to a course. He'd chosen a path. He owed it to himself and to the future of the tribe. "And you might ask why I am taking us so far afield. I guess I should say simply that I am telling this story this way because . . . well, because I can. You are without your gun. Gagged. A helpless hostage. This is the true meaning of power, is it not? You've felt it more than I have. But I guess at this moment I do feel powerful. And you must sit there and listen to me do things my way.

"I was talking about how strange Minneapolis is when it comes to parties. How I feel so far out of the partying crowd. There was a time, to be sure, when 'party' was my middle name. When I ripped the streets with the dexterity of asphalt. Could smell a party days away and be there with my bell bottoms and stacked heels when the lights were turned down low and the music cranked up.

"Back in Philly where I grew up, house parties had become a lot like Minnesota performance art. People screaming all over the place. Chaos. A lot of people acting like they should be the center of attention when a quiet seat in the back of the theater would do just as well. Maybe better.

"The room would invariably be mostly dark with maybe a single blue or red light bulb burning in a corner. The people would be crammed into the living room. It would be hot. The music would be thumping off the walls. Sweat would be the air. Short skirts. Tight pants. Swishes mixed with sways and then someone would begin the chant.

" *'Par tay. Par tay. There's a party over here.' "*

Ichabod broke into an impromptu attempt at the cabbage patch, a dance he'd done in a steamy basement before coming to Minnesota.

"And somebody on the other side of the room would holler back, *'There's a party over here.'* And it would go on like that all night long. A call and response that was woven into the music. At some point some drunken heavy-voiced man would bring new power, *'The roof the roof the roof is on fire. We don't need no water let the motherfucka burn. Burn motherfucka burn.' "*

Ichabod stopped dancing and craned his face close to the detective's. "It was a curious chant to be sure. The first time I heard that it was the same year they bombed MOVE out of West Philadelphia. You remember that shit? Dropped a bomb on a whole bunch of black folks. John Edgar Wideman told us the story. Fire charred the dead babies and the dead. Fire charred everything. *Philadelphia Fire* was hot.

Of course Lieutenant Bloom had heard about MOVE. It was legend among big city cops. One of the few times when a standoff ended in an all-out assault, including the use of some experimental munitions developed specifically for urban unrest. He'd heard the guys from the SWAT team joking about it.

"But you just know that somewhere in Philadelphia there were a bunch of black folks having a party when the bomb went off. They were probably sweating and singing like gospel and dancing and were so churned into the rhythm the sound of their voices was like magic.

" 'The roof the roof the roof is on fire. We don't need no water let the motherfucka burn. Burn motherfucka burn.'

"Who would ever expect the police to bomb a whole city block?"

Ichabod stood up and began pacing again. "So when I say that there was a party going on here, I should be a little more circumspect. What we had here wasn't that kind of party. First of all, there were white people here. And most white folks put a damper on a good party. They get upset if the music's too loud because they've got important pressing political issues to discuss. And then you got the black folks who forgot how to dance or even that dancing is something they could actually do as opposed to going to see Alvin-goddamned-Ailey. I'm sorry, it agitates me just a little. Just a little agitated. I get real pissed off when I see black people who act like dancing doesn't mean anything to them. Like they can take it or leave it. Anyway, we had some of them here. And then there were some Asian American folks and some gays and lesbians. We had all kinds of folks up in here. Native folks. Some Latinos. I mean, you know, the successful multicultiboho tribe. They were all in the house.

"Now, while we may not have those steamy, dance-oriented parties like the ones I remember from home, we do experience something special, unique. Something you can only feel in a room full of people of different colors and cultures. Especially if there's alcohol or drugs, and even more so if there's a good balance of men and women. The sexual dynamics between the races can be white phosphorous. Hotter than a serrano chile pepper.

"But the truth is that we were being righteous because deep down inside we love each other. Really. I know there's a dead person here. And I know there was a huge ruckus and all, but, I swear to you, when oppressed people get together there's a powerful magic unleashed. It floats like ribbons in a breeze. People feel strong. Powerful. They feel, for a minute, like people who feel like people.

"Not like the folks that were at this party were lacking in self-image or anything. I mean the multicultiboho tribe is the vanguard of the intellectual, I said the intellectual not ineffectual, the serious brain power of the multiculti movement. And yes, I do firmly believe it is a movement. And we all know there is murder in every movement. So it shouldn't surprise you that I have to tell this story in the same room with a dead body."

Again Bloom's eyes widened. He nodded his head in the direction of the garbage bags. He tried to ask the question again with his eyes. But Ichabod—lost on his emotional gamut—ignored him. Up down slang formality resignation aggression. At the moment, he thought it all extremely important.

"Kind sir, please give close ear to this story. We have cried so much. Suffered so much indignity. How shall we struggle through this mess? How shall we struggle? Can we struggle together? Can we all just get along? I should like to believe as much, shouldn't you?

"For one thing we might make love. There were people here, in this very room tonight, who wanted to fuck each other. I'm sure of it. I could read their eyes. And I was watching. You should have seen it. The sexual tensions swirled around us. I know there was unchecked lust here."

He stared at the lieutenant. His face slowly softened. "Okay, it was me. I found myself almost immediately listing the women in the room I wanted to know better in that special Jordache way, if you get my allusion. I refuse to be made to feel guilty for this. What am I supposed to do? I'm a single black man in an O.J. Simpson world. Guilt is my first lover. And yet my libido continues to taunt me with the types of encouragements that made sense in 1980 but might get you sued or worse in 1999.

"Suffice it to say that no matter who I wanted to have sex with, under the conditions of our presence it would not have been a good thing. Besides, I was afraid of what the others would have said."

Ichabod grabbed one of the white kitchen chairs he'd brought into the room for the party and set it down two feet away from the policeman. He turned the chair around so that its narrow slatted back faced Lieutenant Bloom. He then straddled it as he sat down again. "Take Marci, for example. She was here. A very interesting young woman she is. You'd be amazed at how many black women living in Minnesota there are who don't want to date white men. It's really strange. They are often and rather routinely ignored by black men and yet many of them will not traverse the chasm and make nice-nice with white men. It's quite noble, really, this deep belief in the strength of blackness. But it makes for roiling anger and sometimes sharp bitterness. This community is not very kind to black women. I've heard too many of them complain of the constant assault they face."

It was transitions like that that worried Bloom. The problem existed somewhere between the rational and the irrational. No man's land. He couldn't tell whether he was in real danger or not. But, if that was indeed a body—and he had to admit that the more Ichabod talked, the more he was sure that there was death in the room with them—then there was no telling what Ichabod would do.

"What is beauty? It's a curious dilemma. Where I grew up in West Philadelphia, beauty was an opal, burnished and glistening in blackness. But after years here in the Land of Ten Thousand Lakes and even more people named Peterson, there is a kind of mocha love banging inside me. A swirl. A mixture of one-part black and one-part something else. Something uniquely American. The openness is confounding. I have been married to two black women. Dated an Asian woman. I've had carnal knowledge with an American Indian. With a Latina. Lived with a white woman. What does this mean? You might think this merely an idle boast, but I'm trying to make a point. That could not have happened in Philadelphia. Opal would have always been the standard. There has been a kind of freedom; a diversity that bespeaks who we really are. But what if you are the opal? And if you are committed to opals?

"You have no idea, do you? You just see a dark-skinned woman. Someone who you are vaguely curious about. But you don't really know her, and there is really no way you could. The souls of black women are hidden from the world. If you weren't born African American you'd have to read a lot of books to even catch a real vapor. So let it be acknowledged here, before I go on too far, that I love black women."

Bloom was also more than a little unnerved by the fact that his cell phone, which Ichabod had not taken from his coat pocket, had not rung. For his part, Ichabod was too deeply into introspection to notice Bloom at all. "But they can get these attitudes, you know. 'Tudes.' Marci had one tonight. She scares me a little. There are times when you can look in her eyes and see the explosion that is building. She has such beautiful big brown eyes. Sensual and vibrant. But there are times when I want to say to her: lose a little weight. Just a little. I mean, that's one of the issues of beauty, isn't it? The 'beauty' of white women includes thinness and here in Minnesota it is definitely a part of the dominant expectation. But you have these black women who complain about how black men ignore them but they won't lose any weight. You get tired of thinking, 'Wow, she's really pretty. If she was just a little smaller I'd be on that, sho nuff.'

"Always a goddamned reservation.

"Underneath it all, Marci is a stone-righteous, serious, black nationalist, clenched-fist sister. On some days I can just tell that white people and perhaps others, but particularly white people, get on her last nerve. It was like that earlier tonight. You could just feel it. She was already doing her best to be *in* the room with this collection of white black brown yellow folks."

The memory of Marci's tense, agitated face caused Ichabod to chuckle again. He focused his eyes on the lieutenant once again.

"I suppose I should mention that April was also here. What's more, I must confess that I have a clandestine desire to sleep with April. Her golden hair outlines a rather delicate face. Hints of affluence and sophistication mingle with a wildness that is virtually intoxicating. And, of course, she is thin.

"And, here I must pause to interject a rather frightening analysis. Frightening to me, that is. What does it mean that I have described Marci thus and April so? What does that mean? It is a perpetual dilemma; perhaps a psychological defect that affects black men who move to the Twin Cities from other places. I have found that we often can enumerate the faults of black women so easily, so blithely. As if we are in a position to criticize. It's an absurdity I think, for us who inherit such a foul history in our relationships to black women, to be so judgmental. Perhaps, I'm thinking now, perhaps I should reconsider some of my statements. I know there exists a tendency to be more fair to women who are not black. The argument among many of my black male friends boils down to 'why shouldn't we date whoever we want to?' "

Bloom longed for fresh air, a glass of water. Relief from Ichabod's rambling. He mumbled again. Hoping to put enough pressure on the tape that its adhesive would loosen a bit. He consciously tried to heat the air in his mouth so that it would soften the tape. But there was no immediate change. The tape held fast. It was then that he remembered that he had a Swiss Army knife in his pants pocket. It had been a present from a former partner of his. The irony was that the knife was one of the deluxe models with all sorts of tools built in; a perfect symbol of preparedness. There was even a pair of scissors nestled in its red plastic case. But, as things stood, it might just as well have been in his locker back at the station.

And yet, it was there, in his pocket. He only had to figure out how to get at it. He thought about all of the movies he'd seen in which bound people had struggled and rubbed and scraped until the ropes broke. And from this he took heart. There was the chance, if he stayed strong and kept putting pressure on the duct tape, that it would loosen and he would be able to get at the knife. He would live for that moment.

Bloom again leaned back in the chair and looked up at Ichabod who was so far outside of himself, so caught up in his own story that he completely missed the flash of discovery and hope that passed across the detective's face.

"Perhaps we are incapable of making such a decision on our own. Maybe dating people of other races isn't the problem. The problem might come in the answer to the question: why? Still, what do you do with the urge to get your zipless groove on with the person who's standing next to you in the supermarket checkout line who also just happens to be white?

"There have been many times when I've been around Marci and there have been interracial couples and she seemed fine. But there are those other times when I can actually see her react. Like peeling paint or something. Watching a white girl flirt with a brother can sometimes unbraid Marci's hair.

"And tonight, tonight I watched her again. She'd been biting her tongue all night and smiling. Almost acting friendly. She was waiting to find out what the deal was. But when she saw April giving me the eye I could tell she didn't like it.

"And then the worst of all possible things happened, April was so busy talking that she didn't realize that she kept lifting the back of her long thick blond hair and then flipping it in the air. I don't know why white women do this but I do know that they often pick the wrong time to do it. When the strands of her hair swished across Marci's face I thought we were in for a fight. This was not the thing to do to Marci. April should have known better. Black women hate that hair-flipping bullshit. I've seen sisters go completely off on white women for that shit. 'You'd better watch that fucking hair. Putting that shit in my face.' I was at First Avenue one night, you know, that club made famous by the Prince film *Purple Rain*? It was funk night. That's the night when all the black people go there. Yeah, and if a white woman gets too close to a group of black women and she's not paying attention and she flips that hair—stand the fuck by. I've seen it. There's a look African women have when they get pissed at white women. It's scary. If anybody starts looking at you like that, you better be gathering up your stuff and heading for the exit. You try to make the dance floor under that kind of pressure you might lose a rib or something."

Ichabod paused and studied Lieutenant Bloom. Suddenly he felt sad. What was he doing? How could this work? This improvisation was, in a way, the truest form of black expression. The interconnected jazzified line of discussion that was the purest form of freedom. His friend, Brother JuJu, always reminded him that jazz was freedom. The clearest, purest moment of freedom for a black person in America was the moment he or she was within the unexpected note in an unplanned solo in a collectively improvised expression. He was trying his best.

But now the sadness was overtaking him. Dewitt McMichael really was dead, sprawled in the corner of a sunny apartment. There were beautiful paintings on every wall. Wonderful sculptures sat on ledges and pedestals. But Dewitt McMichael would never see them again.

"Okay . . . okay. I realize I'm stretching this story out a little longer than I intended. But I just wanted you to know that this is a complicated affair. Nothing as simple as most of the murder cases you will investigate. We are the real thing. Not just a group of stereotypes. Anyway, it got pretty tense in here even before Dewitt arrived.

"The thing is, this wasn't just an average party. Because at nine o'clock, after most of the people had gone, there was a smaller group of us. And we stayed on for a very specific reason. You see, the Shrubbery Foundation—you know the big department store and supreme funder of the arts—was on the verge of presenting its first Twin Cities Genius Grant. Those of us who stayed just happened to be the finalists.

"It was sort of secret. Only we knew that Dewitt McMichael from the foundation was supposed to come by and talk to us. Everyone else thought it was an early kind of party, more of a reception, and cleared out, with our tacit encouragement, by nine o'clock.

"But of those who stayed, there were rumors that Dewitt might even let us know which one of us had won. We're talking big money here. Five hundred thousand dollars. I can tell by the shock in your eyes that you find that hard to believe. But it's true. One of us was in line to get a half-million dollars from the man who is currently lying dead at your feet. The big kicker is that this grant was supposed to go to a person of color. Needless to say, we were all pretty excited. As you might imagine, everybody wanted it, But can you even comprehend what it would have meant to me? No, I don't think you could.

"Now, you know how things like this go. Whenever you get white people with a lot of money waving it in the faces of the unwashed you're bound to have a melee. A scuffle, a struggle, you know what I mean?" Ichabod paused. He thought about what he was saying and realized the thought was incomplete.

"Do you understand what I'm saying? I mean, it's good that this town is so liberal. It's good that there are people here who care about building a community that feels like America. But there is a big difference between the needs of the people and the way grants and programs affect them. It never seems to work out. You finally get someone like Dewitt to listen to you. Someone who accepts that there is a reason to support artists of color, and what happens?" Ichabod let his arm sweep across the empty space in front of him, forcing the lieutenant to survey the wreckage of the apartment. He let his hand, with the index finger extended, stop on the makeshift body bag. "This is what happens. It just seems like they never get it right."

He brought his hand over to his face and gently pulled his skin down. "I've been talking to you as if you are not

them. But the truth is that you are. Aren't you? I mean you
are someone who just happened to stumble into a bad situation. Actually, I lured you here. I mean, I knew if I called
and said I had some information about that poor young
white man that someone would drop by. And, I also figured,
rightly, I might point out, that you would come alone, what
with resources being stretched to capacity as you search for
Ron Abbott.

"I have to admit that I was a little surprised that my
neighbors hadn't called you guys earlier. I thought that
when they saw all the people of color coming in here they
would have been on a sharp lookout for any abnormalities.
This is one of those neighborhoods where people fancy
themselves as being upscale post-yuppie parka-wearing
Saab-driving salts-of-the-earth Americans. Don't be different
than that and try to live around here.

"And don't even try to be black. Of course, only I could
actually try to be black. I sometimes practice it out in public.
It's complicated because in truth I'm really black to begin
with. So I think the idea of practicing such a refined and
highly demanding art in public is to be commended. Don't
you think so?

"I can tell by the twinkle in your eye that you agree
with me, although I know that, were it up to you, you
would deny me the right to say it in public. But once again,
may I remind you that this entire statement is done under
the strength of my being the one in power. I have the gun."

ichabod walked over to the garbage bag and grabbed the end where its yellow plastic drawstring was gathered. A small piece of rope choked off the opening. He dragged the two loops of the bag into the center of the room. Bloom was feeling faint now. He had no idea how long he'd been there, taped to the chair and gagged. He thought it had been at least an hour and a half. He cursed his stupidity. He cursed his routine. None of his co-workers would think it all that unusual for him to be out of radio contact an extra half hour. Everyone disappeared into a strip club or a massage parlor now and then. Everyone had occasional affairs.

"I suppose it is time to begin my story in earnest. It starts with a smile and ends with the body of Dewitt McMichael dead, as you see him here." Ichabod opened the bag just slightly. Bloom caught the flash of hair and a swatch of pale skin. He stared at the shifting images of the corpse as Ichabod purposefully let Dewitt's lifelessness linger in open air. Ichabod was handling the dead man as if he were dirty clothes and he was searching for a T-shirt that had been put there by mistake.

And then Ichabod began talking again. "It was such a needless thing. As you can see, he was a rather handsome man. His wispy, dirty blond hair thinning there at the back. Stringy over the crown. His love of formality. He almost always wore a suit. In the summer they were always white. In the winter they were black.

"Usually by Halloween, today, DeWitt was already deep into his black wardrobe. Although it must be said that his suits were not of the highest quality. Indeed, they were often tattered, as if he bought them at a vintage clothing store. Which in itself is not a problem, but when you remember that this is the man who has the responsibility of doling out millions of dollars in arts funding throughout the country it becomes a little disconcerting.

"But even worse is the fact that he always stank. The suits were almost always dirty. Look at this one. Notice the velvet piping and lapels. What is that white stuff there? Icing? Cum? Ugh. And those stains. The cuffs of the pants are frayed. I'll bet you the hem is secured by Scotch tape. This is a foundation executive. The man who held my future in his hands.

"I'm not, in this explanation, attempting to imply anything about other grantsmakers. They are a group of people with the handicap of diversity saddled upon their backs and when they give money to me, which they haven't often done, or to someone I think merits it, I tend to agree that they have done important work.

"But in this sweet town a fair amount of money is offered to writers and artists who take that money and create a fair amount of useless art. And this, perhaps, is how it should be. But if you pay close attention, the artists of color don't usually get the big chunks of money. We can get money to dance and sing or do performance but when they start doling out that 'here take this thirty thousand dollars and relax for a year' money, it's not usually going to us.

"So when somebody starts talking about giving up big dollars just for the coloreds, we all just start salivating and foaming at the mouth. I'll admit to you that I definitely wanted that genius money. Desperately."

As he spoke the word 'desperately' Ichabod felt his stomach lurch. "You see . . . ah . . . the truth is, I don't have that long to live. Don't ask me how I know, I just know it. Each day is so important to me. I needed that money. I needed it for my peace of mind. So that I could live out the rest of my days free of money worries.

"Now, don't take this lightly. I mean this in all seriousness. I'm afraid. We were all afraid. But, by my own estimation, I was the only one who knew I was going to die. They wanted the money, yes, but none of their needs were as great as mine. Without it I will die sooner. I just know it. Don't ask me how I know, I just do. So many people are dying so young. And if you are a black man your life is barely a long scream before you are extinguished."

Ichabod pointed to the body. "Why would he do this to us? Why would he torture us like that? He made us believe. We trusted him because really we loved him. No, really, I can see the skepticism in your furrowed brow, but its true. We complain, we shout back in anger. We defy. Sometimes we actually showed hatred in response to his inherent racist arrogance, but in the end we loved him. There is no other way to explain it. History shows our love. We've fought and worked and believed. We must love. But for a moment consider that we are in something of a bad marriage. A relationship built on promises that were never kept. You've been in similar circumstances, I'm sure. You know what I mean? He caused this. He did this to himself."

The detective now tried to avoid eye contact with Ichabod. Before he'd seen the body, Bloom had tried to calm himself by convincing himself that Ichabod really wasn't a murderer. But now, how could he deny the concrete evidence right in front of him?

"More outright skepticism? Disbelief? Then let me approach this a different way. Would you prefer to have your own voice? Do you think you could exercise a measure of responsibility in your freedom? I ask this because I must admit that I'm a little nervous in doing what I'm about to do."

Lieutenant Bloom snapped his head in Ichabod's direction. He nodded vigorously.

"You look so pitiful sitting there. I am encouraged to bestow a measure of freedom back to you. Besides, I just couldn't continue such a one-sided discussion. I realize that it is a question of power. You can become quickly and completely drunk from power. Something as small as a gun can have such a profound effect on someone. I look at you there, your mouth gagged like that, and I realize I can no longer hold you in complete silence. It was starting to get to me. I know what it's like to be forced into silence. I do, and it's not pretty. I mean I've been talking all this time. Talking and thinking. Processing. And you've just been sitting there, watching me.

"You just happened to be the one they sent here. You've been forced into this little drama. And it is, indeed, a drama. Not quite so little, what with Dewitt rotting here. But every man needs a voice. And even though men who become police officers could use profound and intense counseling before donning the badge, it is clear to me that if I continue to marginalize you this way, you will do what any human being will do who is forcibly denied a voice—what I often want to do—namely kick someone's ass.

"And I would be wholly disingenuous not to admit that

I know that eventually you or one of your comrades will do exactly that to me.

"I understand that. When I pulled this gun on you I knew that no matter what, the least I could expect, even if you believe my innocence, the least I can expect is an ass kicking. Makes sense to me. If somebody pisses you off you get to do something about it. You just have to frame it in a legal context. But I have known no relief from being pissed off. It's a common complaint among men of color. No matter how criminalized we are, there are countless times we let shit go just to live another day. I can't go around threatening or beating the shit out of all the people who represent a threat to my well-being.

"And you would be correct in assuming that if I truly did act out of this edginess I would be forever embroiled in a series of tête-à-têtes leading to my ultimate end. And that, in the final consideration, is why we have people like Mike Tyson, Dennis Rodman, and Latrell Sprewell. They can do it and suffer the public vilification because people will pay handsomely to validate their myths of the angry primitive. It soothes them."

Ichabod leaned over and carefully picked at the edges of the tape. He knew it would be painful. The ripping of this three-inch strip from the detective's lips would probably take some skin. "To be honest, I'm hoping against knowledge that when it's all said and done, you will speak leniency on my behalf.

"This will hurt. I'm just going to yank it off."

Bloom was huffing now. He'd tried to modulate his breathing during Ichabod's tirade. "Here goes." Ichabod ripped the tape from the lieutenant's mouth. Bloom stiffened at the shock of pain and sat like a statue, stinging and stunned. He was still bound tightly. But there was new air in his mouth. His spirits pulsed up and he instinctively flexed his thigh muscles until he felt the pressure of the knife in his pocket.

"There." Ichabod put his softest voice into Bloom's ear, "I knew you were coming. I called *you*. Remember that. Just don't forget that. I know the story. And I also know that if I don't participate in its telling, I will most likely be the one who suffers. Besides, who better to tell it to you? As I told you earlier, I can tell it so sweetly."

Lieutenant Bloom calculated his first words. He didn't want Ichabod to gag him again, but he was absolutely out of all patience. Flowers of anger bloomed all about him. "How long were you going to keep me taped up like that? I could have suffocated." His voice was almost calm in complete contrast to his facial expression and the anger in his gut.

But Ichabod was only momentarily thrown by it. As he looked at his captive he realized that police officers were trained to sound sweet when they were under duress. Still, he knelt down and said, "I wanted to make sure you were sufficiently restrained before I decided how much freedom you could safely be given."

Lieutenant Bloom stared at Ichabod as if he were an evil witch or an inappropriately lecherous uncle. After a moment, he closed his eyes. When he opened them he scanned the room, casting his glance like a searchlight across the room. The remnants of the party and the ensuing conflagration were everywhere.

"What's with you? Are you crazy or what? What the hell did you say your name was?" Bloom's words were large rocks dropping on the floor.

"My name is Ichabod Word. How many times do I have to tell you that?"

"And . . . you live here?"

Now it was Ichabod's turn to stare at the lieutenant. He

watched Bloom's eyes as they settled on the covered body.
"Who is that?"

"Damn, Lieutenant. Don't you listen? I told you that he
was Dewitt McMichael. He was one of the most powerful
foundation executives in the entire country. He worked for
the Shrubbery Foundation."

"Ichabod, I want you to remove the tape from my arms
and legs. Let me go."

"Why should I do that?"

"Because the longer you keep me all taped up like this
the more harshly you're going to be treated when this is
over. I give you my word. I will not try to escape. I promise.
You can call all the shots. I'm not interested in being a hero
or nothing, so you don't have to worry about that. I just
want you to let me go."

"I took the gag off. What more do you want? I'm the
one who's in jeopardy of going to jail . . ."

"In jeopardy? Ichabod. I've got news for you, friend. If
you walk out of here alive, you are definitely going to jail."

"Well, Mr. Policeman. In this great country of ours that's
not how it works. It all depends on the way this thing plays
itself out. Remember O.J."

"I try not to. But I can tell you with relative certainty
that there is no way in hell you're going to get out of here
scot-free."

"I wouldn't know what that was. Scot-free? What the
hell is that?"

"What's with all this wordplay, Ichabod? Why can't we
just have a conversation?"

"Yes. I assumed you'd want to get right to the heart of
the matter. The bottom line. The nut of the issue. The point.
But as I've tried to convey to you, power is an amazing
thing. And this gun is one of the most powerful instruments
a person can have."

"You think so?"

"I know so. You wear one."

"But it's my job."

"You get paid to fuck with me. And they give you a gun to boot."

"Will you undo me?"

"I'm thinking about it." The muscles in the detective's jaw twitched. He didn't know that reflected the strain from trying to stretch the duct tape. Every time he said *no*, Ichabod could feel the tension in the detective's body grow. He could actually feel it.

Lieutenant Bloom nodded toward the body, "Was there a fight?"

Ichabod swung his gaze to Dewitt. "You might say that. We had an ah . . . argument, you might say. I mean, there was this intense debate. You know how we are . . ."

"We? You mean you and him?"

"No. I didn't say it was me and him. We, Lieutenant. We. There were a bunch of us here."

"Well, Ichabod, tell me what happened." Ichabod could hear the exasperation in the officer's voice. He liked it. It tickled him to see Bloom so impotent. "Yes, there was a room full of people here, although only a small group was involved in the . . . how shall I describe it . . . the ah . . . heated discussion."

The two men locked eyes. "There was a violent, vicious argument, you mean?"

"Technically, for your purposes, the purposes of police investigation, I suppose one might describe it as an argument." Ichabod felt a moment of eloquence seeping back into the exchange. Civility knocked at the door but unfortunately, a corpse shared the room with them. Ichabod really wanted to make a pot of tea and some sandwiches but he knew Bloom would not be a willing tea companion.

"Listen, Ichabod, from what I can see, you're in serious tro . . ." The sentence was broken by the muffled sound of Bloom's cell phone.

Ichabod smiled at him. "What is that? I missed that, didn't I? You've got a telephone."

"Yes, Ichabod. And on the other end of that phone is probably another police officer who's wondering where the hell I am."

Ichabod heard him but was busy trying to get the device out of the lieutenant's inside coat pocket. The telephone was lodged diagonally in the small pocket and refused to budge. "Goddamnit," Ichabod muttered into Bloom's ear as he ripped the phone and the pocket out. "There. Now, let's see." The telephone rang again. "What shall we do about this? I wasn't ready for outside contact."

The presence of the cell phone actually heightened the likelihood of disaster. If it really was the law on the other end, the situation would escalate faster and quicker than he had anticipated. He decided instantly to open the line on the phone. He hit the button.

"Hello?"

"Bill? . . ." The woman's voice on the end surprised Ichabod.

"No, this isn't Bill. Who is this?"

"This," the woman said indignantly, "this is Iris Hirsh. Capt. Iris Hirsh. Who is this?"

Ichabod took a deep breath. "It doesn't matter right now who I am. Let's just say that I have your beloved Bill right here." Ichabod brusquely pushed the phone to the lieutenant's face and barked, "Say something."

"Captain?" Bloom had been watching Ichabod's face. He could tell that they were at an important crossroads. He knew that when his superiors realized that he was being held hostage, things would change. Now he would find out how strong Ichabod really was. The detective intended to find a way to tell Captain Hirsh exactly where they were when Ichabod snatched the telephone away. There were times when Ichabod behaved just like the hostage takers in the training films he'd seen. But there were other times when Bloom almost forgot he was taped up. Times when he was caught in the grip of Ichabod's voice and lulled into a kind of hypnotic state. Now, though, he wanted to be cut loose. And he guessed it would happen soon. He hadn't given up on the knife yet.

Ichabod spoke into the phone, "Would you call us back in a couple of minutes? There are a few things I need to discuss with Detective Bloom."

"Who the hell is this and what the fuck is going on?" Iris Hirsh's voice seemed to open new holes on the telephone's receiver. "Listen, scumbag, you'd better tell me what the hell is going on or when I get to you I'll rip your fucking head off."

Ichabod held the phone away from his ear. He looked at Bloom.

"I woulda warned you if you'd asked. She's a holy terror. Women don't get to be captains all that easily. She'll chew you up and spit you out." For the first time Bloom felt like smiling.

"Listen, Captain, I have your detective here and he's safe right now . . ."

"Where are you?"

"You'll have to call us back. Give us about, let's say, well . . . give us about fifteen minutes, would you? I'd most appreciate it. In fact, Captain, I'm just going to deactivate this thing as soon as we're done." He switched the power button to off.

He placed the telephone on the coffee table that sat between them. "There. I didn't expect that but . . . well . . . you can't plan for every little thing."

Lieutenant Bloom softened his features. He wanted Ichabod to trust him. Maybe that was what Ichabod needed to see. "Ichabod. Ah . . . son, you're in quite a bit of trouble here. Look around you. This . . . this is a crime scene. Somebody died here."

Ichabod sprawled back in his chair. The detective was securely taped down and posed no threat. He could listen to him without any great fear. So he did.

But Bloom was suddenly silent. They sat there like that for about thirty seconds. And then the detective began again. "This is a crime scene, Ichabod. Now, I'm not saying you've done anything. You may be as innocent as you claim. But somebody did something."

Ichabod could feel something change as Bloom began to speak. Somehow his position of power didn't feel so solid. So complete. "Wait a minute." He waved the gun once again in the detective's face. "You're supposed to be listening to me. If you think just trying to scare the shit out of me is going to get you untied and me in jail, you've got another think coming. Besides, I didn't exactly say I was innocent."

Bloom choked back his anger, settled himself and asked calmly, "Do you know what you're doing?" Ichabod shook his head.

"I've heard some motivational speakers say if you don't know where you're going, you're sure to get there. That's me. Hellbent and clueless. I don't want to be doing *this*, if that's what you mean. I really don't. But what choice did I have? It happened in my house, for Christ's sake. You were going to come looking for me no matter what."

There were times as Ichabod spoke that Lieutenant Bloom almost felt sorry for him. He really didn't understand what was about to happen. The police officer smiled, "Ichabod. Ichabod, listen. My name is Lt. Bill Bloom, Minneapolis Police Department, Homicide. Do you understand that?"

Ichabod did not appreciate his tone of voice.

"You're just making things harder on yourself." Lieutenant Bloom felt somehow stronger. He could also feel the growing presence of others around them. He wasn't completely sure but he'd swear that the tactical teams were already setting up outside.

But at this moment, Ichabod was oblivious to the outside world. The arrogance. "Harder? Yes. Like lead. As hard as that, I guess. Yes, I know how hard things are. Look at me. Don't you think I know how hard everything is?" He paced again. But this time he, too, felt the energy gathering outside.

He slowly walked to the window and carefully peeked out. He could see that his street was barricaded at both ends by patrol cars and scattered along the street were a bevy of other obviously official, but unmarked vehicles. At a closer glance he could see the shadows of people. A steady dance of movement and the murmurs filtered through the shroud of midmorning.

Ichabod came back to Bloom. "You're going to have to tell them to stay the hell out of here."

"Listen, Mr. Word . . ."

"No, Lieutenant, you have to listen to me. I've got the guns. Yours and mine. Or are you going to try to overwhelm me with your physical prowess and your stolen knowledge of ancient Asian arts? I thought you didn't want to be a hero. But you do, don't you? It's in your blood. You bleed hero blue don't you?"

As Ichabod talked he slowly moved around his captive, much as a cat would that had captured a moth but wasn't ready to kill it. Ichabod swatted at the man with words as the cat would its paw, intending to draw out the anxiety, the uncertain certainty.

At first, when Ichabod was easily within his vision, the lieutenant had tried to follow Ichabod's movement. But, as Ichabod passed out of sight, behind him, he abandoned it. Instead, he lowered his head and tried to appear unconcerned.

Ichabod continued, "You know what, Lieutenant? I don't think you're brave enough to really be a hero. No. I don't think so. Can I tell you a secret? Something you know I know but would never admit in public? I don't think there are actually that many white men who are that brave. I mean individual white men. Regular white men who without a crowd of other white men, would challenge another man with two guns. I mean John Wayne, Sylvester Stallone, Jean-Claude Van Damme, and probably five or six other motherfuckas would probably kick the shit out of me. Probably would have already squashed my ass. You know? But you? I don't think so. Then again, it's also true that most of our contemporary heroes are media creations. Men who really can't fight but look like they can. Killers who look like lovers. Women with plastic just beneath their skin. It's so much bullshit, isn't it? And yet there are people who make the mistake of believing that they are heroic in the grand tradition of Sean Connery when they probably couldn't beat Madonna in an arm wrestle."

He swung around in front of the detective once again. "So when I put the telephone to your mouth again, I want you to tell them to stay back while we deliberate the next phase of this discussion."

Lieutenant Bloom was caught off guard by Ichabod's continued insolence. He had expected that as time passed and the presence of the police outside became known, Ichabod would fall apart. But so far, he had been surprised by Ichabod's strength. He seemed enraptured by a spirit.

The detective masked his considerations and instead asked blankly, "What discussion?"

And this pissed Ichabod off. "Naw, now, Lieutenant. You can't just ignore all of the eloquent meaning, not to mention beauty, of all I've been saying to you. I think that's one of the primary problems we're facing here. White America, mainly you, only listens to part of what I'm saying. Don't you think it's a little odd that after all I've said, the whole thing about power and struggle and especially having these two heavy-ass guns in my possession, that you would focus on the definition of our little tête-à-tête?"

Ichabod stormed over to the dining room table and sat down. He stared at the shrouded body. "I don't give a fuck if you agree or don't agree that we are in a discussion. The point is, I'm going to blow your motherfucking head off if you don't tell them to stay out of my house and off my property. Do you understand that?"

Bloom was not prepared for the outburst. Nor the threat. It was really the first time since the initial abduction that Ichabod had directly threatened him. "Okay, all right. Don't get excited. I'll tell them. Cut me loose so I can get my people on the phone and I'll tell them to pull back a little. Give you a little time. That's what you want, isn't it? A little time?"

Ichabod again felt the patronizing edge of the policeman's words. "It's bizarre how people who are used to having power fail to realize the times when they don't. When someone else is holding the gun on them. Lieutenant Bloom, I'm not asking you to give me anything. And I'm not cutting you loose."

"Then how am I supposed to communicate with them?"

The tone of superiority in Bloom's voice agitated Ichabod. Throughout his life he'd become accustomed to feeling that way when he interacted with white men, so he let it go. In fact, Ichabod now found himself thinking about television and the fact that there were probably news crews out there, waiting for them to leave the house. Waiting for Ichabod to be blown away or Bloom's body to be removed. Or both. Good thing he'd unplugged nearly all of the electronics in his house. No music. No television. Nothing to distract.

"Lieutenant?"

"Yes, Ichabod."

"Can I tell you something?"

"Ichabod, you've been talking since I came in here. I can't stop you. Please . . . be my guest."

"I didn't want to become famous this way. I am a writer. One of the ink-on-paper guys Vonnegut talks about. A literary artist. I believe in the power of the pen. Writin is fightin, as Ishmael Reed says. But with the sugar of Maugham or Lawrence. I'm a part of that gang. We may not be able to affect things while they're happening. But we can make a big fuss in books so people of the future will know exactly how powerless we felt."

The lieutenant had only understood part of what Ichabod had said.

"What I'm going to do, Lieutenant, is pick up your telephone and bring it over here. And then you're going to talk to whoever is out there you need to talk to. Okay?"

Bloom was in pain. His legs hurt. His arms hurt. His back. He was constantly trying to make little adjustments in the way his body was situated in an effort to relieve, however slightly, his intense discomfort. And, of course, there was the never ending struggle to retrieve the only weapon he still possessed. It just seemed improbable that he'd ever get it. He closed his eyes and leaned back.

Ichabod grew impatient. It seemed to him that Bloom was ignoring him. "Lieutenant? Lieutenant?"

He slowly opened his eyes. "Yes, Ichabod?"

"Will you talk to them?"

"You know what, Ichabod?"

Ichabod couldn't help but let out a big sigh which Lieutenant Bloom heard. "What, Lieutenant?"

"I will talk to them. If that will make you happy. But I want to appeal to you right now—before this goes any farther—to just cut me loose, give me your gun, and let's just walk out of here." His face softened. No lines of stress or anxiousness were visible. "What exactly do you want me to say to them?"

"You were right the first time, Lieutenant. I'm not asking for helicopters and money or anything like that. I simply want the opportunity for us to sit here and talk. For me to tell you about myself and those who were here last night. About the struggle and the end of Dewitt's life. I want to do that without all the eruptions of violence that I know are yet to come. I speak not only for myself but also for those who left me here as their unofficial emissary." Ichabod paused. He felt a flourish of fear rip through his body without warning.

Ichabod realized how lucky he was that the detective could not know exactly how frightened he really was. True, there were distinct moments when he had absolutely no fear. When he could wave the gun in Bloom's face without the slightest thought of anything that might threaten. But then, within seconds, Ichabod would have to fight the urge to surrender. To hold forth his hands so that they might be bound together just as he had done to him. There were times when he wanted to drop to his knees and beg Bloom's forgiveness.

"What I want is for you to tell them to give us some

time in here before they start acting crazy out there. That's what I want."

"And if they agree, you'll walk out of here with me?"

"That's the deal, Lieutenant." Ichabod's spirits rose a little. Bloom's voice seemed upbeat and promising. But Ichabod now began to feel his power over the detective slowly lessening. He walked across the room and retrieved the cell phone, returned to the detective and restored power to the unit. Instantly, it rang out in a jarring tremolo, a sudden scream from the outside world. Ichabod caught the gaze of Bloom and held it. "I'm going to answer it."

"I think that's wise, Ichabod."

"You just tell them to back off right now. You got that?" He pointed the gun at him again. "Just tell them. I'm not joking."

Ichabod opened the line. "Yes?"

Captain Hirsh's voice was right there. "Ichabod? Ichabod Word. Is that you?"

"Yes." He'd guessed that they would know everything there was to know about him very quickly. He'd been right.

"Is Lieutenant Bloom okay?" Captain Iris Hirsh tried to sound calm, emotionless.

"He's fine. Would you like to talk to him?" Ichabod put the telephone to the cop's ear and smiled at him.

"Captain? Yes." Ichabod nudged him with the gun. It was an instinct derived most likely from watching too much television.

Bloom ignored him. "I'm fine, Captain. He's got me taped to a chair here, so I'm hurting a little, but basically I'm okay. I think we'll be able to work with Ichabod here. Yes, I really do think we can get out of this situation without anyone else being hurt. Yes, I realize what it looks like. But I think I can handle this. I really believe we can get out of this."

Ichabod listened intently. He was somewhat surprised at how smoothly everything was proceeding. It was a mark of the arrogance of the police that they could conduct their deliberations with such disregard for him.

"Don't worry. I'm going to be fine. Just back off a little. Set up down the street a ways. Give us some space." He looked up and smiled at Ichabod. If he could have, Bloom would have given Ichabod a thumbs up.

"That's right, Captain. Thanks. Everything's going to be fine." Again he twisted his eyes in Ichabod's direction, "That's right, isn't it? Everything's going to be fine?"

"Yes," Ichabod said a little too quickly.

And then he was back on the telephone, "Don't worry. This will be over in no time."

That statement dripped with double meanings. Bloom nodded and Ichabod pressed the phone tighter to his face. "Fine," the lieutenant said to the captain, "I'll keep you posted. Don't worry."

Ichabod was suddenly aware that his knees were literally shaking. He was nearly overwhelmed with relief. He removed the telephone from Bloom's ear, put it down, and placed the gun back on the dining room table.

He then sat down again across from the detective and said quietly, "Thank you, Lieutenant. I mean I knew that moment would happen. That moment when I might not have been able to keep the stage. Everything always comes down to moments. Your decision to cooperate. My decision to actually do this. A series of moments and the decisions we make within them."

For the first time Bill Bloom could feel the fear that was welling inside Ichabod. He noticed the increasing moisture on the black man's skin. Ichabod's body had a voice. It whispered to the detective whenever he was close by. It was full throated. Sweet and pungent. And as the tension grew,

Ichabod's body spoke louder and louder. Bloom knew it was fear. Ichabod was beginning to understand the force that was there to bring him down.

And the lieutenant could smell it and see it in the way Ichabod sat in front of him. A little of the swagger had dissipated.

"What do you want from me, Ichabod?" the policeman asked.

For Ichabod that was indeed an important question. A tremendous challenge lay ahead of him and Lieutenant Bloom would be an integral part of his future. They were now bound together. In that house. Instinctively he snapped at the cop, "Don't call me that."

Bloom studied Ichabod's face quizzically. "I thought that was your name."

"It is. But I hate it. My friends call me Icky. Call me that."

Lieutenant Bloom was silent for a bit and then he said, "Okay. I'll call you Icky if that's what you want. But I want you to cut me loose. This is very uncomfortable for me. I've done what you've asked me to do. Now, you can do something for me."

Ichabod stood up and began to pace again. He had decided not to answer Bloom's last question. He didn't think he could afford to cut the detective free. He didn't think he could tell the story and worry about keeping watch over Bloom at the same time.

Lieutenant Bloom had waited for Ichabod to respond. He realized after a while that Ichabod wasn't going to answer him. "Ichabod, ah . . . Icky . . . ah, what is happening here? We've got a dead body. A gun. A hostage. The police all over the place."

But Ichabod would have none of it. He snapped back at Bloom, "I know at least as much about what's going on here as you do. And isn't that the way it almost always is? You guys come barreling into situations that you haven't the slightest idea of what's happening. You come with your guns drawn and your faces fixed and you see some spics or niggers or gooks arguing—or just clustered together for warmth—and you start barking like fucking dogs. 'Get over there . . . hands over your head . . . up against the car . . .' You know, shit like that."

Bloom narrowed his ocean blues at him. "You know, Icky, you're starting to annoy me. If there weren't someone dead here I'd think this was some sort of Halloween prank."

Ichabod leaned his backside against the table's edge. "I'd almost forgotten. Halloween. Halloween used to be a special day for a black boy like me. I got to put on a mask and go to white people's front doors demanding food and they gave it to me. They weren't nervous or scared or anything. In fact, they'd say stuff like, 'My, aren't you a cute young man.' Yeah, those were the days. On Halloween a black man could be a monster and still get paid."

The lieutenant didn't seem all that interested in Ichabod's reverie. "Listen Icky . . . why don't you give me the gun."

"What happened to Halloween, Lieutenant? I mean young black boys now can't do that, can they? They'd probably be shot for banging on a white person's door nowadays."

Bloom had decided to engage Ichabod in conversation, hoping to convince him that he could be trusted and the tape could be removed. "Times changed. Listen, Icky, how long is this going to go on?"

The lieutenant had spent all morning listening to Ichabod talk and still he felt that he had no idea of who the man was. He didn't understand what Ichabod was talking about half the time, and he definitely had no better idea of who had committed the murder, or why. He did know that it was evident that Ichabod was willing to risk his life on this approach. That, in and of itself, was quite compelling. He also knew that Ichabod carried a chest full of anger.

"How long is this going to go on?" Lieutenant Bloom repeated himself.

"What?"

"This! I don't know if you're tracking here with me but you are in a lot of trouble. There's a dead man here among other things. By the way, you might want to retie that bag if we're going to be stuck here for awhile. Or drag it into a different room."

Although tired, Ichabod agreed with the lieutenant. "All right. I'll reseal it." Ichabod muttered as he tugged the bag and tried to seal it closed again. "The dumb sonofabitch should have known better." Afterward, Ichabod again loomed over Bloom, "Anything else, Lieutenant? Can I do anything else for you?"

"You can cut this goddamned tape; give me your gun and then we can sit down and talk." The detective sensed that Ichabod was weakening, so he continued, "You need to talk to me. I'm the only one who can save you now."

"Save me? Save me from what? I've done nothing." Ichabod almost smiled when he said it.

But Lieutenant Bloom tried to maintain his increasing power over Ichabod. He simply nodded in the direction of the dead man.

Ichabod got the message. "That? I didn't do that. You can't pin that on me. Just because I'm the only one here and just because I have the gun does not mean I killed that man."

"Icky, can I talk to you? Can I really level with you?"

"Lieutenant, this is one of those really special moments in my life when I have equality. This." Ichabod held the gun up in the air again. "This makes me equal to you. Maybe even better. I mean, people talk about violence and guns and all that but I'm really kind of surprised here. You have to listen to me."

And then Ichabod saw it: in a heartbeat Lieutenant Bloom changed. He had been so compliant. So conciliatory. Suddenly now his whole countenance changed.

"I don't have to listen to shit, you stupid asshole. Are you crazy or what? You think you have power? Equality? You don't have shit. There are probably fifty police out there by now, probably the SWAT team. And let me tell you, Icky, they hope like hell you shoot me or something because they don't get to open fire on a live target that often and no matter what any of them tells you, in each of them there's the heart of an assassin. They would love to bag your ass. And if you're not careful, they will. If you kill me it'll only be a wisp of pleasure in your body before they shred your black ass. Power. Don't fool yourself, my friend. You're as good as dead."

It was like a bucket of cold water. An electric shock. A bee sting. Bloom's voice brought a wave of dread that washed over Ichabod. He swallowed a gasp. What had he gotten himself into?

"Okay, okay . . . I mean . . . Look, I didn't kill this man. I'll tell you everything. I don't know why I've been acting like this. I really want you to trust me. To understand that I don't really mean you any harm. I mean, I'm a fucking writer. I didn't begin this whole scene with the intent of dying, although I realize that's a possibility. I just want you to know that I'm not normally the kind of guy who'd pull a gun on a police officer. I don't have a death wish. I mean, actually, I have a lot to live for. Especially now. There is so much at stake for us."

"Who is he?"

"His name is Dewitt McMichael. He works for the Shrubbery Foundation."

"Who killed him?"

"I'm not sure. Really. Lieutenant. Listen: I'll give your gun back. I'll untie you and surrender. But I have so much to tell you. You've got to see the entire picture before we walk out of here."

Bloom stared at him. "The way this is going, Icky, *we* are not going to walk out of here."

"Artists have to present the truth. We have to. We have to say what we think is true about our own lives."

"No more lectures, Icky, okay?"

Ichabod felt the sting of tears behind his eyes. "How can I talk to you without lecturing? You don't understand the pressure I live under. What choice do I have but to lecture you? You just keep interacting with me in the same old tired way."

"I don't hear lectures, Icky."

"And you don't care, really, that that makes me angry, do you?"

"I don't really care about you, Icky. I mean, don't get me wrong here. I don't feel *anything* about you."

"But that's not true, Lieutenant, and you know it. Are you trying to say that you'd treat me the same way—if I didn't have this gun? You'd be soft and diplomatic? You'd want to know where I grew up? What schools I'd attended? Listen to what I had to say?

"Icky, are you going to give me the gun?"

"Yes. But, please, before we do that, can I just tell you what happened?"

this all started about two years ago when Dewitt walked into the monthly Shrubbery Foundation board meeting determined to convince his board of directors that it was time for a change in direction. He'd been the vice president of the foundation's Art of the People Program (also known as the App) for the past four years. I knew Dewitt pretty well from hanging out with him at parties and art functions. He was like an honorary uncle to the multicultis and the bohos. All roads to the money went through him, so if you were an artist you cultivated him.

And, for the most part, Dewitt was well liked. He had a sharp, quick tongue, an eye for the phony, and a grand sense of drama. Dewitt really thought he was at the center of whatever artistic movement was going on at the time. And there was, indeed, a movement: All of the colors and cultures of the Twin Cities were trying to define an aesthetic. Maybe we're stupid and it can't be done. Maybe the western thing will always be it. You can't help but wonder when so many people of color uphold the artistic and cultural values of the people who oppressed them.

Anyway, Dewitt fancied himself a part of our little crew. And we liked him thinking that. Of course, we argued about it all the time. How close should the artist be to the source of the money? How close? But Dewitt was also a gifted benefactor.

He'd funded programs and events that had actually been the subject of *60 Minutes* and *20/20*. Not of course for their overwhelming political or artistic significance. Although it must be said that much of the stuff he'd funded had a powerful impact on the public consciousness of the Twin Cities. Dewitt's first desire was to challenge, to disturb. He believed that that was the essential purpose of art.

He'd studied long enough at Columbia to earn a master's degree in art history but he had devoted his entire professional career to discovering artists, mostly performance artists who were doing everything they could to "disturb" American audiences.

Dewitt had provided moral and financial support for shows, exhibitions, and performances of explicit sexuality, of mutilation, of angst-filled diatribe, of racial animus, of anything and everything that would shock the Midwestern audiences of the Twin Cities.

One work in particular had attracted national attention, becoming the target of a band of would-be censors. It was an "installation" art piece by a man named H.A. Long. H.A.'s work always involved dead animals, film, naked bodies, and blood. H.A. was a mess, his mind was a cesspool, but for some strange reason people with money and influence were coming to his shows. Which meant, of course, that Dewitt was interested in him.

Dewitt had found him in a small studio space in the Chelsea section of Manhattan on one of his regular trips to New York, to look for art and performances that would make hardworking Minnesotans blanch. Naturally the peo-

ple in New York knew what he was there for so they'd line
up the weirdos when they knew Dewitt was in town. Usually some jobless wanna-be curator would meet him at La
Guardia Airport and take him to a series of undiscovered
artists that teetered on the verge of notoriety.

On one such trip, Dewitt was led to a mammoth loft
space. The visit had been planned well by H.A. When Dewitt walked into the space he immediately felt faint. All
around him were dead chickens, freshly killed, and sus-
pended by the tips of their feet upside down throughout
the large loft space. Blood dripped from the carcasses, splat-
tering on a white plastic-covered floor. The floor itself doubled as a screen for a Tarantino film which was projected
down on it. At first he thought it was *Reservoir Dogs;* then
he thought it was *Pulp Fiction;* and then he realized maybe
it was *Jackie Brown.*

The air was stifling. And then, at the opposite end of
the loft, walking toward him were five naked women. Blood
pattered over them like rain. Sitting in a corner with a rain-
coat on and a smirk on his emaciated but still delicate face
was H.A. Dewitt suspected that H.A. was naked underneath
the coat. He turned around and quickly stepped out of the
space. He heaved right there in the hall. Everything he'd
eaten since the previous night's dinner, including the North-
west Airlines breakfast of a ham and cheese omelet, came
flying up and added to the totality and the artistry of the
moment.

When he recovered he signed H.A. to a massive contract
to construct his installation at Minneapolis's John J. Whip-
persnapper Arts Domain or the J-WAD, as it was affectionately
known in the arts community. A week before the installation
opened, the local press went wild, publishing reports that H.A.
had ties to some chicken blood-worshipping cult. That caused
a stir. But when the reports of the bloodsoaked naked

women started to come out, the sleepy cosmopolitan Twin Towns erupted in an uproar. It was only a matter of time before the press figured out that even though H.A.'s installation was primarily funded by the Shrubbery Foundation's private money, it had also received support from the National Endowment for the Arts.

This led to further outrage and renewed calls to end the use of government funding for arts programs. Over the next year and a half Congress drastically slashed the arts agency's budget, which in turn squeezed the artists and local arts groups that depended on government funding. What's more, sensing a changing public attitude about arts funding, even the private funders, including Dewitt's own Shrubbery Foundation, suddenly began to ask more questions and to offer less money.

Unfortunately, the people who suffered first and most, who were now literally shut out of the funding game, were the artists of color. Dewitt would readily confess that a visit by a coalition of artists made him aware of the issue. I had been among that delegation.

Our argument was simple and direct. We felt that Dewitt's reckless financial support for what some called offensive art had polluted the funding atmosphere. Dewitt had expected the reactionary backlash he received from many white artists, but he never once thought that the artists he most wanted to support would be penalized for it. After our case had been made, Dewitt agreed with us. He said that he could see how we, the group of artists who were really on the fringe, culturally speaking, were being hurt by some of his groundbreaking artistic projects. We were the ones who were really about upsetting the status quo.

It was almost a revelation for Dewitt when he realized this. He'd spent so much time focused on issues of sexuality. Supporting artists who purposely challenged the tolerance level of the Twin Cities community and by extension the country. He stood against all things that had been done before. Against all forms of the status quo. He supported any artist who took sexual chances. Any artists who were willing to take their clothes off in public. Anyone who made people turn away, made them sweat, Dewitt had considered a worthy grant recipient.

He also had to admit that until recently he really hadn't been particularly interested in art by people of color. Why? Well, it just never seemed that significant. He liked us. He liked what we were doing. Rather, he liked the idea that we were doing it. But he had never really considered our work in the same way that he did the work of people he thought were important. Of course all of those people were white. Now, however, it was clear where his priorities needed to be. So Dewitt decided to put the strong-arm on his board to do something no one ever would have anticipated.

That realization led Dewitt to stand before his board nearly two years ago and challenge them to create an ambitious and groundbreaking program.

"Why," he said, "would you be so content to follow along in the shadow of every other foundation? We give money and it blends into the fabric of this community and it becomes harder and harder to identify what we've actually done. I don't know about you but I want to make a difference and I want the world to know it was us who did it."

The fifteen people who sat around the long conference room table stared at him. Nobody moved. Dewitt wasn't sure at first how to take such rapt attention. But he was good at picking up the sparkle of an ignited interest in a person's eye. And he saw it in the eyes of Sheila Best, a middle manager from a local computer company. He saw it in Early Shaw, an attorney. He saw it and he knew instantly that by appealing to their need to feel distinguished and recognized, they would consider his request.

"I would like you to authorize me to make a one-time grant of $500,000 to one artist in the Twin Cities. Perhaps it could be to an artist of color."

He hit them hard with his line. And they bit hard. He walked out of there knowing he was the straight-up Minnesota Kingmaker. And, unfortunately, that was the way Dewitt dealt with it. He realized how much power he held. But he was not impervious to the nefarious power that was inherent in the decision. He could play us like musical instruments. Manipulate us. Tease us. Any one who offers money to artists and writers and such people engages in this game. The more money available, the bigger the dance people will do for it.

At a preliminary meeting in his office, Dewitt gathered together as wide a range of cultural representatives as possible. His first list had thirty-five names on it but he realized quickly that he would never be able to carefully consider so many candidates. He just as quickly decided that there really weren't thirty-five artists of color in the Twin Cities who he thought should legitimately be considered for such a rich prize. So, even at the first meeting, the total number of artists under consideration was only seven. And the sad truth was that by the time Dewitt called us together, he was already having serious doubts about the whole idea.

I watched him sit back in his chair and say, "I could have invited any number of people to this meeting. But I chose you. Each of you represents something I value greatly in our cultural landscape." And each of us felt special. Chosen. Nobody at that point could have foreseen how this opportunity could turn against us. How it might actually end in such tragedy.

At the first meeting there were seven people sitting

around the conference room table who were eligible for the
half-million-dollar grant. It eased Dewitt's growing anxiety
to limit the number. There was me, the aging fledgling, Ichabod Word, novelist, and token black man, of course.

There was, representing the original Americans, the Native Americans, hailing from just outside TooLong Lake
Minnesota, Herm Strong. Rarely acknowledged outside the
misappropriating hands of rich white museums, Herm was
a sculptor of growing renown. His work was increasingly
being singled out as the definitive Native statement of the
nineties.

Dewitt also selected Marci Gone to serve the function of
African American woman. Marci came to Minnesota from
Atlanta, Georgia, and was, as was earlier discussed, drilled
in the expectations of her people and her place in that struggle. She was also a gifted painter.

At Asian American, he chose a poet who has made more
than one person cry in public just by being there, Jennifer
Grimm. Jenny was a soft voice, a penetrating eye, and the
manifestation of command when it came to language. And
most important, Jenny was not ambivalent about being a
woman of color. I didn't know that much about her private
life until last night, but it was clear that her desire did not
lie in whiteness. This alone would have been enough to
create a bond between us.

There was April Tryin who confounded nearly everyone
as to how she even qualified. April, as was also mentioned
earlier, was white. So her presence here was quite upsetting,
particularly for Marci. But you had to give April her props.
She might have been white but she was also a wildly cre-
ative, indeed powerful aberration of culture and energy, a
jazz musician who was known to have made even black
people swoon. She'd even appeared live on a BET jazz set.

There were two other artists there as well. One of them

was Jesus and the other Brother JuJu. I knew both men fairly well and was actually happy to see that Dewitt had been savvy enough to recognize Brother JuJu's talent as a poet. Jesus, on the other hand, I thought was rather weak in his chosen field of dance.

I'd seen Jesus perform numerous times and at first his movements and style were quite stunning, but after a few performances I realized he didn't have anything else in the bag. What you saw was what you got. No matter what the topic of the performance was. No matter what the music was. He choreographed it the same damn way. The first time I saw Jesus dance I was floored by his willingness to incorporate Latin style, salsa, rhumba, and cha-cha into what was otherwise a fairly classical modern sensibility. But he never grew from that. It was always the same little movements that invaded whatever else he tried to do. It got boring and, thusly, at least to me, diminished his significance as an artist.

Still, I must say that I had a renewed sense of respect for Dewitt. He had made a reasonable attempt at full cultural representation.

When the letter first arrived, I was surprised. It didn't seem like most of the other mail sent to artists of color, inviting us to some meeting the purpose of which is usually to discuss the fact that we are artists of color and what on earth can be done about it? Invariably you find yourself at a long wooden table with ten or twelve other people talking incessantly and inconsequentially about how to attract more people of color to some reading or play or exhibit by someone who has no real idea anymore of what it means to be a citified person of color because they've been living in Coon Rapids for the past ten years. Coon Rapids. There are black people living in a city named Coon Rapids in Minnesota. I guess that's not as bad as suffering through four years as a student of Cretin High School. Yes, it's a state with a high school named for a word that means fool. I guess that's at least accuracy in advertising.

I discard many invitations to panels, conferences, and committees, as I've said. Being a writer means actually doing it. Writing. Not meeting with people. Particularly people for whom meetings are their work. And I don't apply to a lot of grants and fellowships. I can't take the pressure of waiting and I most especially don't suffer the inevitable challenge to my own self-confidence well. It is the seed of my discontent. I languish in a white world that really has to be nudged to look sweetly upon my face. I feel those glances askance. Quizzical. Fearful. Rageful.

But Dewitt was skillful in his approach and was bound to net us in his little game. The letter I received begged me to open it. After closer inspection, I realized that it wasn't some inconsequential piece of postal litter that dominates our mail boxes these days. Coupons that alert us to missing children. Discount pizzas. Workfare-priced furniture. It came in an envelope normally associated with a check. One of those envelopes with a window, so that when you pick it up your breath seizes. The kind of an envelope your job would send your last paycheck in. Or your severance. A tax refund. That kind of envelope. It whispers, "I got some money for ya. Right here. Open this bad boy up rat now. Do not delay." You know what I'm saying? That kind of letter.

And even after I ripped the envelope open, he had typed this note on a long (shockingly similar to a check) card. I still have it. Listen to this:

Dear Ichabod E. Word:

As you know I am a great admirer of your work. I have read and thoroughly enjoyed the short stories you've

*published in various local and regional literary magazines.
I know that you remain frustrated as a published novelist.
I realize the difficulties you're probably facing in this re-
gard. I know also that your time is very precious to you
and I don't want to waste any of it. So I will come to
the point.*

*I have selected a short list of people who will be eligi-
ble for the Twin Cities Genius Grant to be given by the
Minnesota Shrubbery Foundation of which I am thrilled
to announce that you are one. I would like to invite you
to a preliminary meeting on September 10, 2 PM to provide you with all the necessary details. If this time is
acceptable please RSVP in the next day or so. Thank you.*

Sincerely,
Dewitt McMichaels

I could not ignore the implications. I didn't know what
to do. Who to call for aid and comfort. At this point I'd
only heard the rumors that were circulating about this huge,
new Shrubbery grant program. Everyone that I thought of
calling was probably also under consideration. And, you
don't want to call someone who's not being considered, all
hyped about some money they definitely can't get. People
don't like that shit at all. The thing is, I never win these
types of competitions. There's something about me, I suppose. Not every writer would hold a gun on a cop, eh?

Well, there has to be an answer to constantly being
ignored.

Anyway, I just closed my eyes and said a little prayer
to the money God. Don't look at me that way. I can feel
your disdain. The honorable artist should never engage in
this rush for the buck. That's what you're thinking. I can
see it all in your face. Well, fuck you. You've got a god-

damned uniform on. I don't have that. Well, my skin color—but that uniform is the one of the enemy, isn't it? Yes, I want to be paid. I'm tired of seeing all these mediocre white people make tons of money and win goo gobs of special prizes and living testaments to their genius when I can't get my funky little murder novel published. And don't think that just because I write about murder and know a whole hell of a lot about how to do it that I had anything more than an indirect role in Dewitt's death. So don't even play with that.

I want to be discovered one day. I admit it. And I want to be rich one day. I admit that, too. I immediately got on the telephone and called Dewitt. He was so nice to me that day. A soothing, gentle, almost fatherly voice eased through the telephone receiver. It surrounded me like a pillowcase that slips gently over its lover.

"Icky." He said, "I was so much hoping you'd call. I wasn't sure. Your reputation is so . . . ah . . ." I remember feeling his discomfort. He'd talked himself into a small corner of a room where he hadn't intended to go. Dewitt was a nice enough guy but he couldn't resist the opportunity to define you. And if you let him do that he would always talk to you as if you were a child. Always evaluating. You had to learn to overlook it, which most of us did.

I was about to rescue him when he found the thread he'd lost, "Your reputation is almost intimidating in the way you have refused to sit on boards and committees. And of course I know you've never won a major grant. So I just wasn't sure whether you would go through this process."

I was impressed. He did know me pretty well. All of my concerns he addressed as a package.

He continued, "But I decided that the payoff of this grant was large enough to take that chance."

"How much is the grant, Dewitt? I was kind of surprised that it wasn't mentioned in the invitation."

"I did it that way for a reason, Icky. I'm not announcing the amount until the September 10 meeting. I know it's not normal but this grant program is going to break a lot of rules. In the end, I'm hoping all of the unorthodox things and rule breaking I'm going to do with this grant will make it especially valuable and noteworthy. You should also know that there aren't that many people left in contention."

I was silent, but my body was already commencing the fifth alarm. My heart was racing. I felt palpitations. Trembles.

He was talking to me. Me. He wanted me to come and sit at his feet and stroke the soft fur of his cat or dog or something in the tradition of any great patron, and then he was bound to bestow upon me the salvation I craved. True, I didn't know how much money we were talking about at the time, but I knew it had to be substantial. He was being way too mysterious for it to be another $7,500 grant. That's just enough money to fool artists into thinking they can make a living from their artistic endeavors.

I was stunned. "I'm very happy . . ." I knew I was stammering. My body wouldn't be still. I was pacing. "I can't help but feel honored that you'd choose me as a candidate."

"You'll get to know all you need to know at the meeting."

I hung up the telephone twenty pounds lighter. Just the potential that my financial problems would be solved lightened my load dramatically. Hope is an amazing drug. It holds us in its grip so completely. I can live off hope; it's better than love that way. You can sleep peacefully when your heart and mind are full of hope.

For a week and a half I puttered in this apartment waiting for that damned meeting. I mourned the end of summer. And you know as well as I that summer is all too much of an hallucination here. Don't let nobody pinch you. You wake up and it's snowing.

I also had to begin thinking about the start of school. Mupster University would begin in the middle of September and I had to have my classes planned and syllabi prepared. But no matter what I tried to do all I could think about was how much money Dewitt had to give away and how he would do it. As I said, I talked to no one. Which, for me, isn't that unusual. But I was conscious of this silence. I didn't want to talk with anyone and be prevented from expressing my hope that my future would be safely nurtured and guarded by the Shrubbery.

I have been unattached for the last five years. I don't even date that much. I'm pretty pathetic that way. Such a handsome and flirtatious man as I am. People must think I'm fucking all the time. I will flirt with you. But I don't have time to develop good relationships. And I hate bad ones. Anyway, I had no one to talk to. Feel sorry for me?

"No Icky," the lieutenant said, "I'm just trying to fulfill my promise here so we can get on with this."

"You're not making this very easy. It would be a better story if you actually wanted to hear it."

"I do want to hear it. There's no question about that. But I'm very uncomfortable sitting here like this and you are completely incapable of coming to the point."

"But Lieutenant Bloom. I've been trying to set the situation up so that you could understand the whats and the whys of our predicament here. All I have are the points of this story. You can't actually relive my whole life nor the lives of everyone that was here."

"Okay, Icky. I said, okay. Will you just get on with it?"

Finally that day arrived. I remember going to my closet that morning and surveying my wardrobe. Who knew what was important? What would Dewitt be impressed by? And what of the others? At the time I didn't know who was invited. I wanted to be noticed but I didn't want to make whoever else was there think that I was trying to show off. The persona of a starving artist can be so complicated.

The Shrubbery Foundation offices are in a smoked-glass building out on a suburban strip. The drive there was a blur of brown grass and Saabs. You don't have to travel far from the nearest lake to understand Minnesota. Corn stalks. Smoked glass. Brown grass. And Saabs. Don't let me get started about the Minnesota climate and the way people deal with it. But keep in mind that it will be hard to tell you this story which takes place here in this white chunk of frost without revisiting this topic.

Anyway, I arrived as close to on time as a black man is allowed and was shown into the conference room by a man who I quickly assessed was gay. He only smiled and gestured. He never said a word. I just sensed it. Okay, I was working off of an old stupid stereotype. I can't believe how ridiculously easy it is to marginalize people. All you need is a desire to feel superior.

I sat down, the eighth person at the table. Joining Dewitt were Herm, April, Marci, Jesus, Brother JuJu, Jenny, and me. We were so beautiful there together. From black to yellow. All brown. Even April with her blond Irish features found her browness among us. Even Dewitt with his pasty white skin found a context within the brown for himself. We just made everything brown. Wherever we were. We made it brown.

Again I thought about how hard Dewitt worked at trying to get it right. It must have been an awkward and uncomfortable task. He had to take one from column A and one from column B and so forth. The food groups. Any program that involved all of the food groups was eminently fundable. Black. Asian American. Hispanic. Native American. If you added gay, lesbian, transgendered, and bisexual, you hit the proverbial jackpot.

Dewitt opened the meeting by saying, "I thank all of you for coming. I want to say a few words and then I'd like to hear each of you introduce yourselves after which I'll finish up. We shouldn't be here too long. I just wanted you all to get together."

I looked around the room. Brother JuJu smiled and nodded at me. Marci was whispering to Jenny. I was surprised that they seemed so buddy-buddy. Jenny was not known to befriend many people. Indeed, Jenny was just this side of communicative.

As was his habit, Herm sat staring at a wall. He was a large man. Not fat but thick. Strong. Like a tree. He wore a warrior's necklace of long beads. Like a white shield it nearly covered his entire chest. He always wore such adornments when he sat in meetings with white men. If you weren't observant you might think he was dumb. He spoke very carefully and softly at the same time. Looking at his body you'd expect this booming voice. But even after a couple of beers (when he drank; which he didn't often do) his voice never reached the register of someone like, say, Brother JuJu.

Brother JuJu brought the whole history of blackness into the room. He presented a more authentic picture of African Americans than either Marci or I did: Brother JuJu actually worked at a community center and conducted poetry workshops all up in the hood. Like I said, I respected him very much. White people need the presence of people like Brother JuJu to remind them that there is an unrelenting fierceness out there on the street corners. He was not the mediating type.

Truth be told, I benefit from the energy of people like Brother JuJu. It makes me a lot more acceptable. And even though Marci will get up in people's faces when she's agitated I think she's even more acceptable than I am. It's a dilemma: You know you can never be fully accepted by white people, but if you don't try you are virtually shut out of mainstream opportunities.

The pecking order of people of color is very significant. Who makes white people feel more comfortable; who makes them laugh; all of that makes a difference. And I swear, nobody ever acknowledges it, but I think that the more comfortable white people are with you the more successful you'll be.

I can see you surveying my apartment. I know it appears I'm successful. In the past five years, I've carefully appointed it in the way an artist would want to. I have a stylish, relatively new car. But let me emphasize that I don't consider myself successful. I've published a number of short stories, but I'm still trying to find a publisher for my first novel. How many living African American novelists can you name? Anyway, I have to hustle to make ends meet. So please temper any impressions you might have about my bougeois existence with the knowledge that I have no future security. I am really very vulnerable.

Anyway, Dewitt began his introduction. "First and foremost I want you to know that everyone here is, in my estimation, an amazing artist. Each of you has accomplished a lot in your lives and each of you deserves to be supported. But, unfortunately, that's not possible. The Shrubbery Foundation's Twin Cities Genius Grant will go to one of you. Actually, I should say that I'm going to narrow the final group of candidates down to five. So two of you won't be eligible."

Everyone stared at him. It was the first indication that the proposition had a cruel seed buried at its heart. I broke connection with Dewitt's gaunt face and studied the others.

Naturally the first person I turned to was Marci. She was always the bellwether. If I could detect disturbance in her face, I'd know that I wasn't overreacting and that there really was a problem with the way Dewitt was conceptualizing this program. And, sure enough, I could see Marci's eyes narrowing. Some people showed you the whites of their eyes when they were angry. Marci went the other way. She shuttered her lights like a country inn. At the height of her anger there would only be a sliver of white hot fire flowing from her eyes.

She was speaking before I could observe anyone else. "What are you saying, Dewitt?" she asked. "Please don't tell me that I drove way the hell out here to find out I'm not even eligible for this thing."

I could tell that this early objection caught Dewitt off-guard. He was already fumbling with his papers. He picked up a folder and flipped it open; closed it; sat back, and sighed audibly.

"I guess I should apologize for that. I didn't think it would be a problem." Dewitt now looked directly at Marci.

This time Marci's eyes were wide open—an indication that her anger had been replaced by disbelief.

"I hope this ain't no bullshit." Brother JuJu was literally rising out of his chair. It was on castors and creaked as he talked. "The sister is right on it. I ain't gonna be having no trippy-assed plantation massa pulling my chain like this." Brother JuJu was without a doubt one of the most handsome men I knew. He was about six feet tall, thin, with a full head of loosely dreaded hair. In fact, his hair hung more in naturally tight ringed coils than dreadlocks. Having joined the army of black men who shaved their heads largely to camouflage male pattern baldness and gray hair, I must confess that I always envied him. It wasn't a big deal. I just liked the idea of having a choice. At thirty he was five years

younger than I and altogether an intimidating force. I main-
tained a kind of superiority over him based simply on the
fact that I aspired to write the great American novel and he
seemed not to want more than to be known in the community as a guerrilla poet.

Dewitt smiled at Brother JuJu. "Will you guys let me
finish? I realize now that it's a little stressful, but here it is:
Five of you will be eligible for this grant. But this is no
ordinary grant. This is the mother of all grants. This grant
will secure one of you from now to the grave and beyond."

Again you could just feel all of us sitting back in our
seats. Suddenly nobody cared about who was or wasn't eligible. Marci appeared almost as if someone had slipped her
a Mickey. Her eyes were off duty. She was seeing out of
them but I could no longer read them. She passed out of
reality. We all did. It was probably just the dollar signs. The
room was full of dollar signs. They were coming out of the
vents. Underneath the door.

"We're going to make a one-time-only grant to one artist
for the sum of $500,000." With that said, Dewitt now relaxed
in his chair. He considered us. Before that moment he was
the center of attention. It was an environment in which our
suspicions of him governed the atmosphere. Now the tables
had turned. Now we were the objects of concern.

"Do you mean a half-million dollars?" April, the quintes-
sential Minnesotan, tall, pretty, controlled, routinely friendly,
asked with complete disbelief.

"Yes" was all that Dewitt said.

April returned to her silence. Herm stared at a winter
scene print that hung on the wall. He sat opposite me, so
whenever I looked in his direction I'd think, at first, that he
was looking at me but quickly realize that there was something over my shoulder which held his attention. And then
Jenny, whose voice was never more than a whisper unless

she was completely drunk, began talking. She sat on my side of the table and to my left. I was sure I heard her speak but it always took a minute to attenuate your ears to her voice.

And then, suddenly it was in the air, ". . . Can't you tell us how this came to be and what it's supposed to accomplish?"

Dewitt leaned forward in his chair. He was still wearing a white linen suit, even though it was two days after Labor Day. What's more, it was clean. He appeared excited, anxious to encourage our sense of specialness. He was about five feet nine inches tall. A slim, taut package. The blond hair on his head was thinning rapidly and seemed sometimes more like smoke than hair. At the back of his head was a bald spot the size of a racquetball.

Anyway, you could see in his eyes that he was undecided as to how much he was going to tell us. That kind of surprised me because Dewitt was the kind of guy who you'd think would have already guessed at how we would react. But he clearly wasn't as well prepared as I expected him to be. It was another small indication that there was something ugly about this opportunity. Because maybe he didn't respect us as much as we all thought.

He took a deep breath and said, "Well, Jenny, you may or may not already know that I've been lobbying the company very strongly for the past couple of years to make one large grant, like a MacArthur, to one artist of color in this community. And finally, last week, they said yes. One time, one grant. And they gave me complete control over the selection process. All they want to do is approve the final awardee."

He looked at me. My heart skipped. Had he already selected me? I knew it was premature. But why was he looking at me like that?

But he continued, "So I made a list of all the artists of color I knew. And you know there is probably no one in this community who knows all of your work better than I. I've funded projects with each of you. I've read all of . . ."

"Uhhh . . . excuse me, Dewitt." Marci dangled a pencil from the corner of her mouth. In that instant she looked like a pretty reporter for the local paper.

Dewitt paused a moment and turned to her, "Yes . . ."

"Do you mind if I ask a couple of questions?" Marci was smiling but for some reason I didn't feel that what was about to happen would be funny.

"Oh, no. Not at all. Actually I meant to say, please interrupt if you have questions."

"Well, ah . . . I was just wondering who else was going to be involved in making the decision?"

"I thought about it and decided that putting a panel of people together would take too long and would cost too much money. Besides, like I said, I know all of your work."

I could tell that Marci was just getting wound up. "That's my point, Dewitt. Don't you think you should have more input?"

"I don't think so. I guess I don't trust anybody else to make this decision."

"But don't you think it should be made by a person of color?" Her eyes narrowed.

"Not necessarily. You see, this money *exists* because I'm committed to diversity."

Herm shifted his weight in his chair. Dewitt faced him. It was as though each one of us was taking a turn. Herm had a way of talking that sometimes sounded a little whiny. I loved him. He was like a playful bear. He could be so sensitive, so gentle, and then, just like a ferocious animal, swat at you in anger. And if he did get angry at you, you would know it. He was not subtle.

But Herm slowly stretched his arms out, "I just wonder about those who don't get it. What about the six of us who won't get anything?"

Dewitt smiled again. He had obviously anticipated this question. "Yeah, I thought about that, Herm. It's not my intention to draw too much of a comparison but in a way I guess it's a lot like the lottery."

I laughed loudly and said, "Shit, it is the damned lottery. That is a serious amount of money to be giving away."

I heard Jenny's voice in my left ear, "Icky, do you know the short story called 'The Lottery'?"

How could I not know that story? It was in every anthology of literature I'd seen when I was in high school. You had to read Melville. You had to read Hemingway. You had to read Poe and Dickens. I faced her. Jenny had one of the sweetest faces on earth. It belied all of her intensity, the angst that surged just below the surface. She seemed so tranquil, serene. Her hair, her dress, everything about her indicated someone who was at one with the flow of nature and its forces. Only when she began to talk did you realize that her visage was pure facade. She tried to hold things close but you could feel the wild energy leaking out of her. She was confrontational, aggressive, insecure. She was driven. And it all happened in a way that left you staring at her, thinking about her pretty face. Which was what I was doing at that precise moment.

And then I realized she was waiting for a response. I wondered why I hadn't thought about her as a sexual partner. I had never seen her with a man and that, in today's cultural circus, was very meaningful and had to be taken into consideration before you made overtures to a potential lover.

I still hadn't answered her question and I felt her about to shift her attention back to Dewitt. I mustered myself to respond, "Yeah, right. Shirley Jackson wrote that. Small town somewhere in white land where every year they select a member of their community by lot and then stone them to death." As I said that I also thought about how fortunate I was that I had read many of those stories in high school. Not exactly the way it is now. Inner city schools don't produce as many anomalies like me as they once did. There are fewer teachers who will go the limit for their reluctant students. Fewer textbooks. Fewer students from West Philly who have read James Baldwin and Flannery O'Connor.

Jenny smiled. We did connect on the literary level.

"That's not exactly the type of lottery I was thinking of." I swiveled my chair so that I could face Marci again. She smiled as she talked, "Of course, I prefer a comparison to the lotto. I don't know about O'Connor but I know about the lotto." This she said in the inimitable style of Amos from the hated but brilliant radio and television show *Amos 'n' Andy*.

Dewitt ignored all of the frenetic bantering and went back to business. "Herm, I've been thinking a lot about your question. What happens to the ones that don't get it?"

Jenny's small voice rose up again: "Well, that's what I was wondering. Why can't you make the grants smaller? You could give more of them." She smiled. "You could give each of us a hundred thousand dollars."

I hadn't thought about that. A surefire foundation grant of a hundred grand was the perfect answer to what I could already feel was a slow rising tension in the room. The entire situation could be defused.

Dewitt slowly pushed the sparse scattered strands of hair out of his face and sat up straighter. "Like I said we . . . ah . . . yes . . . we . . . the Shrubbery Foundation wants this program to have maximum impact. Something that will find our programs talked about on the national news."

"You're telling me." Herm suddenly sat up, his eyes trained on Dewitt. "So, how will I, we, ah . . . the person who wins it . . . ah . . . how will it be paid out?"

"All at once. One lump sum." Dewitt said flatly, trying to hide his obvious excitement.

"Wow," I heard Marci mutter.

"And you know, I've talked to a lot of people and if I do this there will be some negative backlash."

"Backlash?" I knew what he was talking about. I just wanted to make a point that it was the last thing he should have been thinking. Who cared?

"Yes, Icky. You know I've got to deal with all of that. But that's okay. If I don't get flack I'm not doing my job. But I didn't expect it would be so nasty."

Again, I knew what Dewitt was talking about and I suspect so did Herm, even though he asked, "What do you mean?"

"Well, there's a growing feeling out there among the white artists that you guys are already getting more than your share of the arts dollars."

This sentiment drives me straight up the wall. What kind of bullshit is that? Dewitt knew how I felt about stuff like that. All of us. We all struggled against the idea that somehow we weren't worthy artists. "It kills me when white people complain about what we get. They have no concept of history. Of what our struggle has been all about. We don't get shit by comparison."

I could feel Marci's anger. "Well, you can't tell Lena and Ole that," she said, referring to the regional Scandinavian roots and the stand-up people who were connected to them. Marci barely took a breath as she touched her skin and continued, "They think this shit is like some sort of back-stage pass. Like all we have to do is walk in the door and say 'Here I is, I'm the nigra y'all was lookin far,' and bang, there goes the money."

When she finished that thought, I expected to hear some-one else continue. Sometimes we moved as one. Sometimes we could anticipate what each of us wanted. But, alas, some-times we were simply a group of people serving different masters. Individuals who could be played against each other.

I watched Marci's eyes cut quickly to April's. I felt it before she even said a word.

Marci sat straight in her chair. She wore tight-fitting jeans and a tropical print blouse that hung on her like a drape. As I've said, she can be quite stunning. Her face often glowed like a photo from the cover of *Essence* magazine. If Marci had introduced herself as a gospel singer with the glory of God sewn to her soul I would have believed her. But she was no singer. Couldn't hold a note. She was, how-ever, a magnificent artist, like an African Realist. Her pic-tures were mostly colorful acrylics. And for the past two years, she'd only painted the faces of black women. She called it her ME period.

Anyway I could tell when Marci looked at April and then at Dewitt that something was about to jump off.

"By the way," Marci paused, "can you tell me how April here qualifies?"

Dewitt didn't flinch, "Because I think she's a part of this whole mix. I didn't want to penalize April just because she's white."

Marci again faced April, who looked as if she had been kicked in the butt while bending over to pick up a dropped schoolbook. "But I thought this was about people of color." Marci was not about to let this go.

"Yes, but, to most of us in the community April is a person of color."

I wondered what community he was talking about? We got along with April, she was cool, but you can't consider a white person a person of color. Meanwhile, April had had enough of people talking about her as if she weren't there.

"Dewitt, I don't think I'd put it that way." April brushed her hair out of her eyes.

Dewitt did not appreciate what was happening to him here. He knew that there would be some disagreements but he wasn't prepared to waste time on what he considered to be small shit. And when April jumped in it annoyed him. You could tell that he was thinking, "I'm not the enemy."

He ignored April and shot back at Marci, "Well, it doesn't matter. *I* considered her a person of color."

"Oh, snap." I heard Brother JuJu say.

Marci leaned across the table, "So now you can *achieve* colorhood, huh?"

"Like I said, Marci, it really doesn't matter. I don't care about that and I don't care about what the other white artists are saying, either. They can complain all they want. I know how to make noise. I know how to have impact around here. And if I announce this grant, every artist in the country is going to want to know my name."

"Excuse me, Dewitt, but there's one other thing I was wondering about . . ." Jenny's soft voice broke the rising tension. Herm was still staring into space.

Marci was so agitated that she turned on Jenny, too, "You just a wonderin child, ain't you?"

But Jenny ignored Marci and directed her attention to Dewitt. "Who helped you select us? I don't know about anybody else but I think there are more important artists in my community than me. Why aren't they being considered?"

"Jenny, I told you. I made a list," Dewitt said softly.

"Yes, but we are only the people you already knew."

"But I know everybody. And, after I went through a

much larger list, you are what I ended up with." Dewitt was clearly agitated.

I was wondering where Jenny was going with this. She was just so damned cute to me all of a sudden. Her humility was surprising. Unnerving, actually. So I wasn't surprised when Marci struck back at her.

"What do you care, Jenny? Jesus Christ." Marci collapsed back in her chair and sighed.

Jenny looked at me and continued, "I just think there are others equally deserving of consideration." I knew she was right, but I really didn't care about that. There are always people who are more deserving. I am usually among those people. This was supposed to be a time for me. For us.

When I looked at Dewitt I could tell that he was ready to end this meeting. "Well, Jenny. This is just my way of doing things." And with that he passed out a short application form, asked us to fill it out, thanked us again for coming.

there were times when Lt. Bill Bloom thought he was going to pass out. He'd be sitting there, fighting the intermittent shooting pain in his legs or in his chest—pain that was buffeted only by a steady ache that coursed through his entire body—and think he had indeed lapsed into unconsciousness.

He had no idea what Ichabod was talking about. No clue as to why God had sent him to this address in this well-to-do community to meet an insane black man who was causing him such real physical and emotional pain. He would have never expected to encounter an Ichabod type here. This community was one of the blessed of Minneapolis. Along Lake Calhoun where joggers and skaters and bikers and walkers with dogs performed the steeplechase over squawking mallards and Canadian geese. The area where everyone wanted to live. Where you could find gourmet grocery stores and the best private school. Where the police patrolled as if their lives depended on it. Where the snow was removed first.

There were, of course, black people in the neighborhood, but they were state supreme court judges and basketball players, entrepreneurs and architects. Not failed writers with guns. What was this about?

He tried listening to Ichabod. But although he understood the story as it was progressing, he didn't yet know why he had to be tied up to hear it. Perhaps that wasn't true. In fact, he knew why he was taped to the chair. It was precisely because if that were not true he'd have definitely gotten the hell out of there. Ichabod was right about that. If he hadn't been bound, the unfolding of this story would be happening in a totally different way.

He hated being silent. It was so humiliating. Demeaning. How dare he brandish that weapon as a way of trying to deny him the right to speak. While Ichabod talked, Bloom thought about his wife. He knew that she'd be standing out there right beside Hirsh or whoever was running the show, giving them an earful of advice. Making sure they didn't do anything that would jeopardize his life. That was the way Connie was.

They'd been married for seventeen years. Mostly crap filled. Mostly his crap. She believed so much in the idea of love that he'd eventually just given in. He'd quit drinking. Quit gambling. Quit his mistress. He'd quit everything except Connie. Basically because Connie overwhelmed him with her belief in love.

He'd been on the force for four years when he'd met her. He was a patrolman on the South Side of Minneapolis. It was rather light duty. But they'd met at a laundromat. He walked her back to her apartment. From the first day they'd met until the day they were married, he spent almost all of his free time with her.

He remembered the day he proposed to her. He knew why being taped down to a chair, being held hostage, made him think of that day: It was also a day when he was frightened.

He had talked Connie into riding with him up to Duluth where he had to take a class. Halfway there they got into a discussion about the war in Vietnam that ended in her silence the last half hour of the drive. When they reached the University of Minnesota–Duluth's campus, she quickly slid over to the driver's seat of his Buick Electra and sped off.

Bill remembered how fervent he'd been about bombing Cambodia. America had to win the war. That was all there was to it. He'd known when he said it that she was going to flare up. He knew all along she didn't believe war could solve anything. All day long, he fretted over their argument. He could barely focus on his class.

He had no telephone number to call to apologize. No way of contacting her. And then it was five o'clock and Bill Bloom marched his way to the parking lot where she had let him out. As he came out of the door his heart sank. She wasn't there. Ten minutes later, no Connie. Now he began thinking she'd driven back to Minneapolis in a fit of anger. And if that were true, then he knew their relationship was over and he suddenly realized that he didn't want that to happen.

At five-thirty, just as he was about to head back to the administration building, he saw her pull into the driveway. Suddenly he felt like a little boy. He was so happy to see her there were tears in his eyes. He'd always been a big man. Always tough. The tears, the emotion, caught him completely by surprise.

Ironically, Connie was also overcome with joy. She'd gotten lost and had been frantically trying to find her way back. She'd made so many wrong turns, she lost count. When she got out of the car she literally leaped into his arms. They held each other tight. He whispered to her, "I was so afraid I'd lost you."

"I know. I felt it. I knew you'd feel that way. I think

that's what made me so nervous and upset. I didn't want you to think that, Billy."

"You've got to promise me that we'll never lose each other. That there will never come another day when I see you driving off like that leaving me standing somewhere wondering if you'll ever come back. You have to promise."

She smiled and craned her head back. "Are you asking me to marry you?"

"I think I am." Bill stumbled in his speech and in his mind. "Yes. That's exactly what I'm doing."

"Then, Mr. Officer William Bloom, my future husband, know this . . . I will never drive away and leave you standing anywhere. My definition of love is 'through it all.' If we are to be man and wife then it must be through it all."

So he knew that Connie would be out there. And he knew that Capt. Iris Hirsh would do what she could to bring this to a peaceful conclusion.

In the brief moments when Ichabod was silent, Bloom thought first about his wife and then about Ichabod. About what had actually happened. Had Ichabod killed the man in the garbage bag? Was this a simple case of murder? Usually, the details of his job were pretty straightforward. Somebody kills somebody and he and others like him were dispatched to find the guilty parties.

It wasn't brain surgery. People who kill people weren't usually that smart. In the movies or in novels, the killers were usually people who wanted to rid the world of some scourge or had voices playing in their heads or a combination. But in his tour in the Homicide Division, Bloom found that most murders were crimes of the moment, crimes of opportunity. They were not often premeditated.

He studied Ichabod, sitting at the dining room table, smoking a cigarette. Ichabod was a piece of work. Words poured out of his mouth like water rushing down Minne-haha Falls. Ask him one question and you got a goddamned speech. Bloom wasn't much for speeches. But he wasn't a pinhead, either. He didn't believe that people, especially black people, had the right to use what had happened to them historically as a reason to commit a crime. He'd seen it too many times. If Ichabod killed Dewitt, then Bloom wanted his ass locked up. The dead man and his family deserved that. That's the way he figured it. No breaks to the guilty.

But he had a suspicion that Ichabod was telling the truth. That he really wasn't the murderer. If Bloom hadn't felt this way, he would have already given an okay for a sniper to pick him off. Ichabod had no idea, but they had had his ass lined up an hour ago. They could have taken him out any-time. Ichabod wasn't your normal hostage taker. He'd been mindlessly walking in front of the window.

Bloom almost smiled. It was so ridiculous. The only rea-son Ichabod was still breathing was because he'd asked them to hold off. Used to be, back in the old days, they'd have filled the house with lead. They would have opened fire on this place and they wouldn't have thought twice about brushing off Bloom in the process. His wife would have gotten a whole bushel of flowers and his two children would have had their college paid for, but they would have showered the place in lead. But things weren't done that way anymore, and thank God for it.

He didn't think Ichabod was capable of murder. He was so self-absorbed, so caught up in his own need to assert his existence, that he was unaware of how tenuous it really was. Sometimes, as the black man paced in front of him, Lieuten-ant Bloom would close his eyes and try to follow the convo-luted road that was Ichabod's pathway through the world.

If waiting another hour, while Ichabod tried to—as he called it, "tell his story"—would end this standoff peacefully, he could abide that.

The lieutenant didn't want to see Icky die. And he knew that at any moment his life could be snuffed out like the last damp match at the evening campsite. To Bloom, Ichabod was just another confused black man who'd had so much garbage rolling around inside him he couldn't think straight.

Bloom had played on football and basketball teams with black guys. He thought he knew them pretty well. He'd matured through the age of civil rights and understood the difficulties of racial prejudice. He couldn't help telling his comrades when someone made an unflattering racial comment, "They're no different than you and me." He said it often, and he meant it.

But he also believed that most of the black men he'd known had something inside them, something which crippled them. The list of black men who ran aground on the shoals of life was legion. Mike Tyson, O. J. Simpson, Michael Jackson, Marion Barry, that Espy guy at the Department of Agriculture, that Chicago congressman, Mel Reynolds; the list could be pretty long. If there's a famous black man somewhere doing something wrong, you can bet that it'll find its way into the news. As he watched Ichabod strut in front of him he wondered why, if you were a writer or the world heavyweight champion, and you knew everybody was going to be looking at you, why wouldn't you try to be on your best behavior?

But not them. They flaunted it. They didn't know how to handle success. Bloom had come to believe that most black men were so flawed by their history that they were doomed to self-destruction. They're here in this great country, he thought, with all this opportunity, and they're strung out on crack and fighting among themselves. Bloom wanted to say to Ichabod, "I'm more surprised when I meet a black man I can really like. I don't blame them. I mean, look, my folks came over from Hungary before the war. They struggled like hell. They were discriminated against. So I know about being different, about being teased. About having a weird-sounding accent. My parents had it hard. I'm not insensitive about that. But how long are you going to blame your problems on history? How long can you do that? You can't expect me to keep paying the debts of white people I'm not even related to. I have never been a slavemaster." This was what he wanted to say, but he thought better of it.

His thoughts were interrupted by the sound of an approaching police siren. It brought him back to the reality of what was probably happening out there in the streets. He was sure the Tactical Team was in place. Ichabod was vulnerable on so many levels. The apartment was a duplex so there were probably people already on the roof. There were police strategically positioned all around them. And they were not being particularly quiet out there.

Bloom watched Ichabod carefully as he now stood over him. Sweat was flowing freely from Ichabod's head. His sweatshirt was wet under the arms. Bloom eyed the gun. The flash of it in Ichabod's eyes. The sunlight hugging them all.

The lieutenant weighed his urge to speak and then decided to go with it. "You're getting a little nervous, aren't you, Icky?"

"What? I didn't say you could interrupt me."

"But you are feeling a little more nervous than you were before, aren't you?"

Ichabod stared at him. Yes, there was panic bopping to the music. Yes.

"And you know what? You should be getting nervous. Everybody out there thinks you're just an ass hair away from blowing me away, which of course means you're an ass hair away from getting blown away yourself."

the people began arriving at my apartment a little after six o'clock last night. It was more of a reception than a party. Or what a Minnesotan might call an open house. People moving through, staying forty-five minutes or so and then making a beeline to a coffee shop or a place that served dessert. And that had to happen pretty early in the evening because there were virtually no restaurants open after ten o'clock at night. No matter what anyone tells you about the Twin Cities—like how great it is or anything—remember that if you get hungry late at night, you are shit out of luck.

Still, people wanted to be where the action was. And on an autumn evening, Allhallows Eve for the masses, traditional masquerade parade for the hipsters, the artistes and their followers and devotees were bound for my place. As reclusive as I was, it was very unusual for me even to have such an affair. But the impending anointing by Dewitt called for a show of confidence and style. Besides, all of my friends who were seeking something less Halloweenish were grateful for the alternative.

So they came. Some in costume, others only in the ones

they inherited. Uniforms of life. Draped in the colors of their consciousness. Early on, I was so busy being the host that I barely had time to account for all the people there. Indeed, at its height, at about eight o'clock, there were forty-five people wandering through this apartment. Standing in groups. Commenting on a new black play that opened last week at the Peter O'Toole Regional Theater. The play, the first by a non-European in this august theater, was a controversial number. *Dancing Drunk and Just For Fun*, the challenging story of a black man who loved to dance more than anything in the world, was having its world premiere. Some thought it offensive. Others refreshing. In Minnesota there weren't enough black people to produce a hit or bring it down. Things can just exist in the rich topsoil of humanity that is Minnesota.

There was lots of talk about that. And of course the Ron Abbott story. And the speculation about President Clinton and his alleged dalliances. The multicultiboho tribe claimed the space. This was proof that the world was changing. White people and brown people committing themselves to have lunch together and, further, to create art together. Change the damn world. That's what they could do.

And they whispered in smiles that promised such transformation. And, for a moment, everybody was heard. There was a television anchor woman there, Latina. The deputy mayor was there, Native American. Radio personalities, lawyers, painters, writers, dancers, filmmakers, reporters, all breathed this air. Righteous folk. The folk who set the pace. And Lord, thank you for affirmative action. Let the conservatives squirm while we nibble at their cheesewheel of power. Let their children break out into small beads of sweat as they realize they have to compete with all of us.

Lord, tell them why there were no people of color running the government before now. Tell them why we only read books written by white men. Tell them why we go to jail so often, and the people who pursue us, the people who try us, the people who defend us, the people who condemn us, are all people who thought we did it in the first place.

We are innocent. Tell them that, Lord. But in the meantime, thank you for the guilt that flows in the veins of white bureaucrats who must seek us out. Must scour the blood-stained earth of the great plains of America to find that one Native American sister who can fill a need in their affirmative-action plan. Find that one Latino brother in Mankato, Minnesota, who can fix a computer. That Hmong woman who can translate the songs of her people and bank point-of-service placard copy.

Affirmative action and the truth of future demographics brings the corporate body into the public domain. It must emerge from the shroud of profit-taking to open its doors for others who have no history in the heart of commerce. It has created us. Black men who think that they can grow up to be writers, filmmakers. All of us, in the myriad of colors, here because America decided to become a country that was true to its founding idea.

This apartment was full of such people. In the kitchen, there was a small group of people talking about the relevance of Garrison Keillor and Robert Bly, two famous white Minnesota writers. I stood in the doorway of the kitchen and listened as François Mills, a rather cool young white man, explained how both men did more damage than good in the local community. There were nods all around.

"Keillor has played Minnesotans for chumps since day one and everybody just loves him." I knew that statement would draw a rise from someone. But everyone in the room was silent. "And Bly, well, I have a lot of respect for his work. Even all that crazy let's-discover-our-maleness thing. I respect it. But I heard him read last month at the university and he read every poem three times." François was a waif. His head was full of loose curls. He looked as if he were just about to sit down at a Steinway and play a concerto, bright and eager and incredibly competent. He was included in the tribe because he was one of those white guys who would speak up if he saw something foul.

That should be a part of the defining thing about the tribe. You can only be a member if you reject the same old same old. You can't be a willing participant in the marginalization of someone who is *already* marginalized. It's okay to marginalize someone, such as . . . say . . . a police officer because, well, damn it all to hell, it's kind of a new experience for a cop to exist on the fringe. To be afraid for your own life.

Anyway, François paused and said again, "Three times. Like we were stupid or something. I wanted to scream back at him. I get it already. I get it."

Even among the bohemians there was deep respect for poets. So the comment about Bly was not entirely welcome. There was a nervous laughter, a quick shifting of positions. Some exited the kitchen. Some came in. As I turned away I walked into Brother JuJu, decked out in a beautiful multicolored dashiki. It wasn't kente cloth but it was a traditional garment of West Africa.

That's the thing about Brother JuJu. He could pull off the African persona even though he was born right here in Minnesota. An African man nurtured in the Midwestern wilderness. And make no mistake, Brother JuJu was often the uncompromising voice. He could afford the luxury. He worked for a social service agency in one of the fledgling slums. They needed him. He had carte blanche freedom of movement. In the morning he could walk into his boss's office and say something like "I need to go to this place or that place." And they would say, "Okay. Fine."

Not many black men had it like that. They paid him a decent salary and in the final analysis, he passed judgment on them from the point of view of an authentic black man and they thanked him for it. He could basically come and go as he pleased. What more could you ask for?

If he thought somebody was doing something wrong to the black community, he was the first to organize folks. Brother JuJu would march twenty-five angry people down Nicollet Avenue, all the way to the mayor's office, to protest anything from slow garbage removal to police brutality. He claimed *this* was the work of a poet. Not be some simpleton who only wrote poems for the fifty people who bought their funky chapbooks.

He had so much freedom of movement he often behaved as if integrity were a given. Brother JuJu could say what he wanted and he often did. But I knew he would have nothing to contribute about Keillor and Bly. He never wasted time talking about white people if he could help it. Of all of us, he was less a true member of the tribe than any other. Even April belonged in ways that he didn't. At least she believed in equality. Brother JuJu had a healthy respect for everybody but he definitely believed that black people were put on this earth to lead everyone else out of the tar pit of barbarism.

"What's up, Icky?" He said to me out of the side of his mouth. He smelled as though he had been on a Jamaican beach all day, baking his chocolate ass in coconut oil. His African garb was big on his thin frame. But it was as though he needed the extra material to hide his troubled expression.

"Not a thing, JuJu," I said before I had a chance to think about it. But after a second I knew that response would not suffice. "Well, I guess you know as well as I do that that isn't the truth." I smiled as I stared into his bloodshot eyes. I knew there was a problem. "Tonight could be a big night for one of us."

He rolled his gaze away from me. It caught me off-guard. I knew that everybody was nervous about the Shrubbery but I thought it was a rather good kind of worried. We, at least, could hope something great was about to happen for one of us. But Brother JuJu seemed as though he was about to descend into tears. "Naw, man, Dewitt fucked me."

"What do you mean?" But I knew instantly.

"He talked all that shit. Bout how much he thinks my work in the community is so great and my poetry is the shit and all that, but he was just playing with me."

I'd had a hunch all along that Dewitt would eliminate Brother JuJu. I think the honor, if there was any, was in his even being considered. I curled my arm around him, trying my best to be sympathetic. I mean, I did feel for him but I can't lie, I had this growing intuition that the Shrubbery had my name on it. "That's fucked up," I said. "He shouldn't have had that meeting with all of us like that."

"He called me a couple of days ago and I guess he tried to let me down easy. But I was like, why did you do it this way, Dewitt? This ain't right."

I nodded my head. "That dude's on a serious ego trip."

Brother JuJu looked at me as if he were seeing me for the first time. I knew he was thinking that I probably wasn't feeling all that bad for him. I was but . . .

"Anyway, I'm happy for you and Marci. Maybe one of ya'll will get it. I can't see how April can get it. And the Asian folks been getting everything around here for the last few years."

I hated it when people, especially black people, let their petty jealousies show. I believed that the only way we could actually neutralize the mainstream power of the white people who had control over our lives was to forge a strong coalition that would stand together. It is so difficult to believe in your own greatness without thinking someone else

is the child of shit. But I'm always heartened by the children
of the multicultis. They are the proof that things can never
be the same. And you know as well as I that this state is
one of the trendsetters when it comes to race matters. People
are always yapping about New York as the center of this
or that. But Minnesota can boast a knowledge about the
intermingling of cultures that is, ah . . . bizarre, perverse,
and truly American. I'd bet anything that the number of
little mixed-raced babies at any given time in Minnesota is
greater. This state leads the nation in the number of stunned
and freaked-out white parents.

"There's still Jesus and Herm. Either one of them could
get it. The Hispanic community gets almost nothing here,"
I said, hoping to demonstrate my sense of justice and
democracy.

"You can forget Jesus. Dewitt cut him loose, too,"
Brother JuJu said softly.

"Damn." I wondered why I hadn't seen Jesus. Now I
knew.

"I'll catch you later, Icky. I'm gonna get me a drink." I
slapped him on the back as he turned away.

The plot was getting thick like a motherfucka. It was
going to come down to me, Herm, Marci, Jenny, and April.

I remember thinking this as Sharon Fulworth walked in.
She was the daughter of the daughter of a wealthy department store magnate who broke tradition and married the
son of a Pullman porter. I didn't know Sharon's parents but
time stopped when she walked into a room. Women and
men turned to see what the line of time was snagged on.
And they would see this vision. And for a second we all
paused there in recognition that among the beautiful there
were levels.

Vonnegut says that no beautiful woman can live up to
that beauty for any significant amount of time. He would

have to revise that statement if he'd ever met Sharon. She was a photographer of frightening skill. Her photographs were mesmerizing, haunting. Her beauty was barely equal to her aesthetic sensibilities. The only reason she wasn't being considered for the Shrubbery was her age. At twenty-five it would have been a sin to give her that much money.

Her personality had its own interesting dimensions. She was often very animated, almost hyper. She talked fast and sometimes when you were talking to her, you had to hold her arm to keep her from walking away in the middle of a conversation. I'd come to realize it wasn't because she wasn't interested in the conversation; but simply that her mind and her body were gone already. In constant motion.

I watched Herm make his way over to her. He had the silliest expression on his face. I timed my approach to coincide with his and I could see that his expression wasn't so much silly as it was predatory. He was moving in for the kill. We both said hello at the same time. When he saw me his hungry expression changed.

Sharon smiled at us and glided right by. Nearly passing through us. Herm and I were still staring at each other when Marci joined us.

"When are you gonna kick these slackers out of here, Icky?" she said. "I can't wait for the real party to get under way."

"I know what you're talking about, Marci. But it's still early. Dewitt can't even get here until nine-thirty or ten."

"So where did he have to go so bad? I mean, this whole party is for him, isn't it?" Herm sported a really beautiful embroidered white shirt. On the collar was an intricate pattern done in white thread. He had a large arrowhead bolo tie on and a black blazer over tastefully faded blue jeans.

I rushed to correct him. "No no. This party was not for Dewitt. I decided to have a party because we need more opportunities where we can socialize. It just happened that Dewitt wanted to come by later."

Herm looked at the ceiling. "Yeah, right."

"No, really," I continued. "This was supposed to be like a salon or something. It wasn't about Dewitt."

"Funny how it suddenly seems that everything is about Dewitt." Marci took a bite out of a celery stick.

"So, really—where did Dewitt have to go?" Herm was nothing if not persistent.

I shrugged my shoulders but Marci just started laughing. "What's so funny?"

"You don't know where Dewitt is?" Her face lit up like a movie screen.

I didn't.

"Didn't you hear about the Throwin Down exhibit at the MoMedia Center?"

"No. What the hell is Throwin Down?" There were more faddish arts events going on in Minneapolis than you could keep track of. Your entire weekend could be consumed in running from one event to the other. And one of the down-sides of being a person of color in the Upper Midwest is that whenever an artist of color comes to town you're sup-posed to go. You have to go.

Marci was almost laughing. "The Shrubbery, meaning Dewitt, funded this exhibit of gang paraphernalia."

I didn't think I'd heard her right. "What?"

"You heard me. There's an exhibit over there with gang shit hanging on the walls."

"Has Dewitt lost his natural mind?" I wondered aloud.

"I don't know what the hell Dewitt is doing. But I bet it's a little more lively over there at the MoMedia than it is here."

dewitt grew up in Albion, Michigan, the son of two General Motors assembly-line workers. Doris and Timothy McMichael were both drive-train assemblers who always marveled at the simple perfection of their only son. He had always been delicate. Indeed from birth he'd been plagued by a variety of ailments, including a slight heart murmur. As he got older Dewitt grew stronger.

His parents worked hard and saved and managed to send Dewitt to private schools. For high school they sent him away to boarding school at Fergurson Academy. Although he wasn't the smartest boy among his peers, he was clever. Sharp-witted and fierce in his own right.

Dewitt was ten when he got Elmer, a little black and white beagle that reminded him of Snoopy. At first he was going to name the dog after the cartoon character but at the last minute he decided on Elmer. When the dog barked it sounded like it was almost stuttering like Elmer Fudd, the famous guy who perpetually hunted Bugs Bunny.

Elmer was a tiny pup when Dewitt got him as a birthday gift. It was love at first sight. An obsession. He hated to be parted from Elmer for even a second. When Dewitt thought about the coming school year he became anxious. It would mean that there would be hours of time that he would have to leave Elmer behind.

Albion was an idyllic sleepy town that provided the perfect backdrop to an all-American childhood. His parents made good money at the GM plant and lived on a quiet tree-lined street in a community that didn't foresee the energy crisis or the rise of Japanese technology coming. To his parents he was perfect. To the children at school and in his neighborhood he was a slow, frail, fearful playmate. He tired quickly. He never played sports. He wasn't even particularly smart. Not brilliant like his closest friend, Josh, a scientific wizard, who at ten could command the powers of a calculator with stunning efficiency. But Dewitt was indeed special.

From a very early age he exhibited talent as an artist. He drew and painted incessantly. And his subjects, from the beginning and throughout his childhood, were not like those of many artistically inclined children. Dewitt never doodled. He never drew pictures of super heroes. Right from the beginning he was captivated by the shapes and colors of real life. He painted and drew houses and parks and rivers and ice skaters on the local pond. And, after he turned ten, each picture had an image of Elmer. The little beagle would be lying on the ground under a tree. Running in the background of a sketch of a statue.

Dewitt spent many days, particularly after he got Elmer, riding his bike, a red J.C. Higgins, around the city. A big wicker basket attached to the handlebars usually held a drawing pad, a box of pens and colored chalk, and sitting on top of that, swaddled in a blue woolen sweater for cushioning, was Elmer. They were a familiar sight. Sometimes Josh would accompany them, but often it was just Dewitt and Elmer tooling around, looking for an interesting house or a tree or group of flowers for Dewitt to capture in his pad.

Dewitt thought about Elmer—which he often did—as he drove through the city now on his way to the MoMedia Center. He was quite excited by the buzz this exhibit had caused. The director of the gallery, Wilma Born, had called him nearly a year ago to test his interest in a gang-related show.

Dewitt liked Wilma. He liked the way she was always trying to find the narrow spaces between the issues of the day and the things people actually thought about. She was a lot like him. Yes, they were white but they weren't like the Harold Blooms of the world who had catatonized into sugared meaninglessness. They were capable of understanding the beauty in the challenge of finding the beauty in the work of people who opposed the status quo. They were capable of dealing with the differences among people without being afraid of them. And they didn't believe that the work by people of color was inherently inferior.

Dewitt chuckled to himself as he crept down Hennepin Avenue in the rush-hour traffic. MoMedia was housed in a warehouse in an old part of the relatively new Minneapolis. There would probably be a correspondent from the *Village Voice* there. This was what the business of arts funding should be, he thought. Establishing new standards. Pushing new boundaries.

He lost his smile as his mind returned to the day tragedy struck. He and Josh were riding their bikes from the library. Dewitt had quickly checked out three books of pictures of the French countryside. Already he dreamed of one day making a pilgrimage to the center of art and culture. Already he dreamed of being a famous artist. Josh had selected six activity books to take home. They were only in the library for fifteen minutes. Dewitt had left Elmer leashed to a pole while they were gone.

When they came out of the library Elmer was gone. Instantly tears brimmed in Dewitt's eyes. "Where's Elmer? Where's Elmer? Elmer! Elmer!" Dewitt screamed. His slight body darting down the steps, his head moving like a light on a police car.

Joshua, physically a more substantial boy, his red hair glistening in the late April sunshine, rushed after Dewitt. He realized how attached his friend was to his new puppy. Together they searched for blocks around the library. Nothing.

"Who would steal a puppy? Who would steal Elmer?" Dewitt asked frantically. Joshua could only shrug his shoulders. Their bikes were still there. Nothing seemed out of the ordinary. Except that Elmer was missing. After about fifteen minutes of walking in circles, the two boys sat down on the curb in front of the library.

"Don't worry, Dewitt. We'll find him." Joshua tried to console his friend.

"What if we don't? What if somebody took him away for good?"

"Maybe he just got away. Maybe if we ride our bikes down by the river we'll find him there. Or over by the park. There are lots of places he could be."

"I guess." Dewitt slowly rose from the ground. He walked over to his bicycle. "Let's get going."

It was then he heard Elmer's faint bark. The dog sounded as if he were miles away. The two boys looked at each other. "That's Elmer," Dewitt said. "Where is that coming from?" They listened intently. After a few moments they heard the bark again. "I don't know. Sounds like it's coming from over there." Joshua pointed off in the distance. "Come on."

They grabbed their bikes and began running. They were oblivious to everything else. Joshua knew how important Elmer was to Dewitt. And Dewitt was frantic, first with fear and now with hope. They heard the dog bark again, closer this time. As they crossed the second street they saw a construction site with a fence around it.

"Elmer?" Dewitt screamed. The dog barked an answer and pushed up against the chain-link fence. Dewitt could see where the dog had wandered through a small hole near the gate but had been unable to exit. In fact, his leash was snagged on the fence. Dewitt ran to his precious. He was crying again. This time with an intense relief. He unhooked Elmer's leash and scooped the dog into his arms.

"I thought you were gone. You. Why did you run away? Why did you leave me? Don't you know how dangerous it is to go running off? You could have gotten hurt. Promise me that you'll never leave me. Promise."

Elmer whimpered. Joshua was now alongside and they all breathed a sigh.

"I was scared." Dewitt said to Joshua. "I thought he was dead or something."

"Yeah. I was getting kind of worried myself." Joshua paused and looked up at the sky. "It's a good thing he kept barking."

"Yeah. That's right." Dewitt then hugged Elmer and said. "Good boy. Good boy."

Dewitt put Elmer in the basket on top of his books. He then hopped on the bike and slowly kicked off. Joshua rode beside him on his bike.

"What are they building in there?" Joshua asked.

"I don't know. Some kind of government building maybe." Dewitt thought he remembered a sign. He steered his bicycle in the direction of the gate at the end of the block. As he neared the gate the cement sidewalk became choppy with potholes and cracks, shaking the bike. Suddenly it felt as if the wheels of the bicycle were clanging against the ground like the wheels of a railroad car.

He could see that Elmer was once again anxious. The dog whimpered. Dewitt could feel his body shaking and then, in an instant, the sidewalk simply disappeared. Distracted, Dewitt had not seen the hole coming, and he hit it hard. The bike's front wheel smashed against the back of the hole and threw the bicycle into the air. Elmer yelped and flew skyward. Dewitt watched Elmer take flight in front of him but he was more focused on trying to regain control.

Just as he hit a patch of smooth ground, and brought the bicycle under control, Elmer dropped out of the sky directly in front of him. The dog landed on the ground just before Dewitt rode both tires over him.

Elmer died instantly. It crushed Dewitt. He'd loved Elmer more than anything. Even now, as a grown man he had a difficult time thinking of the past, of his childhood, without thinking of the three months of his life that he'd shared with Elmer. It always ended with him feeling sad. Lost.

He'd had other pets, including a cat and another dog. But he could never care about any of them as much as he had about Elmer. His parents had tried to convince him that there was nothing he could have done about it. His father had even driven back to the site to help Dewitt see how he couldn't have foreseen what would happen. That he shouldn't be too hard on himself. But Dewitt couldn't think about being young and happy in Albion without eventually remembering the long ride home with Elmer in his familiar place in the basket. Lifeless.

Dewitt pushed back the tear that his eyes promised. Night would soon caress the Twin Cities. A liberal garden. Home of Humphrey and Mondale. The only exception to mad rampant Reaganism. His little laboratory. A place that had given him such great power. Where he had cultivated the garden with fearless and brilliant artists. He was one of the reasons the Twin Cities had so much luster.

Indeed, the Twin Cities were unique in the amount of money available for artists. Artists came from all over, including New York, to wait out the year of residency requirement so that they could apply for money from any number of funders. The Pheromone Foundation. The Dodger Hagens Foundation. The Minnesota Fund. The MisQueen Foundation's Where Do You Want to Go Today Travel Program. Then, of course, there was the Shrubbery. Talented and popular sculptors or composers or writers or even performance artists could conceivably make over sixty thousand dollars in grants if they knew how to package and to present their proposals.

When people from other cities found out that Minnesotans were so generous to their scribblers and doodlers, they often seriously considered relocation.

Dewitt was one of the people entrusted with the responsibility of deciding who was and who was not worthy of the money that would generate the art that would become a part of the tapestry that was Minnesota. The Minnesota Aesthetic, if you will. Applicable—upon closer inspection— to everyone countrywide, including the great metropolitan centers. Why, it was good enough for the legion of fans of that legendary radio show, *Prairie Home Companion*.

He brought his car to a stop at a light and slipped in a Biggie Smalls CD. The light changed and his green Saab leapt forward. He'd been listening to rap music for the past two years. He particularly liked the rappers who were able to talk about the hardcore realities of urban life while managing to make you want to move your body.

Rap music was one of the reasons he had funded the

Throwin Down exhibition. Through the music, he'd come to understand more about black people than he'd ever imagined. The urban black culture was full of energy, excitement, uncertainty. After he'd listened to Tupac Shakur, Public Enemy, and Puff Daddy he began searching for a way to bring the streets and everything associated with them into the established arts venues.

When he made the grant to Wilma Born at MoMedia he'd done it with the hope that collecting gang paraphernalia might become a fad. That was how things happened. A visionary funder. A risk-taking arts organization like MoMedia and, with a little timing and luck, *voila*, you had instant media muffins. Suddenly you had created a trend.

As he turned the corner of MoMedia's block he slowed down. There was an enormous crowd already milling about the entrance. Dewitt couldn't help but unconsciously hit the brake a little harder than usual when he realized that nearly all of the people milling outside the gallery were black. There was a healthy contingent of Latinos, a quiet but significant number of Asian faces, and a smattering of young white boys in baggy pants, but most of the hooded and tattooed and shrouded figures were black. He recalled a comment he'd heard someone black say at a reception for Spike Lee a couple of years back. He remembered the woman saying, when she saw how many people turned up at the J-WAD, that she didn't know there were that many black people in the whole state.

"Amen," he said aloud.

He eased his car into the parking lot across the street. Even the parking lot was full of young men and women of all races. Some in small groups. Some standing alone. But Dewitt knew enough to know that most of them were gang members. There were guys who wore red bandannas and those who wore blue. There were guys throwing hand signs.

There was a lot of commotion and noise. Music that made even the dirt jump. Bass lines whipping the air like an angry cobra. Dewitt turned his own music down. He heard the same CD he had been playing elsewhere in the lot.

He noticed the number of cars with people still in them at the far end of the parking lot. He moved instinctively in that direction. As he approached he realized that most of the people in those late-model cars were white. He saw board members of MoMedia, curators, other grantsmakers, artists, even members of the Shrubbery board sitting nervously in their cars. They were obviously afraid, and each of them was trying to decide whether to brave the throng of hoodlums or to simply accept the fact that they *were* afraid and leave.

You say you stand for something. For diversity, let's say, and you can't get out of your damned car when there are too many black people running loose. His value system wasn't wired that way. He would show them that this fear could be overcome. Had to be.

He parked and stepped out of his car. He hit the car mouse button and his vehicle chirped its status. Locked and alarm activated. He turned again to make sure there was nothing on the back seat. It was the first time he actually had a moment of regret that his car was so slick. So new. So . . . expensive.

He headed toward the gallery, threading his way through a group of people who stopped talking and stared at him. Dewitt figured that probably all the white people trapped in their cars were watching him. He broke a smile and caught the smallest guy in the group. He nodded and said hello. The kid smiled back but said nothing. Made no other gesture. Dewitt felt good. This was the way progress would happen. One moment. One smile at a time.

There was giggling, an intense awkwardness, but he pressed forward to the door of MoMedia. He stood behind a guy who obviously had a pistol in his belt. Dewitt almost lost it. A gun. People were smoking. There was a copper-colored young man standing in a large group of people screaming at the top of his lungs.

"I don't give a motherfuck. Yo. Check the shit right here. Or we can . . ."

Another man, darker, larger, interrupted him, "You don't need to take it there, dog. Just squash it."

Dewitt strode quickly toward the administrative offices. As he navigated through the space, wending his way through the scattered clusters of dark people, he caught intermittent glimpses of the exhibit. There were sculpted hands jutting out of the walls in signs. Pictures of intricate tattoos. Of the faces of gang members. There was a display of guns, various homemade bombs, clubs, customized baseball bats, pipes, knives, and other makeshift weapons. In another area were crack paraphernalia. He slowed his pace when he realized that the large room had been divided in half. One side was blue, the other red.

Wilma materialized beside him. "Dewitt. I'm glad you got here. I was worried that you might not . . ." She seemed out of breath. Nervous.

Dewitt laughed a brief, uneasy laugh. "No. Of course I had to come. I'm sort of responsible for this, aren't I?"

"If you'll take credit, I'll let you." Wilma looked around sheepishly. "Listen, Dewitt. I have to tell you something." She paused and guided him away from the crowd of people, away from the tension that popped around them.

"I think we made a pretty big mistake," Wilma began after they were in a shallow alcove.

"I wouldn't go that far, Wilma. I mean. Okay. It's crowded and a little scary. But we knew that. This is good. This city has never experienced anything like this."

"That's true, but, Dewitt I . . . ah . . . we may have

created a bigger problem bringing all these people together like this. You see, the consultant I had help me on this didn't really understand that by separating the room like we've done it draws attention to the rivalry and the animosity between the two groups. They've almost come to blows three times already. And I haven't even put the wine out yet."

Dewitt stared at her. For the first time he realized he might have walked into an unexpected, volatile situation. One thing was for sure: They didn't need to add alcohol to it. "Wine? Perhaps we ought to save the wine for a future reception."

She nodded. Dewitt was about to say that he couldn't stay long, that he had to go to Ichabod Word's house to meet with a group of artists, when the local cable ace arts reporter, Danny Glint, tapped Dewitt on the shoulder. He almost jumped a foot in the air.

"Sorry there about that," Danny said. "I just want a quick interview." Danny was a very short, stocky kind of guy. He wasn't made for suits although he wore one all the time. He was like a block of wood. Square. All corners and awkward movements. Like Barney Rubble from "The Flintstones." Danny had a local cable arts show that interviewed regional artists about all the great art they were making to support the reputation that Minnesota was an arts hotbed. Danny was a busy, busy booster, propped up and paid for by the city.

"I don't think I want to talk to you right now, Danny."

"Why not?

Dewitt tried to come up with a good reason but couldn't. Besides, he quickly reasoned, Danny was a pivotal figure in the arts scene. "Okay, Danny. Shoot."

"Interesting choice of words, Dewitt. Interesting choice. This is an exhibit of gang stuff. Right?"

"That's right. We wanted to explore these items in a new way."

"Wow. Dewitt. You are always coming up with such amazing things. How did this get started? I mean, who came up with it? You know. Like where did the idea emanate? From? You know? Right?"

"Yes, Danny. I guess I'm the culprit. Wilma and I together sort of put this together."

"I'm going to recommend it. This is real stuff, isn't it?"

"Yes, Danny . . ."

Dewitt was about to provide a more detailed explanation when abruptly Danny Glint looked as if he'd been shot with a new volt of electricity and took off. Dewitt stood dumbfounded as he watched the forever fledgling reporter go out the backdoor. He wished he'd thought about that. He could have gotten in and out much easier. Instead he swallowed hard and turned his attention back to Wilma, who smiled at the space that Danny had just vacated. When Dewitt had mentioned her name to Danny, she felt that he wasn't really acknowledging all the effort she'd put into this exhibit. What did Dewitt know about gangs? What did he know about running a cutting-edge gallery? Nothing.

Wilma Born had devoted her entire life to creating a safe place in which artists could show their work. It was her struggle that had made this moment possible. And what was actually happening? Well, all around her were highly agitated, armed, loud-talking gangbangers who never partook of the traditional gallery experience. It was indeed a seminal moment, and she'd just stood there and let Dewitt take all the credit. How dare he?

She grabbed Dewitt by the arm. "What am I supposed to do?"

Dewitt looked at her and saw how afraid she was. He couldn't help thinking how strange it was that such a courageous woman could fall apart so quickly. He felt for her. He knew she needed his reassurance. "Wilma. Listen to me, sugar. You are a wonder. An absolute wonder. Look at what you've done here. These people will be forever in your debt. They have come here. Here. This is an American aesthetic. And you have brought them here to participate in it. You should be very proud of yourself."

Wilma looked up into his blue eyes. The swirling blues and reds of the interior of the gallery enveloped Dewitt's image and made him seem to glow like the rainbow. "I know you're right, Dewitt. I know. But this feels like it's out of control. Look over there." She pointed at a man leaning up against the wall trying to light a cigarette. He was obviously high. You could see the sweat pouring out of him. His heaving body.

"I wish I could stay, Wilma. Really. Maybe you ought to call the police. Just let them know what's going on here. I mean, I guess things could get out of control. I guess."

"I already did. I got a creepy feeling pretty early on." Again she grabbed his arm. "Where is everybody? I mean . . . ah . . . all . . ."

"The white people?" He chuckled. "Oh, don't worry. They're here. Well, close by, anyway. But I don't think they will actually make it inside. Of course that won't stop them from saying they were here." Dewitt thought about the scene outside. "It's a fairly daunting journey out there. I'm not looking forward to leaving."

"I know. You mean there are people in the parking lot who are afraid to come in?"

Dewitt nodded.

"My board members?" Wilma slowly began to realize what was happening.

"Oh, yeah. And some of mine, too. And, well . . . there

are quite a few of them stranded out there. I thought they'd follow me in but, ah, I guess not."

"Jesus."

"Prayer is indeed an option, sweetheart. Prayer has its place. But I need to go."

"You're really going to leave me here?"

"I'm sorry, Wilma. I really have to go. There is a group of people waiting for me over at Ichabod's." Dewitt paused as he saw Wilma's face go blank. "You know Ichabod, don't you? Ichabod Word?"

"The writer? I don't really know him. I've met him. Rude, if you ask me."

Dewitt was interested in her perception. "Rude? Perhaps. Why do you say that?"

"I don't know him, really. It's just when I have been around him I've felt that he was a little arrogant. A little self-righteous. Isn't he one of those people who's always talking about how being black is so hard?"

Dewitt laughed. "I know that people think that about him. But actually, I like him. I like what he's trying to do."

Wilma sighed. "Whatever you say, Dewitt. But I don't see any of the black artists here tonight. How come they're not here? It's a show about them, for Christ's sake. There's no support here. I feel that I'm doing this alone."

Wilma could see Dewitt recoil slightly. So she felt compelled to add, "Well, I mean, you're here. You helped make all this possible." At that precise moment there was an explosion of activity near the door. Wilma and Dewitt had been completely oblivious to it while they were talking but now they both turned in that direction as a wave of people came at them.

Wilma and Dewitt moved against the flow and found themselves in a clear space at the center of which were two men. One holding a small handgun down at his side. The other glaring at him as if he were made of steel.

"Go on, dog, peel it off."

Dewitt found himself too close to the two men and he heard himself say, "Come on, guys. This isn't the place to be doing this."

"Who the fuck are you?" asked the man with the gun.

"I'm the one who made this exhibit possible. And if you two keep fighting we're going to have to close it up."

"Motherfucka." He pointed the gun at Dewitt. "I don't know who the fuck you are but you better step off."

The other man stood there calmly, an opposing force.

"As for you, I ought to bust a cap in your ass right here for saying that shit about my partner. But I'm gonna let you slide right now." And with that, the man with the gun headed for the door, the crowd parting to let him through. He pivoted, aimed the gun directly at Dewitt's head, sending a beam of red light like a dart onto his forehead.

"I don't like you. You got a big mouth." And then he was gone.

Dewitt took a deep breath. He knew he was flustered. Almost gasping. He let Wilma lead him to a chair in her office, where he collapsed. He felt as though he was near death even then—a full hour before he left the gallery on his way to the party.

ichabod had written hundreds of short stories. He had stacked them in two piles on the shelf next to the top of his bookcase. And there were two partly completed stories on the kitchen table, another one on the floor in front of Lieutenant Bloom. Ichabod saw the detective trying to read the first page of the manuscript even though it was upside down. When he noticed Bloom's flagging attention, Ichabod knelt down close to the cop's face and asked, "Do you have an interest in literature?"

Bloom stared back at him. He held his thought for as long as he could and then said, "I'm very tired, Ichabod. Very tired."

"Do you like short fiction?"

The detective decided on silence for the moment.

Ichabod broke into a large, false smile. "This is what I do, Lieutenant. I write stories. The one you were perusing from your disadvantageous position is a little number I call, 'Can Death Do this?' "

O my emotional self. Possessed am I outright. Distraught, upturned, caught in an upheaval of the mind. Distressed and isolated. Yes, like some soulless body strapped in a white canvas sleeping gown and tucked carelessly away in the furthermost cell, in the most remote of asylums. I am caught in a luckless wrestle. Losing.

Can death do this? Can death freeze each moment, as a burst of breath, like a Philadelphia street in December, where every thought spoken is marked by the effect of winter air colliding with the warmth of our feelings as clouds rise from our mouths? Can death do this?

I sit here, waiting, transfixed, as people pass by me. These days, it seems, I can be transfixed by the slightest of activity. In the past, nothing moved faster than my frame of mind, which now feels sluggish and unresponsive.

And, though this movement of the mind has slowed, there is this constant series of remembrances. Recollections well up unannounced, crowding out what is, replacing it with what was, forcing me to experience anew their presence.

So, I am sitting here, seemingly catatonic from distress, at once freezing each moment and rolling upon the waves of my aging shadows. There are thoughts and images passing through my mind that I had long jettisoned. It is most confounding, I assure you.

At this late hour in my life, I realize that what triggers my memory, what forces me to confront myself, are the images which swirl within. And oddly, it is my memory of smells that stimulates the most intense images.

For example, right now I am thinking about this city. It has a special distinct smell. I have traveled widely and each place, each instant of movement, brings with it a unique odor. I remember when I was about twelve, returning to Philadelphia from a summer away in a small North Carolina town. After picking tobacco, tending chickens on my grandfather's farm, and using an outhouse, I was anxious to get home.

The city gave me identity. It was the smell of the narrow

streets. The absence of space in its natural function. The intensity of the heat in late summer that melted the asphalt and rippled above the cobblestones and cement. It was the smell of people gathered in clusters on street corners. And, God knows, it was the sweet aroma of corner candy stores that sold large dilled pickles for a nickel that they kept in barrels on the floor and from which you got to pick your own.

The smells permeate, serve as guide to the wonders of times past. It delivers me to pain as well as joy.

There was a time, as a teen, when I played with my friends in a concrete schoolyard. This yard was bounded by spiked wrought-iron spears, each lined up six inches from the other, five feet high, and painted as black as a country night.

On one particular occasion, I found myself shoved against this fence with a force that caused my skull to give way. The smell of walking home under the afternoon sun, blood squirting like a fountain from the back of my head, as a parade of fellow players, neighbors, and others interested in the progressive bloodletting escorted me home.

It is the smell of Thompson Street and the fear that swirled around me as I approached my house. Indeed, it was the smell of the house. Collards simmering, casting a vinegar shadow over the house, and the intensifying smell of hot grease awaiting flour-coated pieces of chicken.

There I was lying in a bathtub, the head busybody neighbor hovering over me, pressing my scalp with his thick dark brown fingers, trying to stop the bleeding. All I could think of was death. Was I dying?

I was rushed to the nearest hospital. The pain was strong. The needle, to my young eyes, was too long to believe. And they slid it into my head. Fear grabbed me by the ankles and threw me into hysteria, as the smell of the hospital laughed and caressed me.

The past recedes. Now I am once again peering from the window in my apartment. I watch a taxicab discharge a passenger. Every moment is of concern to me. The passenger is a woman. In slow motion, I see her searching through her blue leather purse, extract money, and hand it across the front seat to the driver. He wears a red baseball cap. As he turns to accept the money I can see a large, curled P on the top of the cap, advertising his affection for the Philadelphia Phillies.

As she opens the door, the driver bolts from his seat and runs around to the back of the car, too late in his attempt to open it for her. I can see embarrassment flush his face as he realizes she has managed on her own. From the distance his features are ordinary. He is a man in blue jeans, checkered yellow-and-green flannel shirt, with rust-colored hair that juts out from under his cap.

He is wearing a blue nylon jacket on which there is a hood. The drawstrings dangle down his chest on either side. He now extends his hand and the woman purposely ignores it. Her back is to me, but I am anxious to see her. She is already highly recommended. I can perceive her sense of history. She motions away his other hand, as it contains her change from the fare. Magnanimity claims her. Her hair is black and drapes her shoulders. The coat she wears needs work, an old cashmere of questionable quality.

She is now crossing the street toward me in slow motion. I can see the bottoms of her feet, as she steps across the street. Her shoes are black with a golden strip implanted around the toe, between the sole and the upper shoe. Her ankles are slender, delicate. I have so much time to do this, it is frightening. By the time she is across the street, I can see the color of her eyes and guess her age. I have been impressed with her walk and her smile. I am dissuaded by her attire. Enlivened by her arrogance. And then . . . she is gone. Turned northward along the street on which I live. Gone, perhaps, never again to be observed by me.

Forgotten observations. Dissipated energies, useless nights

spent twisted in macabre exercises. Can you imagine being caught in a web of distant clouds, breathing different air, shackled by the mind? Can you imagine being a storyteller? Hundreds of taxicabs lie fallow in some stupid region of my brain, never to be used or thought of again. Unless there is some connection to a smell, then perhaps, the taxicabs may traverse my mind like a looping tape, forever recurring.

Even now I sit here, terrified, consumed by this trembling realization of doom and endings. And am I crying? Am I breaking lamps and coffee tables? Am I shooting heroin? No. In my last hours I sit here, writing this story, confronting my enemy. Taking license at will.

If the dead air holding up the walls of this room was an audience of literary critics, I would be no more afraid. I suppose I have reached the ultimate emotion: experiencing death.

The truth presents itself. There is nowhere to hide. Nothing left to use as protection. My mind is a hell-bent traitor, and solace is as far from my grasp as immortality.

There is this place on the Delaware shores called Rehoboth Beach. It appears the happy resort town. On a clear summer Sunday, the smell of fresh salt water rides bareback through the air. It whips about, mixing neatly with the smell of fish, clams, popcorn, and saltwater taffy. I can inhale that smell. I can remember walking into the five-and-ten-cent store to buy a shovel and a bucket. I can remember the sand getting into my swimming shorts.

I am dying.

And, as this happens, as I sit here marking the last hours, people shuffle in slow motion outside my window. This window was created for me. It is not so large as to make a man's presence conspicuous, nor so small as to restrict my vision. I sit here too much. Friends are constantly urging me to push the typewriter away, to leave my chair by the window and venture out there with them. Well, they shall have it to themselves.

Can death do this? Where does this heavy resignation have its beginning? All the stories, the poems, the plots and scripts, the dreams and fantasies—everything? Stacks upon stacks of crumpled, soiled typed-on papers, destined to turn even more yellow, and the spirit and energy used to make them breathe is slowly, painfully evaporating, even as my life seeks to explain itself.

Walter is outside. He is walking toward my window. He is one of the few who realize my presence. But then Walter needs to know. He brings my paper each morning, leaving it on the window sill. Walter is a young black boy. A fine boy. The best I've ever known. He is short for his age, which he tells me is thirteen. When he's finished his route, he always walks back through my street and waves at me.

I can see him approaching. I see him so clearly that I can see him smiling at me. He approaches so slowly. His hair is curly and winds its way around the pate, forming his yellow brown face.

He is plump, robust, full of energy. His jeans are fading and his tennis shoes unraveling. He doesn't know of my predicament. Eighteen cars pass before he is within talking distance. The light at the corner has changed twice. Three people have walked out of the dry cleaners across the street, opposite my house.

I don't care if he stops or not. I haven't time to spend with mindless children. Especially newspaper children.

"Morning, Mr. Flowers."

I nod my head. You can leave now, Walter. Your purpose is served. Misery knows what's best.

"Have you seen Darcy today?"

This time I shake my head to indicate "no."

"See you tomorrow, Mr. Flowers."

One hopes. One hopes mightily. But why mention Darcy, you scamp? Worthless newspaper boys should spend their time delivering papers, not bringing up the names of people who are evil and conspiring.

It was too late. He has thrown me into thought. A dream enshrouds. One that Darcy has figured in in the past. It is a sort of perpetual dilemma, this dream. Haunting. Single-handedly, this particular dream saps the spirit from my body each time it revisits.

This Darcy fellow works for the United States Post Office. He goes to work each morning, gathers together an assortment of letters, packages, newspapers, magazines, and sets about the business of delivering the mail. Not once in ten years has this Darcy brought me anything but bad luck. It is his fault that I am dying like this. Unloved. Unread. A living person, full of hope, reduced by the postal service and freak literary practices to a soulless relic.

Each day I waited for him with love and hope. I sat here, just as I sit here today, anticipating the pure beauty of his body trodding down the street toward me. I knew, simply knew, that he would eventually bring me my release. I was certain. For truth, how long can a person languish?

I trust there are limits, but nothing in my life confirms it. He passed here on days when a bill would have been greeted as a love letter. And on those days when he did stop, and I heard the tinny rustling sound of letters sliding against the metal of the mail slot, I'd clutch my heart.

O my emotional self.

Here it is: I'd open this white envelope with my name neatly typed on the outside. CONGRATULATIONS, MR. FLOWERS.

And then, I'd be on the Johnny Carson show talking about this existence I'd lived—heavy, bitter.

Tell me, who's playing the lead in the movie version?

We're still meeting about that. I want James Earl Jones, they want Sidney Poitier. We've had some meetings. There'll be more. Everybody is excited.

Darcy the mailman is the villain in my life, he is the tool of some party of fools who think I'm an idiot or that I just don't mean that much. Ten years ago, a friend told me that there was a group of publishers, totaling about three, who got together every two months to decide which writers would be published. They made those decisions based on speculation and rumor. They measured acceptability, neatness, poise, and the temperature of the blood. There was a final criterion that had to do with sex and politics, but I've never gotten the full story.

Well, it matters little now, the game is over. Now I am more concerned with the vision of teenagers in the alley across the street, apparently smoking something out of a small pipe.

A boy of about seventeen is standing in the middle of four other boys. He is the hub. He retrieves the pipe and hands it to the next person. In between, he takes a light hit himself. I am amused. It is a strange idea to me. I know what they are doing, but for them to be so close to me, not knowing what I am thinking, nearly makes me laugh. Even as they banter in hushed voices, they have no idea that I am dying.

One by one, as they inhale the smoke, their heads snap back to an erect position. Eyes close momentarily. A sigh. One after the other. Perhaps my writing is a waste of time. Perhaps there is a sharper, more easily obtained euphoria. If there were time, I might investigate.

But this life of smells draws nearer to the truth. Why should I be spared? All I have are thoughts and feelings and unseen experiences. All I wanted was to stimulate, ever so gently, some exploration. But, even as I accept my fate, I am still struggling to write my story. Even now, I battle what is happening to me, trying to reconcile all those things that have taken place. I must be brave. I must be special.

Now. There. See. This black car that has just parked in front of my house. Inside it sits a black man of fifty-five. There, now, the door swings open and he climbs out of the hearselike car. He is graying, distinguished in his deep blue three-piece suit. Very dapper. He is coming for me. Another black man waiting and losing himself. This man carries his black bag with bravado. Here he is, a big educated man, trained to save lives and minister healthful bromides.

Hospitals manufacture their own smell. It is as distinctive as the smell of a new car or the aftermath of gunpowder explosions. I have this image of an aerosol can of hospital smell. If used carefully, it could create intense and inexplicable inner fear. One could spray it at union negotiations or in church. On contact the victim would begin to have deep misgivings and general discomfort. Eventually, the victim would agree to anything, as long as they could be saved.

"Flowers? Open the door! It's Dr. Andrews."

I do. I have to stop soon. He'll be taking me away. No typewriters there. No time to dream. We are bound to a building of fear and death.

"How are you feeling today?"

O my emotional self. "How now?"

"I see you've been working. Good. I think you are going to be just fine."

I try to knock him over with my eyes. Push him away with my voice. "Doctor, how can I be fine? My work is not finished and you are taking me away." I am near tears. I didn't expect to be so weak.

"You should be back here in three to five days."

He was smiling. The unfeeling mannequin of a man. "You keep saying that. Why won't you tell me the truth? I'm dying. I can take the truth. I am intimate with the spiritual and mystical aspects of life."

"Mr. Flowers, this operation is just not as serious as all that. As I've explained to you, there is a small tumor that has to be removed. You'll have some pain. Perhaps a few months of fairly bad headaches, but nothing more serious than that. Oh, yes, and of course, I mentioned there will be some loss of smell. But I've gone through all of that with you before. It's nothing we can't recover from."

We?

The countless words that have stumbled out of my mind now dance on white paper. The art of writing waits again for others to catch up. O my emotional self. Damn the Darcys. Damn the Darcys. Establish this silence where there was once unheard noise. O . . .

Can death do this?

ichabod flopped down in the chair across from the lieutenant, as high as he'd ever been. This was happiness. Telling stories. Seeking the truth in a convoluted maze of reality
and fantasy.

Bloom stared at him. "Ichabod, this is madness, you
know. It can't go on. They're not going to wait all day and
night for you to come out of here."

Ichabod searched once again for a cigarette. He found
the pack, lit one as he walked to the bookcase. "They will
wait, Lieutenant. They will wait. And do you know why?
They'll wait because they don't want to do anything that
might further endanger you."

"I told you before, they will eventually get tired of
waiting and they will swat your ass down like a weak-
ass fly." The detective paused to gather himself. "Cut me
loose."

"No, Lieutenant. I can't do that. I don't trust you."

The telephone sang out, startling Ichabod. Bloom could
see fear instantly appear on his face.

"Should I answer that?"

"Ichabod, if I were you, I'd answer it. And I'd beg them to let you give yourself up."

"But I'm not finished. You don't even know what happened yet."

"That's not my fault, now is it? You've had plenty of time to tell this little tale of yours. We could all be going home by now."

"You forget, Lieutenant, I am home." After four rings the telephone was once again silent.

"Yes. I . . . ah . . . I didn't forget. But, you know, the truth is, when you leave here—and you will leave—you will not be coming back any time soon. You've ruined that."

Ichabod turned away from the voice. He rested his head on the bookshelf. Spoke to the books themselves. "I know. I know this was totally stupid. Self-destructive. And I know that no one will understand why I'm doing this the way I am. It would be so much easier to take the white-boy way out."

He cut his eyes back to Bloom. "You do know, don't you, that no matter what kind of ambient fears you may have about me, about my being black or whatever else, there are no more violent people on earth than white men? Immoral, unscrupulous, vicious, heinous. The kind of people who shoot up schools and fast food restaurants. People who worship the gun. Who sacrifice their own children for the stupid right to bear arms. What kind of people would do that?"

The lieutenant looked at him. He couldn't believe his ears. "Are you talking to me?"

"Who the hell else would I be talking to, Lieutenant?"

"Well, forgive me for not being sure. I mean. I'm the white guy here, right? I'm unarmed . . ."

Ichabod hastened to correct him. "*Dis*armed. I disarmed you."

Bloom blinked quickly. "You disarmed me, Ichabod. You did. And you've bound me down with duct tape. And you brandish a gun over me. Threaten me." His whole body seemed to cramp. He groaned and continued. "There's a body over there. Did a white man kill him?"

Ichabod covered his eyes with his hands. Now he was tired, less certain of what he was doing. Less sure that there was a point to this course of action. He wondered who was outside now. He guessed that the whole world was watching by now. He was sure he knew at least four people who were waiting to see how things turned out. Were they out there, too?

It was an inbred sense of guilt which drove him in this strategy. The whole thing had been his idea. And now he was losing the sense of what was to be accomplished. He sighed. The telephone rang again. He walked over to the table and opened the line.

"Yeah?"

"Ichabod, this is Captain Hirsh. How are we doing?" Her voice started out fast and then abruptly slowed like a tape first played at the wrong speed and then quickly brought to its proper level.

"We're doing fine, Captain. Just fine. I've been telling the lieutenant here a story. It's taking a little longer than I first expected but I'm doing the best I can."

"I'm sure you are, Ichabod. I'm sure you are. But I want you to think about what I'm up against out here." Iris Hirsh paused an extra beat. "It's not easy holding these guys back. We need something from you. A sign of cooperation. Something."

"Like what, for instance?"

"Well, Ichabod, you could let Lieutenant Bloom go. That would be an excellent indication of your willingness to help

us get out of this situation without any further ah . . .
confrontation."

Ichabod steeled his voice. "I am in the middle of something in here. In fact, I was just telling your detective that I
am not some kind of wacko white boy freaked out by his
wife's infidelity or the increasing numbers of women in the
workplace or some intense sense of inferiority that would
lead to a suicidal explosion of violence. That is not who I
am. So I don't want you to be treating me like that. Understand? I want respect."

"I'm not treating you in any way, Ichabod. I'm just trying to get both of you out of there safely."

"Then let me finish. That's the only way this can end
peacefully. Give me a little more time."

Ichabod heard the woman's heavy breaths. She wanted
to reach through the telephone wires and snatch his ass out
into the streets. He could feel it in her voice. But she was
well trained, the soul of restraint. Hostage-scene negotiator.
All the guys had seen her operate. Listened as she spoke
honey drops to crazed or drunken men barricaded in some
simple A-frame house, armed to the teeth and willing to go
down in a blaze of glory.

Iris wondered why those guys didn't realize there was,
in fact, no blaze of glory. Just the acrid smell of gunpowder
and singed flesh. Such confrontations were often the onset
of eternal quiescence. The only salve, perhaps, for a
twisted soul.

But Ichabod, though a mite twisted, was no suicidal su-
premacist. No survivalist counting the days until the feds
set foot on his property so that years of planning and
hoarding and stoking the fires of insane paranoia yielded
the perfect killing machine. No. This story would unfold in
an entirely different way. From an entirely different
impetus.

"Can I speak to the lieutenant again?"

Although hesitant, Ichabod wanted to show that he was open to negotiation. He held the handset to the policeman's ear. His eyes locked onto Bloom's, trying to read the other side of the conversation.

"No, Captain. No," Lieutenant Bloom said calmly. He was trying his best to sound steady. Brave and collected. Besides, he was ready to make his move. He'd been quietly but firmly putting strong pressure on the arms of the dining room chair and the tape had finally loosened enough so that he thought he could reach and open his knife.

He decided to wait until Ichabod had finished talking with Hirsh.

Ichabod pulled the phone back. "You will just have to be patient. We're getting very close and everything has been fine so far. Your boy here is fine. Just give us a little more time." He killed the power to the phone and turned back to put it on the table.

Bloom pulled the knife out of his pants, and used his thumb to pry one of its blades open. He sawed the tape, an awkward maneuver that applied just enough pressure to the tape to make a cut. Still, it took less time than the cop expected. Once started, it ripped easily.

He drew a deep breath, snatched his arm free, and lunged at Ichabod all in the same motion. Bloom's sudden activity completely startled him. Ichabod knew instantly that everything was about to change.

Bloom was still securely bound by both legs and one arm and at first Ichabod saw his portly captive swinging his torso wildly. It was like a painting magically come to life. A swirl of colors and the sweat from his panting white body.

It was only then that Ichabod saw the knife flash. It was like a lightning bolt sent from God. He watched, stood there as if his feet were nailed into the hardwood floors. As if

they were the floor itself as he watched Bloom flail. He
heard the duct tape snap as Bloom cut his right leg free.
Now he resembled a screen door flapping in a summer
storm as he wheeled around and began hacking on the tape
that bound his left arm.

Ichabod's mind tried to send all kinds of panicked mes-
sages to his body. It was no longer an intellectual exercise
and no longer possible to keep the physical relationship between the two men on the same level as it had once been.
But Ichabod had figured that would happen. He was actually a little surprised it had taken the policeman so long to
marshal his outrage into a plan. So far, Lieutenant Bloom
had only seemed interested in the facts of the situation. Who
was dead? Who killed him? How long was Ichabod going
to continue his game? All questions about people and issues
other than the detective's own safety.

Ichabod had wondered about that. Could Lieutenant
Bloom be so selfless that he would never break down and
simply strike out in a singular desire to free himself? Wasn't
that the point of life? This thirst of the soul for freedom?
Wasn't that why Ichabod held Bloom under restraint?
Wasn't that why Bloom, after being confined beyond his
comfort level, was hell-bent on breaking free? Ichabod
thought so. Everything he did was designed to create a
greater manifestation of freedom for himself. Even holding
Bloom hostage was done with a clear sense of ensuring his
long-term ability to feel free. In the end no one would probably accept his explanation for this debacle. They would
probably not understand.

But that didn't mean he shouldn't be doing exactly what
he was doing. What is leadership anyway? Besides, he was
an artist and he agreed wholeheartedly with John Gardner:
Art leads, it doesn't follow. Who knew what revolution he
was in the process of kicking off? Alas . . . it would all have

its value located in the space just over the horizon. The blush would eventually and inevitably reveal the smile.

And yes, he had anticipated some form of rebellion. But it had taken so long to erupt that it almost caught him off-guard. He ripped his feet from the floor. Freed himself from his sluggish mind and purposefully walked to the bookcase. Bloom was close to hacking the last of the tape that held his left arm down. Ichabod grabbed the gun from the book-case and spun around just as Bloom was on the verge of freeing his other hand. The red handle of the Swiss Army knife, with its tiny white cross, painted a red streak in the air around the lieutenant.

Ichabod leveled the gun at the detective. In his mind, Bloom was talking. Screaming. He had mustered everything, every moment of disappointment and emptiness to stoke his anger. His stillborn career, his limited experience with peo-ple who were different from him, his dislike of pepper and yet its continued prevalence in nearly every dish by nearly every culture. Yes, pepper. He hated pepper with such force that he'd once threatened to kill a waiter who'd, without asking, angled his phallic pepper mill over a sweet spinach salad at one of those fancy hotels downtown.

"Who gave you the right to put pepper on every god-damned thing? Who?" And with that Bill Bloom had jumped out of his chair and grabbed the startled waiter's lapels and yanked him close enough that the waiter could hear the beat of his heart.

His wife, Connie, had slowly stood up and walked over to Bloom and gently placed her hand on his back. With that gesture she reminded him that he was a peace officer, sworn to uphold the law. To protect and serve. With that gesture she asked him to think of his future and their mutual safety. She had, after all, invested in his career just as much as Bloom had.

When he let the poor man go and sat back down he carefully began searching his salad, looking for the largest pieces of cracked peppercorn so that he could pick them from his plate. He muttered as he did this. The muttering was a sign of anger. Of a kind of tough resolution that he would never bend. Never end up "liking" pepper. No matter how many times he was tested. He would never relent.

And now he muttered as he chopped the vinyl-coated duct tape. If he unloosed himself he knew he'd have to throw himself at Ichabod with all the fury he had. He'd been passive long enough. There was such a thing as honor.

Ichabod broke his stance. He was conscious of feeling like a thug on an eighties detective show. *Baretta,* for example. All he needed was bell-bottom pants and an afro. And bad "funky" music playing in the background. He held the gun down by his side for a beat. The pot was about to boil over.

He again leveled the gun at Lt. Bill Bloom. He flipped the lock. He'd made himself promise that he would go that far. He'd pull the trigger if this foolish white man wouldn't or couldn't sit still through this exercise. It was just a game. He wanted to shout at Bloom to act his age. Understand that it was just a game, that it was Bloom taking it to the next level. If Ichabod had to shoot him, then the police would burst through the door in seconds.

"Lieutenant," Ichabod said calmly.

Bloom stopped abruptly. He'd completely retreated into himself. From the moment he'd realized that his knife was finally within reach, he'd lost consciousness in a way. He sort of forgot about Ichabod and his ranting and slipped into a place where the only voice he heard was his own. And he was angry. He heard himself saying how if this was the way his life was supposed to end then so be it. But he would not go out tied down by some insane amateur. He'd struggle and fight and flail and do whatever he had to do to be true to himself. He was an officer of the law and a man. Ichabod had crossed the line. And for what? Bloom had no better idea of Ichabod's story than when the sorry episode had started.

But somehow Ichabod's voice pierced through his jumble of thoughts. His eyes met the stare of the nine-millimeter pistol trained on him. When he flashed on Ichabod's face it was clear that his captor was also under a challenge from his own spirit. Bloom could see that Ichabod had checked out. The gun and the moment had conspired against one man's quest.

"Stop." Ichabod ordered, his voice stone.

"Or what?" Bloom snapped free his left arm and then instinctively bent lower to work on his left leg.

"I said stop. Put the knife down." Ichabod stepped closer.

Bloom took a deep breath. He let it run wild within him, this breath. It circulated through his brain and drained the depth of his body—each available molecule found a home.

"What do you want from me, Icky? I've been patient but I can't just sit here any longer."

"Lieutenant?"

"What?"

"Would you take a good look at me. Look at me." Ichabod spoke through his eyes. "I'm prepared to die. Right here. Right now. Are you?"

Bloom slowly turned around. Ichabod could see the four-inch blade of the knife sparkle. It looked new, unused. "I don't want to die, Icky. I really don't. That's why we've gotten this far. But I'm tired and sore. I'm hungry."

"Do you want to die?" Ichabod knew he had him. The lieutenant blinked. To be free today, he must be willing to die. Willing and resigned. Only then was there the slightest chance that Ichabod would back down. His punishment was certain. This was a political act. Unfortunately, he was sure that no one would understand the political nature of his actions. When black people made a fuss it was always so easy to find the cliché in it. To be a person of color in America was to give yourself up to the cliché. If you strived, you were trying to be white. If you struggled, you were a victim, just like your daddy. If you were angry, well, hey, what the hell was so wrong that you should be so angry? And weren't all of you angry, anyway?

"I told you. I've been trying to stay alive."

Ichabod took a step closer. "It doesn't look like that to me. I turn my back one minute and you produce a knife." Ichabod smiled to show he was reassuming control. "Let it go. Let it go and sit your fat ass back down before I light you up."

Bloom stood, half bent over, his leg still firmly tied off, his suit a sweat-drenched smock. "Icky . . . I . . . ah . . ." Bloom knew that Ichabod would stop him from cutting all of the tape. It surprised the cop that Ichabod had waited so long. When the detective turned his back on him to get at his bindings, Bloom had expected the worst. But Ichabod had stood and watched.

But now that he had a weapon in his hands and was almost free, Bloom wasn't about to just give up and allow himself to be tied down again. Then again, he had to accept the reality of his predicament. A mistake now could easily cost him his life. He didn't really think Ichabod was a killer, but at each turn the black man seemed capable of the violence Bloom wanted to avoid.

He looked into Ichabod's eyes and saw a man who was enraptured by the unfolding events. Then, deep in his body, he tasted a fresh rejuvenating cup of water. It soothed his soul and strengthened him. He straightened up, put a faux expression of resignation on his face, while his heart flared with power.

"Okay . . ." Lieutenant Bloom let all the air drain out of his body. He made himself thinner. Stronger. He became facile, able to do what his mind hoped. Strong enough to overcome. He felt his muscles release and for a long moment he was at peace. "Here." He held the knife up by two fingers. "I guess I didn't really think I was going to make it anyway."

Ichabod reached for the knife. "It was a little stupid. Here I am with this big-ass . . ." Ichabod's sentence was cut short. Lieutenant Bloom had regrasped the handle of the knife and faced its blade at Ichabod. He sliced it through the air. Instinctively Ichabod raised his right arm to ward off the blow—to keep it from hitting his throat. But the knife was sharp enough and Bloom strong enough to penetrate his arm. The knife grazed his wrist, drawing blood.

"Oh, my God. You fuckin cut me. You fat-ass motherfucka." Ichabod stepped back and brought the gun up. Bloom had thought he was close enough to grab him, but Ichabod had managed to sidestep his swipe and jump back just out of reach. Both men had miscalculated. And now they stood face to face.

Ichabod was hurt. There was an immediate stinging in the palm of his hand. The gushing had slowed a bit after he grabbed his arm. He struggled to hold his gun as he backed away from Bloom. "What the fuck is wrong with you? I should shoot you right now. Blow your stupid ass away."

For some reason Bloom felt stronger. "You know what that will mean, don't you, Icky? You're not getting out of here. And if you shoot me you're not getting out of here alive."

"Suppose I don't care about that now? Suppose I assume that's the way it's going to be?"

The lieutenant kicked his leg out from the chair as his answer. It creaked loudly but remained intact. At that instant Ichabod realized he was dealing with the unmovable force that he'd first thought Bloom represented. He would talk. He would indulge whining for a while. The truth, however, was that Lt. Bill Bloom would never vouch for him. Never do anything but attempt to bring him under control. Make him submit to his will. His law.

"Lieutenant, I'm only going to say this one more time. I'm just about ready to bust this cap in your ass. I will shoot you. Drop the fucking knife and sit down. It's the last time I'm going to tell you." This time Ichabod didn't wait. Even with his bleeding arm, he rushed at Bloom, kicking him sharply in the groin and clubbing him on the head with the gun. Bloom dropped like wounded game and lay motionless on the floor.

Ichabod quickly retrieved a bundle of clothesline rope from the kitchen. Before he'd decided on using the duct tape, the rope was to have been his tool of bondage. He scrambled to bind Bloom's hands and feet in what was traditionally the method of tying hogs for slaughter. He knew he couldn't lift him into the chair so he let him lie there. When the officer came to, Ichabod would maneuver him into the cherry wood chair.

And then he had to attend to his bleeding arm. The wound had slowed just slightly but it still produced a steady thin stream of blood. He wasn't sure but he thought the knife had actually cut a vein. Although the wound was clotting, it still hurt. He walked to the linen closet and removed a stack of towels. He sat down at the table and waited for the lieutenant to regain consciousness.

His eyes wandered to the lump of flesh swaddled in

plastic curled up in the corner of the room. He knew the smell of Dewitt would not long be confined by such a flimsy coffin. Like Bloom, Ichabod was tired and hungry. And now he was injured and bleeding.

On the floor, Bill Bloom lay still but not unconscious. He half expected Ichabod to pull the trigger. After a moment Bloom slowly turned to face Ichabod. "You could have killed me."

Ichabod looked up from his arm. The towel he'd wrapped around his wrist and arm slowly reddened. "You are one stupid sonofabitch. What the hell were you trying to do?"

"You know what I was doing. You should have expected it." It was then that Lieutenant Bloom realized that Ichabod had been wounded. He saw the blood puddled and smeared on the hardwood floor. "I got you, didn't I?" He couldn't help but chuckle. His groin was on fire and his head thumped. "I got you. That's something."

"Oh, so, you're proud of it?"

"I needed to try, Icky. I'm a cop, for crying out loud."

"I should blow your ass to kingdom come."

"I thought you would. But you didn't. You didn't. And let me tell you why you didn't."

"Why, Lieutenant?"

"Because you were afraid."

Ichabod's temper flared. He almost screamed, "I am not afraid of you. I am not afraid of you. I wouldn't be here if I was afraid. I am capable of killing you. I truly am. But that's not what this is about. You are insignificant. Historically you only matter because I do. Right now, all of your energy is being used to survive my presence. *My* presence. This is about me. And I'm not afraid. It just wasn't the right time. I want to finish my story and I want you to be alive to hear it. Do you understand?"

The lieutenant stared at him. The clothesline rope that Ichabod had used to hog-tie him was bruising his skin. He had expended a lot of energy. He was very tired. Exhausted. Hurt. And now he was more frightened than ever. More sure that someone else would die.

"Do you understand?" Ichabod fought the rising frantic.

"Yes. But what are you going to do about that arm of yours? Looks like I got you pretty good." Bloom smiled again.

"You got me pretty good, all right." He held the arm up for the cop to see. "But I'm tough. I'll live."

"Icky? I'm not going to ask you what this is all about again. Every time I do you go off into some long tirade. I don't feel like I know anymore than I did before. Except maybe that you're even crazier than I thought you were."

"Do you want to sit up again?"

"That would be nice, seeing as how it looks like you're not about to let me go."

"No, Lieutenant. We're at the best part of the story now. This is where it gets fun. Now you get to hear the intimate details of the events which transpired here. And, of course, you'll have the opportunity to learn more about the ways and manners of the bohos and the multicultis. I'll even get you something to drink, Lieutenant. A glass of water? If you'll lie there, or sit still from this point on, I can assure you that the worst of our ordeal is behind us. The rest is all story—if you'll let me tell it. And if I don't bleed to death first." Ichabod paused. "But I'm confident I'll live long enough. We will survive. You and I. Just like old times, eh? A white man and a black man locked in some eternal dilemma, waiting for something that will help us see the sense in our embrace. You and I, Lieutenant. We are archetypal Americans. We *are* America. And, unless the warriors and the generals get too antsy, we will survive together."

as Dewitt motored through the city on his way to my house, the party was already shifting into its next phase. People were leaving—actually I was encouraging people to leave. We wanted the house clear of everyone who wasn't eligible for the Genius Grant by the time Dewitt got there.

I'd been making the rounds, whispering to my comrades that they should also urge people to consider another venue for their Halloween revelry. To be sure, there were countless places where they could take the party. No regional population could celebrate meaningless and created holidays better than Minnesotans. They marched in parades at the slightest provocation. They have this thing downtown called Holidazzle or something like that where there is a parade every night between Thanksgiving and Christmas. Every night. These are cold Minnesota winter nights. And the streets are thronged. And then in February, when human flesh is susceptible to flash freezing, they have the winter carnival that also features ridiculous activities, not the least of which is marching to music in subzero weather. Minnesotans will drink themselves senseless at the mere hint of a celebration.

But maybe there was nothing else to do in the midst of a harsh winter. It made you want to be with other people. Lots of other people.

So nearly every bar was advertising some special Halloween event. There were plenty of places to go. Not to mention the Smoking Entrails poetry reading at the trendiest of night spots, the Scrounge Lounge.

Sometimes we'd go there en masse and heckle the poor young wanna-be kids who sense the mysteries of poetry circulating around them, but struggle to find the thread which connects their souls to the sound of their voice. We know that it takes either insanity or courage to stand up in front of a crowd and tell them about your abusive father, or the way white people's hair smells when it's wet, but we go and throw shit at them anyway. And when I say we, I mean the obvious and clandestine members of the multicultiboho crew. Many of the same people who were at the party. Of course, some of the people who were here last night were also some of the same people we've heckled. Our grudges aren't long-standing. A couple of weeks and people who were mad at each other are talking about collaborating on a performance project. Especially if the Pheromone Foundation ("We smell out good art") or the Macmammon Foundation are offering some money.

This was happening more and more: Foundations and other arts organizations were offering money to coax people who were culturally different to work together. It was an admirable goal. Suddenly everybody wanted us. We were the vogue. The thing. The theaters wanted to do plays by writers of other cultures. And they wanted to cast white plays in a "color blind" way. Performance-art venues scoured the terrain for unknown cultis they could "discover." Not unlike Dewitt. Suddenly, we were the shit.

And we liked it. We watched the faces of our white

counterparts, the artists and writers who had previously held the power, and we knew that for this particular moment in time, we had shaken their smug belief that they would always and forever be the center of the universe.

At that moment, however, my main concern was clearing the house. By the time Dewitt arrived, I wanted everyone to be gone except for Herm, Marci, Jenny, and April. The way I pictured it, we'd be sitting quietly sipping wine out of the fine crystal I kept in the kitchen cupboard.

There are times when I can be the consummate, considerate host. But last night I was on edge. I knew I was being a little rude but I couldn't stop myself. I walked up to François, who was once again on a jag about the local poetry scene, and tapped him on the shoulder. I can only guess as to why I approached him first. He being white and all. I suppose I felt I *could* be rude to him and he wouldn't get all bunched up about it. And you can't ignore the fact that if you can get a white man to do something, other people will follow.

When I peered over his shoulder I realized he was talking to Dotty Enpointe, the only black woman on television in the area. She was a statuesque chocolate woman with a perfectly tight, but slightly sexy smile. Some people called her "the Lips," out of admiration. She always made me think of Donna Summer. In 1974, *Esquire* magazine named Donna as the "white man's burden" in their annual Dubious Achievement Awards issue. Dotty sent more white Minnesota men to bed happy after the news than anyone will ever admit to. I figured François was struggling with this burden even as he tried to sound intelligent about the local poetry scene.

There were about five other people clustered around them, listening to François drop his particular science. "You have to support the righteous words. The poetry that's about changing things. Breaking down walls."

That made me mad. Knowledge was one thing. I granted François that. He knew stuff. But don't be telling people of color they have to be doing this or that. Not when you're basically a rich white boy and you could, if you had any initiative at all, do any damn thing in the whole wide world you wanted. I couldn't stop myself from saying, "François, you're always talking some revolutionary bullshit. What exactly have you ever done to bring this system down, or even into alignment with your political instincts?"

He turned around and what had started as a smile quickly transformed into a puzzled look. I'd never cracked on him before. But I was tired already of his pompous revolutionary ass.

"No, really." I continued. "I don't mean to be on your shit or anything, but don't you think it would be more important if white people like you, white people who could see, could even admit to themselves and a higher power, that there was something wrong in the way people of color were treated by white people and the systems they controlled? That they would actually do something themselves to change the world instead of expecting it of those of us who feel put upon?"

"What would you suggest, Icky?"

"I don't know," I said quickly. "But whatever it is, it isn't going to get done in my house tonight. It's about time for ya'll to get on up out of here."

That wounded him. At first he'd just thought I was being provocative. Confrontational. But now he could see that I didn't really want to engage him. I just wanted him to go. "But don't take offense François, I'm kicking everybody out of here."

As I said that I caught Dotty's eyes. They were even

wider than usual. I realized then that I was in danger of being mentioned on her weekly news segment called "UGH!" This was not the best way to get into the news. Dotty would list all of the bad movies, restaurants, boorish and notable people who in some way had committed a social or criminal faux pas. I smiled at her, hoping to defuse any ill will, leaned around François and said, "You are welcome back any time. I'd love to spend time with you." The confusion in Dotty's face slipped into a smile.

"I'm tired, anyway. Maybe we can get together sometime and talk."

"I'd like that," I said.

François was already drifting his way to the front door. I knew I had gone a little overboard. But before I could do anything about it, my apartment filled with Gloria Gaynor's "I Will Survive." I took off in the direction of the CD player. There I found Don Tweed and Steve Deed. Those really were their names. And they were best friends. Never saw one without the other. I didn't know whether they were gay or what. But Don was diminutive and as black as asphalt, while Steve looked like the six-million-dollar man. A chisel-faced astronaut-looking kind of guy. Together they appeared at nearly every function. Don was a banker by profession but had a growing collection of art made primarily by black and Latin artists. And Steve worked as the executive director of the Filmmaker's First Film Support Group. He'd helped a lot of people think that they might one day make their first film. But I secretly suspected he was being paid by somebody to actually *stop* people from making their first film. You'd meet people of all stripes who thought they had a good idea for a film before they talked to Steve. After he was finished with them, they always talked about how they had to take a class in scriptwriting or read a book or something. Nobody ever actually made a film.

They were standing by my stereo, flipping through the available CDs. "Hey, guys," I said, "I'm sorry, I don't want to get this party going in the wrong direction."

Steve looked at me with that Paul Newman in *Hud* stance and said, "So you can't handle a little boogie? I thought you were the guy from Philly who had been to all those great parties."

"Yeah, yeah. I know what I said." He had me there. That was one of the reasons I hardly ever had people over. I hate being seen as a hypocrite. I don't hate being a hypocrite. I just hate people knowing it. "But," I reached between them and flipped the stereo off, "this was only supposed to last until eight. And it's almost nine. You understand. I've got some important business to take care of." As soon as the music died I heard a few moans in the background. I'd gotten there just in time. A few more beats and people would have been dancing.

They looked at each other and, without exchanging a word between them, they pivoted in unison and vanished. Maybe I turned my head. Maybe there was a trapdoor suddenly present in my living room. I don't know. But I didn't see them leave. Tweed and Deed were an interesting couple. I'd heard that they were actually heterosexual. That they actually used each other to seduce women. You know, like Dan would use Steve to be in places where white women were. Places where, if he went unescorted by Steve, he'd be made to feel uncomfortable. But with a white man, he was accepted. It brought him untold benefits. And Steve got a conscience. He got a defender; Dan would never let any of us talk about Steve too much. Anyway, they were gone.

When I looked around, I could see that other people were retrieving their coats and sweaters and were making their way toward the exit. I tried to get to the front door to properly send my guests out into the world, but I must confess that I said goodbye to only a few people. The rest simply drifted out into the fall night air.

Of course, after a moment or two of hesitation, and a nod from me, Herm, Jenny, Marci, and April tried to hang back. There were a few suspicious stragglers who sensed that something else was going on, and tried to linger. But I quickly concocted a story about how we needed to talk about a potential performance piece that we were planning. Sometimes you can see a groan before you hear it. The stragglers heard the words "performance piece" and beat feet to the door.

And then we were alone. I remember I retreated to the bathroom and on returning walked into an obviously agitated Marci. "What's wrong with you?" I asked her.

"Why do you think something's wrong with me? Oh, I guess just because I'm a black woman you think I'm always pissed off about something." I couldn't detect a smile so I decided to play it smooth.

"No, Marci, you just look like you're angry at somebody."

"Oh, excuse me. I just look like that." She sat down on the couch. "I'm sorry, Icky. I didn't mean to snap at you. I'm just tired of people fucking with me. Tyrone was here. Did you see him?"

I hadn't. I assumed she was referring to Tyrone Jenkins. He was a goofy guy who seemed to be stuck somewhere in graduate school. The perpetual student, a horrible intellect; almost bogus. Whenever I saw him in a discussion he never made sense. To make matters worse, his last girlfriend had had to put a restraining order on his ass for stalking her. I didn't like stalkers. Cowards. Mama's boys. That's how I saw him. A whiner. Women thought he was handsome, but when I looked into his eyes I saw emptiness. What he really needed was counseling. "No. I missed him. Why?"

"That's one slimy dude." She sipped her drink.

"What did he do?"

"He tried to get me to go home with his sorry ass."

I laughed. Tyrone was worse than a whiner. He was stupid. "What did you say to the brother?"

"I cursed his ass out. He's been sneaking around with a friend of mine and everybody knows about that problem with his former girlfriend. Like I'm going to mess around with him. It just freaked me out, that's all. I feel like I want to go home and take a shower."

Herm walked up behind us. "Did he try to kiss you? I thought I saw him with his arm around you."

Marci cut her eyes in his direction. She actually smiled as he was talking. "Maybe you saw his arm on my shoulder. But I guarantee you did not see him kissing me."

"I didn't say you kissed him," Herm's smile was *so* big, all-encompassing. I knew he was an angry man deep down, but when you faced him all you felt was warmth and all you saw was teeth. You couldn't help but like him. "I said I saw him trying. If he'd been successful, I might have had to step in."

"Oh, now," I said, surprised at all the attention Marci was getting. "What's this? You were looking to defend Marci?"

"If she needed it. I would have." Herm swung away, still smiling. I looked at Marci who was also smiling. Or swooning. I wondered: Marci and Herm?

"So you're leaving?" I asked her.

"Who said anything about leaving?" She repositioned herself on the couch. In the background I heard April putting her favorite CD on the machine, *Cloudbusting* by Kate Bush. I happened to have it because April had brought it for me the last time she visited. Of course no one knew that we had actually spent quiet time together. But when Kate

Bush's haunting voice filled the air I felt other eyes tuning into me. Marci looked directly at me. "I'm not going anywhere." And then she shifted her voice into a round-the-way-girl mode. "Ain't this the place where the money is? Shit. I'll put up with anything for a half-million dollars."

"Why do you think I volunteered to give this shindig?" I was feeling strong and upbeat. I wanted her to know that I wasn't stupid. That I knew how things happened. "I know what time it is. You can't get nothing in this town if you don't woo the powers that be."

"Is that what you do?" she asked between sips.

"You've got to know how to play the game." I said, smiling myself. I was proud of my position in the community, even though I was as confused and conflicted as anyone else. One moment I felt guilty and angry and dangerous, and the next I was happy, healthy, politically savvy.

"But it's phony."

"Yeah, and . . ."

"C'mon, Icky, I know you better than that. I know you want the grant. I do, too. I'd have given the party myself . . . shit . . . baby, I'd have made my mother leave her house and have given the party there for a grant this big . . . if I had thought about it, I would have. Dewitt would have had to come over to my house and sit at my table. You just thought about it before I did. That's all. I mean, if I had thought about it, and if I thought it would have made a difference, I would have rented a goddamned hotel ballroom if I thought it'd matter. But this thing ain't based on social bullshit. They're going to give this to the top colored artiste in town."

I considered what she said. I hoped she wasn't that naive. "And what determines that, Marci? Talent? Bullshit. It's who they feel the most comfortable with. You know that. Don't forget that Cecilia won a Shrubbery Foundation

Artist Grant last year. Cecilia. Don't forget that shit. She got thirty thousand dollars for those weak-assed 'I'm black and I'm proud' poems."

Marci twisted her body and slowly stood up from the couch. I saw the outline of her butt under her snug jeans. Forget everything I've said about her. I loved her at that moment. I did. I remembered being back in West Philadelphia, embraced by blackness. Visions of black arms and butts and breasts fluttered before my eyes. I smelled early Saturday morning blackness. I smelled the particular perfume of blackness circulating in corner candy stores and bars and beauty salons and barbershops and all the places where I learned everything I know.

There are moments when it doesn't matter where you are. In France. In Russia. In Minnesota. Anywhere. If you are black there are moments when it doesn't matter where you are, if you were raised in a black environment you are instantly propelled back there. You can't escape it. Not that I wanted to. The unfortunate part of it, though, was that you couldn't control when it happened. Sometimes you might be about to kiss the prettiest lips on the prettiest white face you've ever seen and bam! you can't get that smell out of your nose or the curl of caramel out of your eye.

But as Marci wheeled away from me I felt close to her. I knew a lot about her, as I did about Herm, Jenny, and April. But I knew Marci differently. Even though she was born in Atlanta, I felt a kinship that was special. We never talked about it. I never asked her about her family per se. She never asked about mine. But we knew intimate details. Specific things. Like I knew that she'd been teased a lot by the kids in her neighborhood. In one way she was fearless, a fighter. In another she was always hiding. Trying to disappear into the woodwork. I knew that she'd always done well in school. That art had always been a passion for her.

We were trying to do things that our parents and relatives didn't understand and couldn't adequately support.

But that ass. It was there a foot away and moving. She faced me. "Well, that's true. I've applied for a Shrubbery six years in a row and they haven't given me a goddamned penny. I figure they must laugh their ass off every time they get an application from Marci Franklin. 'Oh, here's that crazy colored girl's application again. She's one dumb-ass nigger. She keeps applying like we might give it to her. Where's the trash can?' That's how they do me."

I couldn't help but laugh. She even had her hand on her hip. But I knew what she meant. None of us had had success at the corporate or government arts-money trough. "Well, you know I've never gotten one. But this one, this one is mine. I can smell it." I didn't know whether I should have been saying that. I knew it would make the others nervous. But for some reason I felt that Marci would understand because she was just like me. Neither one of us could even fathom someone paying us to do the things we loved to do. The things we felt were important for our people.

She laughed back at me and so I continued, "No, baby, I'm not taking any chances with this. I'm going to be the perfect host."

"I heard that." A serious veil draped her face. "I can't believe it. I just can't believe it."

I knew what she meant: this opportunity was beyond comprehension. "Read my goddamned lips," I said. "The five of us. The five of us. And only the five of us are being considered. And one of us is going to become rich. One grant, one grant to one person of color, one goddamned grant. The goddamned Genius Grant. Only one of us can get it. And every one of those on the final list are in this room."

Her hand dropped from her hip and the veil lifted and

her face broke out into fireworks and her brown skin lit up this room. I wanted to hug her right then. She let out a sigh.

"Damn. And it's going to be one of us. Wow." Her anticipation brought a sadness that settled in the air. I nodded my head and gulped. It was a heavy burden. She continued, "That's a lot of money."

"You got that right." I could see her stacking dollar bills in her laundry room. Standing guard outside the door. Armed with an AK-47. "But don't get too excited. I told you. That grant has my name on it. And even if it isn't me you've got to worry about Herm, Jenny, and April."

She took a step closer to me. I expected her to whisper. Instead, she grabbed my shirt and pulled me close to her. Her voice remained strong and audible. "I still don't understand something. Something that really puzzles me. "Why April? What in the name of God is the deal with that?"

I knew this wasn't the last time we would talk about it. I'd already made peace with it. But I liked April, which made it easier to ignore the obvious absurdity of her being eligible for the grant. "She's on the list." I said flatly.

"But, Icky, what the fuck are you talking about? She's white."

"I know that. But she's eligible. Don't look at me. It's Dewitt you need to talk to about that. Besides, it's a multicultiboho thing. You know what I'm sayin?" I brought the street into my voice and posture. I could tell by her edged stare that she didn't appreciate the humor.

Marci stared at me. And suddenly I knew everyone else was listening. Including April who'd been huddled in a corner with Herm for the past ten minutes or so. "She's white, Icky. I thought it was for us? She can't be a person of color just cause she screwed a black man."

Her energy soured. Marci was like that. One minute cutting a joke, the next the flash of a machete angling down on you. "Relax, she isn't going to win." And then, still mind-ful that we had a long way to go, I smiled and said, "But the boho got to be in it or it ain't whole. It ain't right. This is the way Dewitt wanted to do it."

"Shit" was all she said as she headed to the kitchen.

"A half-million dollars. Think about it, Marci," I called after her.

Herm curled an arm around my shoulder, his mouth full of shrimp salad and crackers. He winked his right eye and gestured with his food plate. "That's a lot of fry bread."

Jenny collapsed into a dining room chair. "I hope that we don't just talk about money tonight." I looked at her wondering what else we could possibly have to talk about. "We should take advantage of the fact that we're all here together. How often does that happen?"

"The last time Dewitt called us together," I snapped.

"You know what I mean. So what if it's Dewitt that brings us together? I don't care. We hardly ever do stuff like this on our own. Why is that? How come we aren't better friends? Why don't we have dinner together or go out drinking?"

I understood her point but Jenny is so damned emotion-ally thorough. She wheedled a point until you felt it as she did. Until you really understood what she was trying to convey.

"We could go out sometimes." Herm had that silly smile on his face again. It was always there when he talked to women.

Jenny stared at him. "I'm talking about community, Herm. Relationships."

"Well, how do you know I'm not talking about relation-ships?" Herm persisted.

She ignored him. "It takes money or the promise of it to get us into the same room." She stopped and turned again to me. "Ichabod, I don't think you've ever invited me to your house before tonight. Right?"

I nodded, knowing that none of the people who were sitting there except April had ever been there before. I liked them. They were as close to being friends as anyone I knew, but I'm just not a social person. But her point, as I've said, would be made nonetheless.

"This is what money makes us do? Isn't it?" There was silence.

She continued, "I know you guys always have parties but I never get invited . . . and now, suddenly, it's please come to my house so we can talk about some ridiculous grant . . ."

"Hold on." Marci joined us there. "What parties are you talking about that you don't get invited to? I'd sure like to know because if there are parties, I don't think I'm being invited either."

April heaved a heavy sigh. "There are no parties. Believe me. No parties."

"That's not completely true, either." Herm said what I was thinking. "We have gotten together a few times and, to tell you the truth, Jenny, I never thought you'd want to be there."

Jenny seemed so small next to Herm. Like a token or an icon. "Why would you think that?"

"I don't know. You always seemed so . . . ah . . . into yourself. You know, like closed. Not like you needed or even wanted people to get to know you."

"So that's the way I come across."

It was true. Quiet. Cute, but quiet. Not capable *really* of fitting into any kind of social system. Of all of us, Jenny, I thought, was closest to acting and maybe even wanting to be white. She dressed like an aging preppie. Had her hair cut like the star of a popular sitcom. She just seemed so establishment.

"He's right, Jenny," Marci was saying. "You always be trying to act like you don't need nobody."

Whatever her faults, Jenny was not afraid of confrontation. She stepped right in. She pointed at me, "I've called you three times at least, just trying to see how you were and if we could get a cup of coffee or dinner or something, and I don't think you've ever called me back. Am I right? Am I right?"

She was right. I hadn't called. I just didn't think we could be friends. If I don't think we can be close, maybe really close, I won't waste my time. So I hadn't called her back.

"And I work very hard . . . in my own way . . . I mean, I've worked very hard trying to keep the channels open . . . across the board . . . I mean . . . I've done my best and nobody ever seems to pay attention to me . . ."

This must have caught April's attention. She had been slathering some of the guacamole on crackers. But suddenly she put down her plate and asked Jenny, "What do you mean? Nobody pays attention to you?"

"That doesn't sound hard to understand to me." Jenny responded to April and then turned to Marci, "Does it to you? No. It's not hard to understand. People ignore me. They act like I'm not really there."

Marci looked at me. I was baffled, too. Jenny always seemed to have money. She drove a nice car. She had things. No poet is supposed to have things. We could never figure that out.

It seemed that Jenny was spiraling. "But for money . . . There is no end to what we will do. Is there? I get this invitation out of nowhere to apply for some ridiculous grant. And then the meetings and now a party. What's going on?

Why am I so popular all of a sudden? Nobody seemed to know I was alive three months ago. How did all this happen? I wasn't going to come tonight. But . . ."

"You came because you want the money just like we do." Marci laid the truth on her. I heard Herm chuckling behind me.

"Speaking of grants. When did Dewitt get this bright idea?" Herm asked.

"What difference does it make when he got the idea?" Jenny's soft voice felt strained to my ear. "It's about money. I find it very confusing. When you decide to become a poet you almost simultaneously make the decision that you will not make any money doing it. I've made it this far. A poet shouldn't be out begging for money. You know that it has an effect on what you do, on your art. You know it does. It's hard sometimes to calculate that difference, but you know it's not the pure truth. Something happens to words when there's money connected to them. Something happens . . ."

Although I knew what she was talking about, I was tired of being poor, tired of worrying about my bills. Tired of my struggle to value myself and my work in the face of my perpetual struggle to stay afloat. I didn't want money to be so significant in my life. But what choices were there? I'd been broke and stumbling. I wanted something different now. "What about getting paid?" I said aloud.

"Each one of us is flirting with real, honest-to-God wealth." Marci snapped her fingers and walked to the window, presumably to see if Dewitt was strolling up the walkway. She parted the blinds impatiently, and with a sigh in her voice, said, "I don't know about you all, but I like my chances. The simple odds are pretty good. I agree with you, Icky. What about getting paid? How long are we supposed to do the work that we do without the support we need to keep doing it?"

Herm chimed in, "Yeah . . . it's about time. I'm tired of seeing everybody else get what I should be getting."

And April, who had listened patiently, finally found a point she could wholeheartedly agree with. She nodded and added, "What we all should be getting."

"Please, April, you can't just put yourself in this." Marci was on the attack again.

As usual, April was not about to take it. She was special in that way. A white woman who had enough strength to stand up to people of color, to prove that she really cared about them. You had to love her for it. What a dilemma for the right-thinking white person. If you believe race differences could be overcome and try to act on it, you are likely to encounter surprisingly strong resistance from people of color. We are just so damned suspicious—suspicions supported by repeatedly half-hearted and insincere overtures. I could see the frustration flash full in April's cute little face.

"Why not, Marci? Because I'm white? Is that it? Because I'm a white woman?" April smiled like it meant nothing to her. The frustration transforming to edge.

"You said it . . . I didn't." Marci crossed the room and ended up standing next to April. I felt the rising tension. We were all getting tired. What had sounded like just a wonderful idea was already wilting like a fallen flower. As the night drew on and we waited for Dewitt, conflict slowly perfumed the air.

But, of course, Jenny intervened. "What's this all about?" she said, facing Marci. "Why are you against her?" Marci and I stared at Jenny. It made no sense that April was being considered for this grant. No sense whatsoever. Naturally, Jenny found the sense in it, anyway. "We're all oppressed . . ." she began before she was interrupted.

Herm stuck his chest out. "But none as profoundly as me. I've been doing my art for ten years and no one has given me a dime."

I did everything I could to keep from laughing in his face. That's what this was about in the first place. None of us had been the lucky recipients of any significant private or government money. And there is a hell of a lot of money available. Foundations and organizations are constantly searching to find emerging artists to reward. I personally know of at least three artists who have received more than sixty thousand dollars a year for two or three years in a row. There are some white artists and writers out there who've made a profession of bouncing from one grant to another. They are totally incapable of earning an "honest" living. Indeed, one of the little side effects of getting arts money is that it is like a little bit of a drug. It eases into your system and suddenly you start to feel that you are entitled to it. And when Dewitt talked about the white back-lash, that's what he was referring to. It must have felt like a seismic shift as white artists realized they had to contend with a larger and more diverse pool of competitors than ever before. I've heard more than one of them say with abject resignation, "You have to be a person of color to get a grant these days."

"We're all in the same boat, Herm," I said gently. But Marci was undaunted. "I just don't appreciate finally getting a chance to get some real money and still having to compete with a white person."

Jenny rushed into the breach again. "Well, I find it a little disconcerting that we have to be the 'people of color.' You know? Like we're different from white people. Aren't we all after the same thing?"

"Yes, Jenny, we are," I said. "But the point is we've never been able to compete for all the money that's available on an equal footing. It's like affirmative action for artists. There's all this money available and we should get our fair share."

"But shouldn't we be better than the white artists? I don't really want charity."

"It's not charity." It angered me when people of color tried to convince me that we actually competed with our white counterparts on an equal basis. I wanted that to be true. Lived for that day. Not that we weren't capable. Or, in some cases weren't even better. But we struggled under significant handicaps. Not the least of which was that it was always white people making the decisions about whose art was better. The historical truth was that for many years the artistic urges of those of us whose aesthetic was some melange of cultural impulses were not even visible to those forged on the Platonic principles of art and beauty.

My colleagues at Mupster uphold these traditions. The glut of mediocre white artists clogs the canon and eclipses valuable contributors to American culture. This is what we are fighting. And we all know that powerful people relinquish that power very reluctantly.

It wasn't charity. We deserved a piece of the money as compensation for our contribution. We were artists of color and in a way, despite the unrelenting efforts of traditionalists and conservatives, our work continued to be the heart of all that was vital about American art.

herm made himself comfortable on the couch with Marci. Dewitt was taking longer than we expected and the energy level was slowly dwindling. It was as though a cloak had descended over us. Each of us found a space. April sitting by the window on a sill that doubled as a narrow bench. Jenny on the floor, curled up by the overstuffed leather chair in the corner, and me sitting at the dining room table.

But I was watching Herm. I sensed that he was about to say something. He yawned and stretched, his voice just below the surface of his consciousness. When he spoke, his voice was tired. Reflective. Nervous. "We are different, all of us. You know. Very different. Sometimes I'm struck by how different everybody is. Even among my people there are vast differences. And between us and the other Indian nations. Little things. Big things. How we dress. Whether we like to hunt or fish or farm. What is in our blood? Who knows where it comes from? But I know it's there."

I looked around at the rest of us. I could tell that no one was thinking of interrupting Herm. This was who we were, too. Thinkers. Feelers. And we respected each other at that level. This was precisely why I thought we could be a community. Because at the heart of it we knew how to respect each other. Although it was hard, we knew how to do it.

"Do you know," he sounded almost wistful. "Do you know that when I walk into a room, especially a room full of Minnesotans, that I can feel people's voices immediately fall to a whisper? Do you know what I mean? Everyone knows that a descendant of the land has entered. There is reverence for me, for the pain of my people's struggle. Reverence because I stand for the thing that white men have tenaciously tried to conquer: the earth. I embody all that is natural. My people are still connected to spirits that others have never known or have long forgotten."

I was wrong. Marci couldn't remain silent any longer.

"So it's only your people who commune with spirits? Is that it? Do you think that Native Americans are more spiritual than Africans? Or Hispanics?"

"Or Irish people?" April added.

Herm smiled a big, strong smile. One which brought a degree more energy into the room. A smile which teased us. Told us he was bound to push us further into conflict and that he would enjoy it.

"But we have not forgotten," he continued. "I could talk about the nations that were wasted on this land, about the poisoning of our air and water, about the poison that was injected into us in the form of alcohol, and the insanity of paleface dreams. It is genocide, to speak plainly."

Much of this we'd heard him say before. But sitting there, waiting for Dewitt, it seemed all the more surreal. I was sure we were slipping into some outside life. A place where this lecture would be like a road that led us somewhere. I could see little smiles lurking on all our faces.

"And yet I am the eagle and the bear. The wolf and the wind."

"Are you kidding me?" April was laughing.

"It's who I am," Herm said flatly. April looked at me to see if I thought it was as funny as she did. I was trying not to think. Trying to just listen. I knew what he meant. But our cultural histories are so overwrought. Sometimes you just want to say "time out!" But I knew he meant everything he was saying.

"It's who I am. I bring the power of my ancestors and their knowledge of this life we have marched . . . I take that and I make sculptures. Big statements made out of the very earth that gave birth to me. I make this art because I cannot imagine what else to do.

"Yes, I could relocate to a rez up north and do what some of my other brothers and sisters have done. I could dedicate myself to the heart of our culture. But I'm trying to prove that a native man who is true to his ways can still make it in this white world. So, okay, I admit that you can see this struggle in my work. There is no more purity, is there? I mean, I make art to be sold. To be held by museums. Its function is different than the work of my ancestors who painted or carved for a reason. To celebrate harvest or a successful hunt. To announce a marriage or a death. To signify the infinite power of the spirits. No. My art is like a hybrid. Like a special little rose that is named for a dead aunt."

He paused and laughed out loud. "Do you have a Herm Strong in your house? Do you?" He looked at me. "It's obvious that you don't. But you should, you know. I make them for you."

I smiled back at him. "Herm, I almost never buy art anymore. I don't have the kind of money you charge for one of your sculptures."

He looked at me and said, "I've been doing this for fifteen years. I gather natural things. Driftwood, rocks, branches, leaves, rope, whatever I find along river beds and in the forest and transform them with color into art that you can understand. I bring our tears to you."

He stared at me and at that moment I felt guilty. It is so hard to know how to support somebody. Herm closed his eyes.

"Fifteen years. Two wives, two children, bankruptcy, emptiness—sometimes, near craziness. And now, when I'm not doing my art, running from committee to committee, the only native there . . . when I'm not doing that, well, I spend most of my time preoccupied with whatever woman is in my life."

Marci stood up. "You know what, Herm? I don't know if I want to know anymore. We all have our stories."

"I want to know. I'm interested." Jenny smiled up at him.

He ignored Marci who replenished her wine and returned to the couch. "Oh, yeah, I still get my share. Women want to get close to this most spiritual existence." April giggled, but Herm was not going to be derailed. "Really. Especially when it comes to white women."

April stopped laughing.

"I am a bridge. I can't tell you how many personal spiritual journeys I have been a part of." He looked at Jenny. "Yes, indeed. And they keep getting younger and younger.

"And I'll tell you the truth. I'm beginning to get a little tired of it. There has to be a better way. A way that doesn't make me sound so lonely and pathetic. So, I have to say that I want this grant bad. I really do. My people were here before everybody. Other people come along and disrespect our lives, our land, and our legacy and then when there are resources to give away, they divide it up amongst everybody but us. So I expect this grant to be mine."

In the sound of his voice growled a deep hurt, a familiar

sound. It almost felt like mine. Or like Marci's. We were all wounded. But Herm, though, had a way of claiming such great pain that it was a struggle to keep from really feeling sorry for him. But you have to try to remember that Herm's sculptures sell for thousands of dollars and that he lives downtown in a tremendous loft space. You have to remember that when you listen to Herm. He'll have you thinking he's living under a bridge.

In a way, too, that was a commonality among us. No matter how successful we actually were, we had a hard time accepting it. We mostly still acted as if we were lumpen proletariat. Rather, we were instead quite middle class.

Herm kept going, "We have suffered more than any other group of people in this country." And then his voice completely changed. It became almost ethereal. "Can you imagine what I could do with a half-million dollars? Or how much prestige it would give me? I could go to my loft and forget about the world. I could crawl into my own world, make my own world all over again. I think I'm getting a little too old to be chasing young girls, if you know what I mean?"

Again the chuckle bounced out of his body and provided a light in the shadows. "Although the one thing this diversity stuff has done is open the field a little. You have more of a choice. I've been dating a Cambodian woman lately. It's great. She says I've got yellow fever. I couldn't help but laugh. Her parents would absolutely freak if they found out about her and me. Here I am a thirty-five-year-old native guy dating their nineteen-year-old daughter."

I had never heard him talk about his dates or girlfriends or anything before. "Where is she tonight?" I asked him.

"Sherry? Oh, yeah, well, Sherry's probably down at the Scrounge Lounge, or that new club, the Florida Room, or something. She's never home at night." He paused. "I can't keep up with her. But what the hell, right?"

"When do you get to hang out with her?" I sensed him trying to get out of this conversation.

"We spend a lot of time together. We do." I knew right away it was a lie. There was a long pause and then he said, "Damn, I want this money. I mean, like, what else can I do? What more can I do? I make great art. I represent the epitome of struggle. It should be mine. I hope the spirits are with me." He stopped abruptly and studied me. For a second I thought he was going to jump up from the couch, but in the same second he must have changed his mind. He sank back into the chair. "You know, Icky, I should have smudged this place. It could have used it. We could all use a little purification around here, don't you think?"

I didn't know if he thought I was supposed to answer that or not. So I didn't. I could tell that Herm was getting tired. He was probably one of those "crack of dawn" artists. People who rise with the sun and envelop themselves in the wonders of daylight. My life is formed from the darkness. I am most alive before the light peeks at the coming day. That is when the words whisper to me and my stories take shape.

Marci broke my little reflection. "So, Icky, how long do you think this is going to take? How long is it going to take Dewitt to make a decision?"

"I think it's going to happen pretty quickly. I just have a feeling about that. Who knows, maybe it will happen tonight."

Herm's eyes opened, "Do you think?"

"Who knows?" I said. "Could be."

"Damn, a half-million tax-fucking-free dollars." Marci was smiling again.

The dollar signs were flying again. Circling our heads. Herm put his head back again, "That's a new life."

"That's for damn sure." Marci said to herself.

It was then I heard Jenny rustling. It had crossed my mind momentarily that maybe she'd dropped off to sleep. But no. She sat up straighter. " I don't know. I mean, why should we want all that money?"

But Marci was all over that one. "You got something against money?"

Still, Jenny was committed to the argument. "What about us? About our lives? Money affects that."

April let her head rest softly on the window. "That's the point, Jenny. This could liberate us," she said. Her words reverberated off the pane and dusted us with her truth.

"Shit." I said. "That kind of money makes the underground railroad look like a mine shaft."

"But isn't anyone worried about what it will do to us? To this group. To our friendships?" Again she cut her eyes to me. And I felt it. "Icky, you're the one who's always talking about the multicultiboho tribe. Doesn't this threaten that?"

I thought about what she was saying. Rather, I should say that I *tried* to think about what she was saying. The dollar signs were still very thick in the air. It is impossible to calculate the impact of any desire. Indeed, desire is the heart of sadness and disappointment. And at that moment I was consumed by personal, selfish desire. Maybe Jenny was the only one of us who was able to even raise such questions at that moment. We just wanted the money.

I stumbled and sputtered and finally said to her, "Maybe. Maybe it affects things. I don't know . . ."

"I'm worried about our relationships." She said, "I don't want a whole lot of money if it will mean any of you will be jealous . . . we're friends and we're all trying to be true to ourselves . . ."

"Excuse me, Jenny." It was Marci with a derisive smile on her face. "I wouldn't worry. Like James Brown said a long time ago, 'Money won't change me.' "

Herm said, "Money changes everybody."

"Then change me, goddamnit," I screamed. Everybody jumped a little. But I think they all, with the exception of Jenny, agreed. "You can just go on and change my ass. I'm tired of being broke." And then, just as I thought the atmosphere had decompressed, April said something that was way too reckless.

"I just want my own money . . ."

And of course, Marci cut her off. "Your *own* money? What does that mean?"

April knew she'd made a tactical error. "Uh . . . well . . ."

April tried to keep it hidden that her parents had so much money. Something had happened in her family and she tried to be completely detached from it. I didn't know whether it was her choice or if she'd been disowned. The penalty in some families for having meaningful relationships with people of color, particularly black people, could be very severe.

And you could see the disgust on Marci's face. To Marci, it was just another reason to be suspicious of April. Marci got up from the couch and turned in a complete circle as if she were sleepwalking. Finally, she said, "Don't that just figure.." She recovered her intentions and asked, "Where's the bathroom, Icky?"

I directed her down the hall. "Second door on the right."

But April said in a very loud voice, loud enough for Marci to hear way down the hall in the bathroom. "Yes, my father has a little money. At least he used to have money, anyway. But my father is a special case. He started out just like any other potato head in New York.

"My father was basically just a hard-working, blue-collar guy who got lucky—if you want to call it that. He started off in the trucking business and it just kept growing. And if you are wondering whether my father was a nice guy, or if we had a good relationship, I have to tell you that the answer to both questions is no."

She rose from the window seat and walked to the dining room table, beckoned by a nice shrimp salad and a fair amount of sushi, which still lay glistening in neat rows. She picked over the food. "And I abhor, absolutely abhor, how he really made his money and the fact that he turned into a crook. I hate it."

I'd never heard about April's father. She talked about her mother all the time. A couple of years ago I'd even met her. Her name was Betty, and she had one of the fiercest personalities I had ever come across. April had grown up in Alexandria, Minnesota, and once, when her mom was visiting, I went with them to dinner at her hotel. And as we walked into the restaurant area I caught the image of an Aunt Jemima cookie jar sitting out in a display of their breakfast offerings. What the cookie jar had to do with breakfast, I wasn't sure. I surmised that they felt that the image of any fat, black, scarf-wearing woman would impart confidence in the quality of their breakfast. While I was trying to figure out what to do, Betty complained to the maitre d'. And when he flustered and stuttered she asked to speak to the food manager. And when this woman walked out behind two swinging doors, Betty dressed her down as well.

"Are you alive? Are you conscious? This is 1997. Why in the world would you have something like that out? What kind of a place is this? I'm spending a lot of money to stay here and I can't come down to dinner with my daughter and her friend without being offended by you. Not some slack-jawed Cletis yokel. But by you. This hotel."

The woman shrank to the size of a pea. I couldn't help but think that if I'd said the same thing it would have settled in a totally different way. Somebody would have felt the need to challenge me. To say that they didn't see why I was so upset or something. But with Betty, there was all silence and contrition. Indeed, this food manager woman was like a little wildcat.

Once, when I was in Kingston, I watched a feral cat, a rather small, scraggly thing sneaking up an alley. It came suddenly upon a larger, fiercer cat. The smaller one immediately fell flat, splayed to the earth, and whimpered. I'd never seen such supplication before. It was stunning. The larger cat passed and the little one jumped up and made a beeline.

And then Betty turned and we all followed her to the front desk where she asked for the manager. By the time she was done, we had her bags and were walking across the street to a different hotel. I couldn't believe it. That was fierce.

But this reflection only made me wonder more concretely as to why I'd never heard April talk about her father. She was in control of the moment now. It was obvious that the stories were weighted with the specter of the money. Of Dewitt's arrival. It was as if we were caught in a bubble of time. Nothing could move until we did. And right now, no one was moving. Only words.

"So, I can't really use his money. It's money gotten from poor people, defenseless people."

"I thought you said your father was a truck driver," Jenny said softly.

"I know. But he was much more than that. He got all caught up with the mob. He did well, but . . ."

"Where is he now?" I was surprised that Jenny was that interested. Besides, whenever somebody tells you they know somebody in the mob, you don't usually ask where they are now. They either don't know or don't want to talk about it. It was obvious that April didn't want to talk about it. I could see it in her eyes as she rolled them back and refocused on Jenny.

"But I can't change things with that money. And that's what I want to do. I mean this whole idea that we can be a force. Us. This conglomeration of people." She motioned at us.

"We can change everything. Yes . . . I know my family's got money. And, yes, they paid for my education, and without their help I wouldn't have had the time to take up the sax and play my music."

We all instinctively turned to the saxophone case that sat by the door. April never went anywhere without it. And no matter what you knew about April. No matter what opinion you had of her at any given time. When the subject switched to music or when you listened to her play, you had to reassess your impressions. Her mother lived in her horn and in her breath. This was one of the most fascinating paradoxes. On one hand, April was Minnesota. Was liberalism personified. She "got it." As they say. We gave her a hard time but we all knew she was more one of us than one of them. Them being all the people who were nervous about the rising influence of people of color in this country.

What we wanted she already had. All she had to do was turn her back on us and give in to the pressure to be white— in all the ways America asked that of its citizens who were not people of color—and she would have been a star overnight. She was made for it. Helen Hunt beauty. Marsalis talent. Need I say more?

But, more to the point, she loved jazz. Loved it as though

it was a person. As though there was no need, really, for men in her life. Or anything. She'd rather play or listen to jazz than eat. That slim body created sounds you couldn't believe came from her.

And where did she get that knowledge? That's what I wanted to know. Jazz was about knowledge. Even more than the blues. Indeed, the blues was a simpler form of jazz. Articulated complexity. But jazz was often a more abstract, more convoluted explanation of the same misery and the same struggle. For black people, jazz was the manifestation of life. The real proof of it. And April lived that life.

"It's my music that matters, baby. The sweet sound. Turns my inside into reality." Marci walked back from the bathroom at this moment. April faced her. Walked up to her and continued, "And my inside is not white. My inside contains the same colors, the same knowledge of all unrealized dreams."

I reeled at the power of April's statement. A white person shouting for recognition from a black woman. Marci looked at her as if she were a complete fool. And perhaps she was for being so direct. So confrontational. But at the same time it was quite exciting. Impressive.

I think Herm saw it, too, because he came up behind me and whispered, "Now who was that guy she was tangled up with earlier?"

"What?"

"Didn't you see her making out with that guy?"

I searched my brain but I couldn't remember seeing April with anybody. So I shook my head no.

"Well, you missed it. But you know the guy. Ah . . . Ricky. You know Ricky, over at the Saturn Theater, he was in *Black Dust*."

Ricky was a big-time ladies' man on the multiculti circuit. He was Hollywood handsome and the women swooned when he appeared.

"He was all over her."

I was surprised. Not at them, but at the fact that I didn't see it. I would have teased April right from the beginning. She was always talking about how dreadful the men were she had to choose from. She spent so much time in dark, smoky clubs that she felt almost everyone was a drugged-out trumpet player or a blunted-up spoken-word artist looking for a combination saxophone player/lover.

I'm sure April hadn't heard our little exchange but she had been distracted by it. Still, she continued, "I understand privilege. I even understand your animosity toward me." I really wasn't in the mood for more combat and that was exactly where this was going.

Marci narrowed her eyes but April continued, "You may not believe me, but I think it's mostly not real, Marci. Actually, you know, I think you like me. How else do you explain how often we get together? How much I know about you? We have coffee at least once every couple of weeks. You don't do that with someone you hate, do you?"

I was watching Marci. There was a smile, a knowing one, creeping across her face. It made me feel good. This was the truth, too. The way we could face it together. Tension was replaced by warmth.

"We've even gone to some concerts together. But you know what?" April whirled around to all of us. "I've noticed that as long as we're alone together we can communicate, relate in a completely normal way. None of this carping and sniping. But if we're in a group, like this for example, it can be very tense. She can't help but try to beat up on me. What is that about?"

Marci was about to say something but April interrupted her, "But it's one of my goals in life . . . to get close to

Marci." And now she returned to Marci. "To lure you into loving me. Understanding me. I mean, I know it's a selfish thing, but I want to prove that a white person can make that kind of a connection with you. That a white woman and a black woman can be friends. Why? Why? Because what hope is there if we can't? What hope?"

I will admit to being completely blown away by what April was saying. She was addressing Marci directly. And she was doing it in a way that Marci had to listen to her. But this was obviously being lost on Herm who was still standing behind me. April had stirred his fire or something because he was definitely zooming in on her.

"So," he said in an even softer voice, "What's her story? I mean, like is she . . . ah . . . attainable or what?"

I looked at him. "Attainable? Are you kidding me? Attainable?"

"Yeah, you know what I mean." He actually nudged me. I could see Jenny watching us out of the corner of her eye. I didn't like being so obvious. That was one of Herm's problems. He could be so damned obvious. He could sit some place for an hour, totally silent, and then, if an attractive woman walked into the room, suddenly he would start winking and nudging and saying inappropriate things.

"I know what you mean, Herm, but I don't know the answer to your question. I know that she and Ricky have been playing with each other for years. I don't think it's anything serious between them. And, frankly, I've never seen her flirt with anyone else." I paused just long enough for him to catch up and then said, "Except maybe me."

I knew it was a little indiscreet. We'd only fallen into each other's clutches once, though she was somebody I did wonder about. But she traveled so much and was never available to just hang out. I was convinced that most of her relationships were started, consummated, and ended, in blazing speed; in some podunk town with guys her mother would be shocked about. It didn't matter. Herm wasn't concerned at all with any interest she might have had for me.

"I was just wondering," he said vacantly.

"Yeah, I'm sure you were . . ."

If April had heard any of that she didn't act like it. She was caught up in her own world. There was obviously something she was trying to say. Something that had been caught in her consciousness and needed expressing. Her usually lineless face was suddenly quite shadowed. It was getting late and it had been a long day, but there was something else creating the darkness in her face.

"The biggest hurdle for me," again April turned to Marci, "see, I knew dealing with Marci, for example, would be hard. And I knew I had a lot to learn about the real, the full history of black, native, and Hispanic people. You know, you have to commit yourself to this kind of learning. You have to have the experiences. Relationships. You have to do the work. People have to trust you enough to let you inside. That's what I learned when I started trying to play the music.

"So I knew all of that . . . but what I didn't anticipate, the biggest hurdle, has been the men. The sexual energy that swirls among and across cultures is unbelievable. Some of it is completely intoxicating and some of it makes me angry."

I got the feeling that maybe she might have heard a little of my conversation with Herm. My apartment, as you can see, is not that big. I was immediately embarrassed.

I could hear the edge in her voice. "I am not a thing. And if I tell you the truth, which I will, men of color, especially black men and Latinos, often say what white men think. They just say it. And the fact that they're saying it, sometimes, is wonderful. I had to get used to that. Sometimes they mean exactly what they say and sometimes they're just fucking with you. But it almost always comes right at you. Not much sideways stuff. And the more I thought about it, the more I came to believe that this is what men have thought and the way they have acted since forever . . . all men. But I swear, sometimes I really wish we could just pull the plug on exchanges which are full of cultural attitudes about gender or sexuality. Just squash those conversations altogether."

Even though I could still feel Herm's breath behind me, I was watching Marci. Her smile was still there. There was even a gleam in her eye. I think she really did like April. I hadn't known that they'd socialized as much as they did. I was also listening to April. I knew what she was talking about. What Herm and I were doing was exactly that.

I don't think Herm heard her at all. His radar was on a totally different frequency because he kept right on whispering in my ear. "She's pretty, don't you think?"

"Yeah. She really is. Somebody is going to get a great partner when she settles down." I don't really know why I said that. I guess I was caught up in Herm's energy, too. I was listening to April, but my interest was definitely flickering between the righteous and the salacious.

Again Herm's voice came from behind me. "You?"

"No. I don't think so. Besides I know Ricky pretty well. I wouldn't want to piss him off."

"But I thought you said that they weren't that big a deal."

I was getting a little tired of this conversation. Of Herm's need to identify something about April that qualified him to make an attempt for her affection. Or something which would disqualify her from being worthy of the effort.

Still, I kept going, "I don't think it is, but I'm really not in the market right now. Besides, I don't really get those kind of signals from her." And this was true. We had that one moment when we'd been out drinking and ended up in my apartment groping each other before we both decided to stop and think about what we were doing. Other than that, I considered April more a flirt than anything else. "And I have to tell you that I'm for sure not going to cross the line with her again, unless I know how she's going to react."

I watched April go over to my CD player. The only person talking now was Herm. And he was becoming a little annoying.

"Scared of her, eh?" He nudged me again. I couldn't believe it.

"Yeah, I guess I am. I don't want my feelings hurt," I said with a chuckle.

"That doesn't bother me. Hell, you never know what you get until you ask for it, or just reach out and try to take it."

I turned all the way around and said to him, "Well, go for what you know, Herm. Go for what you know."

Maybe I said it a little too loud. I was agitated at him. He should have known better. So should I. But he'd dragged me completely into an inappropriate conversation in an environment that was already charged. April was trying to be sincere, open, and here he was plotting a hit on her.

At any rate, Marci heard the end of what I said and jumped on it. "Go for what?"

"Herm's bugging me about your girlfriend over there," I said.

"April?" Marci shot her eyes to Herm. "You?"

Herm smiled, "I was just asking about her."

"I swear to God. Do you just have to be a white woman in Minnesota to get every man's attention? Is that all you have to be?"

April put on *Thembi*, a Pharoah Sanders disc and wheeled around, seeming not to have heard us. Jenny sat motionless, as though she was just there to be a witness and to tend to the fallen.

"But I'm breaking all kinds of rules. I'm a woman jazz musician. No, I'm a white woman jazz musician. You have no idea how hard that is. When I play Trane's "Love Supreme," or even some Grover Washington, people do a double take. I'm not supposed to be doing that. Am I? It doesn't matter that I love the freedom in that music. Or that I've spent all of my adulthood trying to understand the very idea of improvisation. It's one of the things that white people must learn from other cultures. The need for improvisation. It's not chaos but hyperorganization. It's about confidence and collectivism. And when I'm on stage that is my community. Those people are my people. Whether they are from Cuba or Nairobi. And as I said before, I refuse to be isolated into whiteness."

There was a momentary silence. I half expected Herm to say something. I could feel him staring at her. I had never heard April talk so directly about herself before. I don't think the others had either. And she wasn't finished.

"I want the money because I'm the only one here who can afford to use it for the community. Oh, I don't mean that I won't use some of it for my survival, but what I really want is to set up a program for kids to learn how to play music. All races. White kids, black kids, everybody learning the beauty of music and being together."

Marci broke the mood by saying "What in the world do white women have? Will somebody please tell me? I want to know?" She flopped back into her space on the couch.

"What are you talking about?" I asked, but I realized almost instantly that she was still focused on Herm's statement of interest in April.

"You know damned well what I'm talking about. I mean I've been out with her. Just like she said." Marci looked at me. "One time we were in a club and there weren't that many women there yet, but there was a whole shit load of men. Almost all of them black. And who do you think got drinks sent over to her? Me? No, sir, buddy. Not this little ol' pickaninny. Not in this multicultiboho world. Motherfuckas was tripping over me to get to her."

I found myself laughing but no one else was. "Oh, come on, Marci. This is Minneapolis. That's what happens here. Black women have been complaining about that since I moved here. Brothers come here from other cities and freak out at the way they are sought after, pursued by white women. For many of these guys it's the first time that white women are open to them."

"But why, Icky? What's the attraction? Why are white women considered to be so damned valuable?"

Even though I felt the desperation in her voice I couldn't help but come back at her with humor. She knew the answer to her question. It was a part of the thing we were all struggling against. It was why none of us ever felt complete. Whole. We were always being measured against a way of being that diminished us. Even as we tried to fit in. Tried to be what was acceptable. We always came face to face with the truth of the matter. We could never be white. Asian Americans could never be white. Hispanic Americans could never be white. None of us. We were what we were. The only thing we could do was fight for the beauty and the value of that. That was our journey. And if there was to be a miracle it would come in our ability to create a language that all of us could safely communicate.

But, even though I knew this, I said, "So, what are you sayin?"

I said it in a very sarcastic way, because I hated it when black people were reduced to asking stupid questions about the way our world was. Our history of being stolen, enslaved, held back, discriminated against was the answer to all of those questions. The only thing we can do is resurrect the truth about our real histories. The ones that have nothing to do with striving to be white. Resurrect that truth and our wholeness can be restored. As whole people we can stand up next to white men. Shake their hands as equals. Feel strong beside them, without having to measure ourselves against them. Even love them. Every culture has its greatness. Only in the face of social and economic domination does a culture unravel. Slavery did it to us. Women like Marci came into the New World as slaves and servants to women like April.

"Don't play with me, Icky."

Herm looked at me as if I were a condemned man. "I thought you didn't like to get your feelings hurt?"

"I'm just trying to say that this isn't about who people are sleeping with. It just isn't. Besides, you can't tell a person who they should be attracted to." I slowly got up from the dining room table. I thought it was time to break out the hard liquor. I had a bottle of scotch hidden in the kitchen.

But Marci continued. "And I'm just trying to say that I don't exist in this blond-haired, no-butt world. I'm the opposite. My brothers look right through my black ass, like I'm not even there."

Herm walked over and sat down next to her. He put his arm around her and said in the most sincere voice, "I think you're quite pretty, Marci."

As I walked by them I said, "I never said she wasn't."

"You never said I was, either." I looked back at her and she was smiling. We both knew there was a dance of sweetness between us. Perhaps it would never be more than the banter that currently existed between us. Perhaps it would grow.

As I found the scotch, I heard Jenny say, "I think black women are the prettiest women in the world . . ."

And then April followed. "So do I."

When I returned with the bottle and glasses, Marci said, "Thank you for that. I feel much better now." Her voice was soggy with sarcasm.

I gave each of them a glass. Now was a good time for drinks. Herm waved me off.

"You know I can't drink that. You guys can get smashed. But I'm the Indian here. I'd be just another stereotype."

"You can have *one*, can't you?" I asked. But he just turned around and walked away.

At the same moment, as Jenny finished taking her first sip of the expensive single malt scotch, she turned to Marci. "Why does that make you angry? We were saying something nice. But you just threw it right back in our faces. Sometimes I just don't understand."

"You understand, Jenny. You just try to come off with all that innocent bullshit. Poor sweet Jenny. She's not from here. She's always so confused about everything." Marci was back to being cruel.

Jenny smiled at her. "Most of the time I just want to be left alone. At least that's what I tell myself. And if I'm around harsh, steel-edged people, I just want to escape. Get away. That's how I feel right now. I want to get out of here."

"Marci didn't mean that. She was just fucking with you." I said quickly. I didn't want Jenny to leave. I don't know why but I was feeling closer and closer to her.

"Don't worry, Icky. I'm not going to leave. Marci doesn't control my actions. The truth is I feel like I'm compelled to be here. I don't know why really. It's like I have to. My curiosity is so strong. I'm drawn to this. Drawn to find the connection between you and me."

"Yes." April whispered. "Yes, that's it. We've been told there is no connection. No real connection. But there is."

Jenny shook her head. "It's not that simple. We are kind of working against the natural order of things. You know what I mean? You see, I grew up in a rather traditional Japanese American home dominated by the notion that what was ours, our food, our clothes, our customs, were for us. That it was the be all and end all of my identity. Ask no more questions. You will get a good education. Become something respectable. Get married to someone they approved of, which I was never sure what that was. Some days it was a nice Japanese businessman, other times it was any white man who had a job. Even worse than telling me who I was supposed to be is the fact that they didn't want me to acknowledge that there were other people in the world besides white people and Japanese people. No other kind of people were even thought of or discussed. Everything else was outside, the other." Jenny shuddered and held her hands up, "Stay away from them."

"All races and cultures are like that." Herm said through a lightweight yawn.

"But in my family it was complicated by a contradictory energy which pushed me to blend in. Blend in. Blend in to what, I ask you? It was very strange, my parents were completely chauvinistic about our culture and our customs. And yet, in me they wanted a Barbie doll. And what can I say? There are times when I want to be that. Yes, it is quite frightening, I know, but sometimes I really want to have blond hair. Couldn't you just see me like that?"

I thought about it. Jenny had a really soft look to her. Her face held no shadows. It was childlike, fleshy. I couldn't imagine her with blond hair.

"All the guys would be after me, then." She paused.

Her face softened even more. She looked at Marci and then at me.

"Anyway there is a reason I'm here and it's got nothing to do with money. I'm here because when I found out about this grant I decided that I didn't want to be just in competition with all of you. I care about the relationships we create. I care about what people will think about us after this is over. We are special. And, we are all isolated. Separated from the very communities we are connected to by the color of our skins."

I was getting tired, too. This was our style. Each seeking a way to say what had to be said. It was Jenny's style to wait until people were tired and flaccid before exposing herself. This was a woman capable of protecting herself.

"Everybody here is talented. Icky's stories mimic the detective genre but get at so much more. They are explorations of internal chaos. Marci paints colors like you wouldn't believe. She has this one painting called *Reverend Lee*." Marci smiled, anticipating Jenny's attention.

"Wow, I mean, the whole history of the Baptist Church is in that painting. Herm's sculptures blend the old with the new, the spiritual with the mechanical. And when April blows that horn of hers, you stop thinking, you just do. I want this to be a community. I don't want to be so isolated. And, just for your information, I do not want to be white."

Again there was silence. I thought we'd sit like that until Dewitt arrived. I knew everyone was wondering about him. Where the hell was he? I couldn't help but think of *Godot*. Or even the film *Waiting for Guffman*. Were we just bumpkins deluding ourselves?

But Jenny wasn't finished. "I worry about what I think sometimes. How I actually feel. The fact is there is no way a truly multicultural community can be fashioned without, well, you know, you have to sort of go through the black folks."

This statement caught me off guard. Jenny was now looking at Herm and April. What was she trying to say, I wondered? I caught Marci nodding at me. Just when I thought things were slowing down they picked up again. How long was it going to take Dewitt to get here?

Jenny was very tentative. As if she really didn't want to say what she was in the process of saying. "You know what I mean? It's the truth. It just is. No matter what my family tells me about their struggle to get to America, their struggle to speak the language, or get educated or find jobs; nothing seems to speak as strongly as the memory of slavery. In this country slavery, and the half-hearted attempt to erase its stain, has given the ultimate power of righteous indignation to African Americans. No other group can claim such legitimate anger."

And then she turned in my direction, carefully avoiding eye contact with Marci. "Don't get me wrong, I basically agree. Nothing really can change until African Americans are seen as real people and have all the opportunities that everyone else does." At this point I guess she just threw caution to the wind because she looked at Marci and said, "But your anger is so strong it prevents our ability to co-alesce. And Marci and even Icky will say that I'm not angry enough. But how can we truly come together when anger is our only means of bonding?"

Marci closed her eyes for a moment. Just long enough for me to know, for everyone to know, that this comment hurt. We knew how to do that to each other. We were well trained to defend ourselves. To attack. There wasn't much room for honest and meaningful criticism. This line of discussion made me very nervous. Actually, any time we moved toward an analysis of blackness I got anxious. I think

I was more afraid of getting angry myself than what I expected Marci to say or do.

And then Marci was speaking. "You're right about one thing," she said to April. "You do have to come through the black folks. We are the standard-bearers here. We are the ones who were killed and had our heads bashed in and scrubbed all the floors and did the windows and dug the ditches and picked the cotton here. You enjoy a sense of freedom in this country because we put our lives on the line for it. You have to deal with me. We made this goddamned country."

"You can't make what isn't yours." Herm's flat voice smacked Marci.

And she had to accept his admonition. He was right. We were all trampling on land that was essentially stolen from the people who were here first.

"Okay, okay. You're right, Herm. But my mother—you don't know my mother—but my mother is a proud lady. A distinguished lady. And I've seen her completely humbled in *my* life. That's what happens to us. All of my mother's friends, her sisters, they were all bright, capable women. And almost every one of them had to snuff their own aspirations to be wives to wounded, oppressed men.

"My mother was an accomplished pianist, and do you know what? After she was married, she never played again. All of her dreams went up in smoke. My father was a frightened and beaten man. He worked construction when he could. He never let her do anything. After all this time, I've made my peace with him, but for her I can't help but feel this incredible sadness. And I will never let it happen to me."

I couldn't believe it but at that moment tears started rolling out of Marci's eyes. Her voice barely quivered but she was obviously crying. Maybe it was an inside hurt. For which there was no sound. Only pain and sympathy.

"Once, on a Christmas day, I saw him slap her. They were arguing, about what I can't remember, but in the middle of it, he hit her. I was standing on the steps, about eight years old. It was like lightning had struck her. She collapsed into a creaky wooden chair and for the first time I saw my mother cry."

She looked at us. One at a time. "Do you remember the first time you saw your mother cry? Or get hit by your father? Did you even have that experience?" We all made some gesture of inconclusiveness. At that moment I couldn't remember ever seeing my mother cry. I was more bewildered by Marci's show of emotion and vulnerability than by anything else.

She continued, "It was as though the truth came in an open-handed smack from the man she loved. And the truth was that his frustration at being black in America, and her frustration at having given up her career in a futile attempt to make his life mean something, had come down to a stinging pain in her face and an emptiness in her soul.

"I swore then that it would never happen to me. My art is uncompromising. I am uncompromising." She stopped and faced April. "You're damned right I'm angry. Anger is a type of commodity, if you don't have money or the value of human dignity, you must trade in anger. And the only way we *can* be friends is if I look at you and I see that you are angry at the same system, the same racist bullshit that I am. Then your anger buys you my trust."

Jenny looked at her exasperated, "But that is not how I was taught."

"But, Jenny, this is a new school, a new education, a new day. You can't plead upbringing. You are smarter than your parents. At least you know more than they did. And

I hope that you care more than they might have about building coalitions and alliances which cross racial and cultural differences."

Jenny said what I figured the rest of us were thinking as well. Marci was always the most vocal. The most confrontational.

"And what about you, Marci? How much do you care about building these coalitions you're talking about?" Jenny said.

And April joined her, "Yeah, what about you?"

But Marci snapped back at April, "What the fuck does that mean? What about me?" She just had a hard time giving April any ground.

"You're so busy being angry that you never listen. You never feel the pain that other people feel. It's always about you." I was ready to end this tête-à-tête. I could feel Marci beginning to boil. April had used this situation to push her point with Marci farther than she ever had. Definitely past all of our comfort zones. The whole evening was in jeopardy of imploding.

"What?! Wait a goddamn minute, would you please? Where do you get off talking like that to me? Who the fuck do you think you are?"

We were at the spot I'd been afraid we were approaching. The moment before you commit to a course which changes everything. That moment when the emptiness, the white space of fear, inadequacy, exhaustion, or whatever ruled you. Controlled everything. It was where we had always been.

I didn't want to be there. None of us wanted to be there. "Come on, Marci," I said, "Dewitt's gonna be here in a minute. Besides, we're supposed to be here for each other, right?" But I feared we were trapped in a torrid compulsion that would lead us to disaster. This fear was supported by the fact that Marci flashed her eyes on me and held up her hand, palm facing me. I didn't need to hear the words that that gesture referenced.

April felt the attack coming and tried to stave it off, swiveling her head from Herm to Jenny to me at a near frantic pace. What I saw in her eyes was the same fear I was feeling. We had to get out of this. She probably should have just stopped talking but she didn't.

"That's exactly what I'm saying, Marci. I don't hate you, in fact . . ."

"In fact my ass, April. I don't care, okay? I really don't care."

April softened her features. Tried to be like that cat, meek and supplicant, "Can't I just tell you how I feel?"

"No. I don't want to hear shit you have to say," Marci shouted, the explosion in progress. I saw the spray from her words sparkle in the incandescent light. "You can't tell me a damned thing."

Suddenly the movement in the room slowed to a flicker. Their voices became the paint on the wall and the wall. The floor and the furniture. It was either words or dollar signs. Feelings or desires. I wanted desperately to do something that would change our destiny. And you can change destiny. That might be your destiny. But nothing came to mind. We were trapped there in this.

"And why is that?"

"Because you're white," Marci said. The glint on the tip of her tongue would have pinned any of us to the wall.

April pointed weakly at Jenny, who was a little startled to be brought into it at this point. She looked at April as if she would be happy to join with Marci if it meant April would disappear. "What about her? She's not white. She's trying to say the same thing that I am . . ."

"I can speak for myself, April," Jenny said coolly.

"Well, then, why don't you?" Marci unconsciously snapped.

"Why should I? Because you want me to?" Jenny was revved up. Her voice broke into new territory. Her normal voice was so even, calm. But it was now almost shrill. "Part of the problem here is that both of you speak too quickly."

Marci looked at me as if she were about to "lock and load" her shotgun and blow somebody away. "Icky, I think you better tell these folks to step off. I'm not havin it tonight."

I figured that if Marci was asking for help it was the right time to try to end it.

"Yeah. Hey listen . . . what's going on here? We don't need to be fighting like this. You guys need to chill out. It's getting a little ridiculous in here," I said.

Herm shrugged his shoulders. "What do you expect? This is the way we are. We are expected to take pot shots at each other. What else can we do?"

Marci was standing now, her body bent and held in place in a posture that made her seem as though two pipe cleaners were her arms and legs. Her neck was angled at April. Her eyes were on Jenny. There was menace and danger around her like an aura. Her beauty was encased in this hardness that would not relent until she felt justice. But we were incapable of providing justice. We were at the mercy of the court. We could only hope with Marci that things would change.

Jenny was trying to say something. Something about how we just had to work harder at being friends and how she shouldn't be about messing up the relationships we had. But I knew that there was no way out of that place in which we'd ended up. The only thing to do was to act as if we'd never gone there in the first place. To just back out before we couldn't.

I grabbed the bottle, raised my glass once more, and said, "Check it out. I have a suggestion. Let's try not to be too tacky about this. A half-million dollars is a lot of money, we all know that. And it's got us in its clutches. But Jenny is right. That's no reason to destroy our relationships."

Marci wanted a way out, too. I could tell. She didn't want to be in combat with Jenny, or April for that matter. We were all tired.

"So, what's your suggestion?" She broke her pose and became fluid again.

"You agree that the reason we're fighting each other and going through all of this is because of the money, right?" They all nodded. "Then, I say let's try to take the initiative. Suppose we have a plan instead of waiting around to find out what he's going to want to do. Suppose we take control. Do this straight up."

Herm's eyebrows rose. "What are you talking about?"

"When Dewitt gets here, we each take a turn telling him why we think we deserve the money and let it go at that. I mean, he's coming to talk to us about it. He knows how much each one of us wants it. If we all face up to that honestly and then let him go through his process of making the decision, at least we'll know where we stand.

April spoke first, "I guess I like that idea."

Herm nodded. Marci smiled and said, "I know how we can really come together as a group. Why don't we agree to share the money no matter who gets it." I don't think she really meant it. When she said it, my mind flashed on the notion of splitting up that grant and it didn't feel like something I'd want to do. I cared about the group, but that seemed like taking it a step too far. There must be other ways in which people can bond and make a statement. I like Marci's idea about anger being a commodity. But money. Money actually was a commodity and the idea of sharing for somebody like me was not one I took to easily.

Herm's face turned instantly sour. "Oh, no. No. If I get it I would want all of it. That's the point. I think it should be winner take all. We can still support that person." Thank God for Herm. He always came through at just the right time. He said what we all were thinking. Including Marci. She wouldn't want to split that money up if she got it. I knew her better than that.

The smile returned to his face. "I'll buy us a tremendous dinner at the Old Time Minnesota Cafe, or whatever you think is the proper way to celebrate. But I can tell you one thing for sure. I'm not giving up too much of that money."

"That's about what I'd expect from you," Marci chuckled. The tension was easing. We were back to trying to be friends. The collision had been minor.

I was surprised that Herm even responded. But he did. "What's that supposed to mean?" I knew then that there was nothing that would completely relieve the pressure that hovered around us. We each had thorns sticking in our skins and when someone purposefully or accidentally touched them we jumped in pain. And we reached out to flick theirs a little. If one of us was in pain we found a way to inflict a commensurate hurt to someone else.

This too was what we needed to fix. A way to interact in the world without relying on our need to diminish other vulnerable people. The idea that a black woman and a Native American man would be carping back and forth as they were in the wake of opportunity was absurd. It made me think of Chester Himes's autobiography, "My Life of Absurdity" in which he expands on Albert Camus's idea that racism was absurd. Himes wrote in the first paragraph of the book, "If one lives in a country where racism is held valid and practiced in all ways of life, eventually, no matter whether one is a racist or a victim, one comes to feel the absurdity of life." This was what we were now.

And Marci wouldn't let him up. "From what I hear, you give all your money up to your girlfriends, anyway. You would need it all." She knew which splinter to jiggle. I saw Herm's eyes open wide. He couldn't believe that she would go there.

His body kind of trembled. I could tell his anger was stirred. And as I've earlier noted, you really don't want to get Herm too angry. Although it must be said that Marci was up to the task of standing up to anyone.

"You don't hear me saying anything about your personal life," he said.

Marci shot back, "You don't know a damned thing about my personal life."

I had to try again to divert them. "Come on. Damn. Can't we talk for ten minutes without arguing?"

Herm looked at me and then at Marci. "I guess not. I didn't come here for this."

Jenny stretched out on the floor. "I hope you guys chill out before Dewitt gets here. It won't look good for any of us."

I nodded, happy for any help in keeping us in the same room. And then, like a sign from God or the arrival of the devil, I don't know which, the doorbell rang. "That's Dewitt," I said.

Marci broke her stance and became fluid again. It would be good to have Dewitt join us. At the very least it provided a new target. "It's about fucking time. He's got us here like a bunch of yelping puppies waiting for his white ass." She said and then turned to April. "No offense intended."

11

i was happy to leave the room to greet Dewitt. He had no idea of the stress he had inflicted on us. But he was full of smiles. A bit flustered, it seemed, but smiling nonetheless. We hugged. I felt in that embrace that he was very happy to be here. In my home. I couldn't help but feel that I had some sort of special place in his plan. I have to say that I truly expected to be the one to whom he gave the money.

As we held each other there at my door, I was struck by the fact that I had rarely ever held a white man in my arms. Or ever felt held by them. It was a heady feeling. I counted it as a negative that I had no real friends who were white men. It was a significant problem to me. How could we ever achieve the type of society I wanted to live in if I couldn't tolerate the close personal friendship of a white man?

I couldn't help but wish, as Dewitt offered himself to me, that it was not so perfunctory. But I can't lie. White men often reveal themselves as untrustworthy. And friendship is too precious. I'm regularly wounded by the false friendship of people of color. And also from the few white women I will let become close. But to risk it with a white man seems too expensive. I look forward to the time when this isn't true for me.

But, you see, in my book, a friend—real friendship—overrides nearly everything. A person can't be your friend unless they know and accept who you really are. They have to account for and actually love the things in you that inherently make you unlovable. Or at least understand it. Anger, for example. Or a bad habit.

People like Dewitt jump over that part of the issue. They don't think of themselves as being guilty of anything and so they feel that their attempt at warmth and fair treatment should be accepted at face value, proof of their ability to be friends. And it's true that many people of color can accept that. But I can't do that. Maybe it's because I'm an artist, I don't often humor white people. Indeed, as you have discovered by now, I'm sure, I can be quite acerbic.

But, you know the way black people bullshit. We say shit all the time that we don't mean, seriously. We're trained to be that way. I mean, really, nearly every black person I know who has a job, or who belongs to some kind of organization or something, has been over at a white person's house for dinner, or with them for drinks, and thought, "what the fuck am I doing here? These people don't really want to know me."

But we go anyway because we wouldn't get anywhere, no job promotions, no raises, grants, nothing, if we couldn't every now and then, be sociable with white people. And when we're there we're liable to say anything. Lie like a motherfucka. I know I've done it. Said shit that makes it sound like we're friends but, really, you know, it's the old okey doke. It's bullshit.

I was out of town once, up in Bemidji, Minnesota, at this one dude's house for Sunday brunch, and he was trip-pin' over this golf match that was on TV. And this was well before the coming of Tiger Woods. I didn't know shit about golf except that only white men did it. That they kept us out of their clubs. That they tried to act as if we weren't capable of playing a game they thought of as "cerebral." Like what was I supposed to say? "Oh, yeah, I guess I can see how this is exciting." That's bullshit. Michael Jordan and the Bulls were on CBS. I wanted to say, "What the fuck are you doing? There's basketball on." But I stayed and ate their food and made small talk as we watched white men play golf. Cool. I liked the guy well enough but we could never be friends.

It was my shortcoming, but I couldn't help but associate golf with privilege. And I've come to believe that it takes a special kind of white man to be my friend. Haven't met one yet. I'm talking about a guy who is willing to let all his privilege shit go. I don't want to be in a relationship with anyone who can't help but judge me based on his standards. White men always seem to be evaluating me and I never seem to measure up.

I am always surprised when I hear a black man talk about his friend, so and so, who is white. I immediately wonder about the nature of that relationship. I can't help it. How does a black man, born in these United States learn to love a white man? How is this possible? And I'm not talking about that "gettin over" bullshit, where people will say anything to anyone to be liked. Or just to have a white friend (from which there are many benefits).

Every time I start feeling buddy-buddy with a white guy I find myself saying to him, "You know. I've never had a white man as a friend. I don't think it's possible for me right now. I'm too goddamned angry."

Most white men back right off. But one guy I said that to actually said, "Well, I want to be the first." And you know what? He was bullshitting me. He didn't mean it. I don't think I ever saw him again.

Dewitt and I walked into the living room. After all of the happy greetings, he said, "Sorry it took me so long. There was an art opening downtown of an exhibit I funded."

I broke a smile. "The Throwin Down show?"

"Yeah, it was quite something. There was a little problem though." Dewitt paused and seemed uncomfortable. "Ah, we didn't think that many of the gang members were going to show up. There was an awful lot of commotion out there."

Marci burst into laughter. "You might have guessed there'd be problems with a show about gang paraphernalia."

He turned to her, obviously surprised and a little agitated that she would laugh at him. By that point we were all stifling a snigger. I'm sure he was baffled at our response. But he pulled on his shirt as if he were wearing a suit that needed straightening and said, "Well, to be honest I didn't count on the *gangbangers* actually being there." When I looked into his eyes I could tell that he hadn't realized yet that we were teasing him. So I kept it up.

"Ah, who exactly did you think would be there?" I asked.

"Well, you know, the normal arts crowd. It was kind of scary. There was a very large group of black guys hanging outside and a lot of the people who had come just didn't try to get in. I saw them in the parking lot but I guess they were a little too afraid to get out of their cars." Dewitt gulped air and walked to the dining room table. "Ah . . . food. I didn't get a chance to sample the hors d'oeuvres there. We had planned to have this nice spread of food and wine. But it just didn't work out. Most of the people that I wanted to come and see the show couldn't. It was a disaster."

"Black men are so frightening, aren't they?" Once again Marci's sarcasm found a completely exposed target. But Dewitt was so unconscious he didn't notice. He was nibbling shrimp salad and filling his glass with wine.

When he lifted his head from his plate and looked at Marci, it was clear that he had missed her point entirely. This was Dewitt in fine style. He was used to being the center of our attention. And, even more significant, he never doubted his good intentions and would never have guessed that we would make fun of him that way. But this sarcastic banter was our only means of trying to balance his arrogance. Among us it was incendiary and dangerous. Against him, it was all laughs and winks.

Dewitt paused for just a minute. I felt him trying to determine if Marci's comment was negative or not. And then he moved forward, "Well, we just didn't count on all that activity. When I was leaving there was an argument, people screaming at each other. I just ran for my car. I know there were weapons there. I saw three or four guns. They had them tucked in their pants, bulging out of their jackets. I saw them."

He wiped his mouth with a napkin. "What the hell is going on? What kind of people bring guns to an art opening? Can you believe it? I'm talking about an art exhibit. Icky, could you fix me a drink, please?"

I fixed him a scotch. But I couldn't believe that he was acting so naive. And he wasn't, really. Or maybe he was only naive about things like this. About black people in particular. Maybe he thought all you had to do was bring the streets into the gallery and you could appreciate the irony and the pathos and the beauty and everything would be fine. "You're really talking about gangs, Dewitt," I said pouring myself just a fingertip splash of scotch. "Anyway, I'm not so sure that shit is art."

Herm looked at me and shook his head as if to scold, "I don't know. The icons and sounds of the people are art. Who says that the graffiti markings on a blank wall aren't art? Or the slang poetry?"

"But guns? That *is* a little much." Jenny's voice was soft again. After two drinks, her face was very flushed. All of our movements were slower. Our speech less clear. The wine and the scotch were gradually taking their toll.

April walked over and sat down at the table. "You have to understand the power of the bond among young black men. They have no advocates, really. Many of them have no viable family structures. The gang is a substitute for all of that."

"Oh, so now it's like you know so much about black men. Gang members no less." Marci was so revved up that nothing satisfied her.

"I'm not saying how much or how little I know, Marci. But I bet you that I've spent more time walking the streets of the inner cities of Minneapolis and other places than you have in the last five years. You try to be black in your studio painting. When is the last time you were around a lot of black people? How long has it been?"

"I don't know why you keep fucking with me, April, but you are walking on thin ice. You don't know shit about black men. I don't need to know how many 'inner cities' you've been in to know that you still don't know shit about us."

Once again I scrambled to reestablish civility. Dewitt had finally arrived and we were still fighting. It wasn't looking very good. "Hey . . . hey . . . now, why don't we just change the subject. You guys are not going to agree on whether that gang stuff is art or what young black men need. At least not tonight."

Dewitt seemed a little bewildered at the level of energy flowing among us. I said to him, "This has been a long night, Dewitt. We thought you'd be here much earlier and we've been having a very intense series of discussions. So, let me suggest that we all get a slice of this lovely fruit tart here, replenish our drinks, if you want—there's coffee in the kitchen—and let's sit with my man here and have a talk about this Genius Grant."

Everyone jumped up and headed toward the kitchen. I had set the fruit tart on the counter along with forks and plates. I took that opportunity to go to the bathroom. I stood there, my face staring back at me as I relieved myself, wondering what I would do with so much money.

When I returned to the living room, I walked in on a conversation between Jenny and April. They were standing in the middle of the room, each balancing a small dessert. I was about to invite them to sit down when I heard what they were talking about. I decided, instead, to listen for a minute.

"You seem to be so comfortable in situations like this. I can barely keep from running out of here. It's as though there is a desire to be friends, but . . ."

"I know, Jenny, but we have to keep trying. Look at me. They don't trust me." April's voice was tired. Saddened.

But Jenny looked at her very strangely and said, "Who?"

I kept just beyond their sight, at the corner where the hallway leads into the dining room. When I craned my neck I could see them but they couldn't see me. April finally answered her, "The rest of them, you know—them. But I'm not going away. They will have to deal with me. I'm committed to being a part of this movement."

Jenny was tired. I could tell that even from where I

was standing. A puzzled expression was embossed on her smooth, youthful face. "You said them . . . them . . .?"

"Yes, you know, Marci, and Herm, and Icky . . ." April said innocently. I suppose she thought she had an ally in Jenny.

"What about me?" Jenny asked.

April realized a little too late that Jenny was offended. "You? Yes, of course, you, too."

Jenny stepped back and gazed at April. "You don't really see me, do you?" April barely acknowledged her. But Jenny said it again, "You don't really see me, do you?"

April stared at her. Jenny waited but April just kept looking at her without saying a word.

And then Jenny seemed to abandon that line of discussion and asked April, "Do you want the grant?"

"Ah . . . yes, Jenny I do. I have a lot of plans for that money."

Jenny smiled. She had changed subjects just to bait April because she then asked her original question, "You don't see me, do you?"

"What?"

"You don't see me, do you?"

"See you? What are you talking about?"

But Jenny persisted, asking the same question, "You don't see me, do you?" I thought it was a brilliant moment of performance. That was what you had to expect from Jenny. Marci was volatile, explosive, caustic. But Jenny had a sense of the dramatic. It was subtle, manipulative, but in the end just as effective. April knew what Jenny was trying to say.

April responded with her own brand of sarcasm. This time she spoke loud enough to bring people out of the kitchen. "Is there a woman by the name of Jennifer Grimm here? I mean, I thought there was a smart, engaging, quiet woman here by the name of Jennifer Grimm. I could have sworn I was just talking to her."

Dewitt came into the room at that precise moment. A brittle feeling permeated from April's last comment. The vapor of Jenny's silence. I stood transfixed. Even Dewitt could sense that something was dreadfully wrong. And something was. "What's this about?" Dewitt looked a little silly when he said it. As if he knew there was a problem but didn't think it could actually be that significant. He re-plenished his drink from the dwindling bottle of twelve-year-old MacCallan's.

I made myself visible and attempted to rescue them from having to explain it to Dewitt. "The room is full of expectant energy, Dewitt," I said grandly. "We are an intense group of excited artists. We await your wisdom, sirrah." I smiled broadly at the last word. I knew that Dewitt would under-stand my Shakespearean usage. "As I said, we've had a number of unusual conversations tonight."

Luckily, Jenny was ready to get down to business. She nodded in my direction and then said to Dewitt, "So what's the story on this grant? It's getting to be past my bedtime."

Dewitt laughed. "I'm sorry to hear that, Jenny. The night is still very young." He didn't know how wrong he was. Darkness was about to descend over us all. And he would not see the sun again.

"Oh, let's cut the play and the shit, Dewitt," Marci said as she and Herm joined us. Then, to Jenny, as she sat down: "You like that, poet? I made a rhyme without knowin it." And ended with a great flourish with her face directly in front of Dewitt's. "Who's getting the ducats?"

He tried to get comfortable on the chair facing the couch, his thin body sinking into the overstuffed beige cushion. But suddenly he looked ill at ease. "Well, what I really wanted to tell you all was how hard I've thought about this. I know this is an important decision."

It was then that I felt something drop in my stomach. Something thick and tough began to form there. I peered into his eyes and saw the shape of a bird struggling to fly, the reflection of a narrow-winged bird, like a nighthawk or a swallow, flapping its wings. As if it were tangled somehow in Marci's hair. And he was watching that as he formulated his speech.

I could see it and I immediately felt afraid. There was a new energy in the room.

"I've agonized over this so much. And I guess I don't have good news for you."

I tried to still my roiling stomach. There were small eruptions throughout my body. Each of us was immediately stricken with this new uncertainty. Marci was the first to respond, "What do you mean? One of us is gonna get the money, right?"

"Of course," I found myself saying. I saw the bird and I heard Dewitt's voice but I was bent on creating a different reality. That grant was promised to one of us. To me.

For some reason April was not tracking with this new atmosphere. She obviously didn't see the darkness in Dewitt's eyes. Or the way he hadn't responded to Marci's questions. Or the way he averted his eyes from mine when I tried to provide an opportunity for him. None of that had captured her attention. Instead she asked a question that none of the rest of us cared about at the moment. "Why isn't Jesus or JuJu here? Especially Jesus. There's no Latino."

This was a subject he could address, even though he seemed hesitant. I had been rejected by the best of them. I've made that clear. I know rejection. The way people invite you to be a part of things and then, when your hopes are high and you think your life might change, they pull the rug out from under you. I felt it.

His voice was somber. "I considered them, but let's just say this is the group that made the final list."

Herm was smiling. I knew what he was thinking. He was sure that his chances of success were growing with every new piece of information. Jesus was out. JuJu was out. And after Dewitt's first statement it wasn't difficult to surmise that Marci wasn't the one. So his energy was still flying. "That's fine with me. Come on, let's hear the details."

Dewitt held up one thin, delicate arm. "I pride myself on being strong and courageous." He stopped abruptly and swallowed a shot of scotch. It was his third since he'd walked in the door, which was unusual.

"Ahhhh. That's really good stuff," he said to me.

"Yeah, I keep it here for special occasions," I answered absently. And then I looked at him like, "Okay, already. Just tell us what the hell is going on."

And he complied. "Well, anyway, I know you're all waiting for me to tell you something. I appreciate your patience. I wasn't going to do this here, you know. I wasn't planning on making any great pronouncements tonight or anything. But this process has been so painful for me. I had no idea it was going to be this way." Again he took a long pause.

We all sat there like statues. Herm jumped up from his chair in a huff and walked to the window. I knew he was about to burst. Dewitt's eyes followed him there. And then he continued, "So, I'm just going to give it to you straight. Maybe I shouldn't have said anything about this before I knew exactly what I was doing. But I couldn't help it. I know now I should have kept it more quiet until I made my decision. But, I didn't and, well, that's all water under the bridge, as they say. Well, here it is: I've decided none of you should get the money."

I swear the bird flew out of his eyes and out the window. I watched it disappear into the blue dark crepe sky. Dewitt nervously sipped more of his scotch. My scotch. I didn't look at anyone else. Only Dewitt. But I felt other eyes boring holes into him. You could almost see the dents erupting on his skin from the force of the gazes he was receiving.

Herm, who'd taken his plate of half-eaten fruit tart with him to the window, had actually dropped it. It's still there on the floor. Hardened and inedible. But I felt his presence moving back among us. The rest of us, except Jenny, who'd tightly folded herself in a knot and sat on the floor, were on the edge of our chairs.

Marci scanned the room. She looked at Dewitt, blinked her eyes rapidly and then closed them. When they opened again she was staring at me. And then she shuttled to Herm, Jenny, and April. But when she again focused on Dewitt I knew we were about to lurch to another level.

"I don't see anybody laughing." She paused and looked around again. I couldn't tell whether she was actually trying to discern if a joke was being played on her or what. But it became clear that she knew what was going on. "I said, I don't hear any motherfucking laughter. Okay? Nobody's laughing here."

But Dewitt was trying to be "courageous," as he put it. "I'm not joking, Marci. I knew you guys would be upset but . . ."

Marci cut him off. "But . . . my ass. I didn't ask you to ask Icky to call me and tell me to come here tonight. I was sitting in my goddamned house. I wasn't thinking about you or your funky-ass money. I came here because I thought somebody had finally recognized what I have been . . ." She exploded into tears. I'd never seen her disassemble like that before. "I've been working like a dog all my goddamned life and you have the nerve to tease me like this. You're fucking crazy, man."

I'd had enough. I could see Dewitt bracing himself for the onslaught but I didn't care. The dam had been breached, "Dewitt, man, what the fuck is this about? You told me that we were finalists. That one of us, at least, would get the grant. You let us go through all this shit, all this tension, for nothing?"

"I know. But, well . . ."

"Well, what?" Herm was looming over him. There was menace in his voice and in his eyes. His long hair seemed to whiten right in front of our eyes.

Dewitt slowly tried to rise out of the chair. He had placed his plate on the floor at his feet, which he must have forgotten because his foot abruptly slid across the plate and caused him to fall back into the chair. It was then that I realized that he was a little tipsy. I'd never seen him drunk before. And maybe it was a good thing for him. Maybe it numbed him to the tumult that was rising around him.

"I'm sorry," he said about the plate which skidded a couple of feet. He tried again to stand and succeeded. "The time isn't right. The more I thought about it the more I realized . . ." He stopped and straightened himself up. His scotch-and-fear-induced fog dissipated. "Now I know you're going to be upset with me, but this is what I do. My job is to be ahead of the pack."

He started pacing. We were all paralyzed. Dumbstruck. Fixed in that moment. In those positions. A human menagerie.

"I make trends. I start things. You know what I mean." He continued, "Now this multicultural thing was pretty hot there for a while. Still is, I guess. Everybody's doing it. It's everywhere.

"Whenever you want to put together a program or exhibition, you always have to stop and think about this damned multicultural thing. You don't know what it's like. I get a brainstorm, a great idea for a performance series or something, and then I realize I have to think about race and culture and all that shit. Art should not always be concerned with these issues. Life is more than race. Art is more than life."

Herm had slowly backed up to the window. And in a move that captured all of our emotions, he collapsed onto the window seat. What a horribly volatile mixture this was. His frustration, our frustration. If someone had lit a match this entire apartment would have been blown to bits.

"You have no idea, you just don't. Last year I wanted to do something about retro cyberpunk. Do you know how hard it is to find a black person and an Asian and a Latino who is at the forefront of retro cyberpunk? Do you?" And this, to me, sounded a lot like the scratchy popping flaring sound of a match being lit. Dewitt was asking us to understand his pain. His travails as a manipulator of public and private money. Of people and the art they produced. He did this in the name of art. In the name of culture. And we played along because we live in a dream world. A world where we believed that if we could focus our energy on something—our art, for example—that we would be fulfilled. Loved. Supported.

We had suddenly been ejected from the main stage. We were the sideshow, at best.

"Why? Why must I be reduced to this?"

"Because, my good friend," I said, "my great funder of the arts, because you believe in us."

His voice sounded far off, empty of emotion, "I do, Icky, I really do."

"Then close your eyes and take out your checkbook," I

said. Marci had stopped crying but was breathing heavily. I could hear the cadence of her breath, wrapped in the moisture of her tears.

"It's not that simple, Icky. The time has passed. When I first thought about it, this grant was right on the money. But now, now, I'm thinking that well, what's the point? What are you guys really saying?"

"What?" Herm said weakly from the window.

"Well, that's the point, really?" Dewitt faced to Herm, his posture stiff and unyielding. "What are you saying? Tell me the truth, Herm. You don't really give a shit about your goddamned ancestral legacy, do you? I mean, your art is thick but to tell it as it is, you have to admit it's not pushing any boundaries, is it? You have to admit it doesn't challenge us to *do* anything, now does it? I mean, how much do I really want to know about living on the plains? About folkloric images that haven't changed for centuries? What chances do you take, Herm? You're just saying the same tired thing all the time. Anyway, what will you do with the money? Give it away to some young white woman?"

Herm sprang up from the window. His line had been crossed. Alone I was no match for an unleashed Ojibwa of his size. "Whoa, Dewitt. What's up with you?" I tried to reach him before Herm did. But Dewitt was actually walking toward Herm as he talked and they ended up literally face to face with each other, surprising both men.

"You better get your stupid white face from in front of me," Herm said. And then, almost as an afterthought, he hit Dewitt on the side of his head with his open palm. Dewitt went to the floor like a ball, bouncing against and knocking over the coffee table. He ended up sprawled in the middle of the floor. April rushed up to grab Herm's inactive arm and I stood between him and Dewitt. No one went to Dewitt. He just sat there with his hand on his head, staring at us. His face was flushed.

April and I held Herm, who had actually stopped struggling. Jenny and Marci were now standing with us. "What's wrong with you?" I screamed at Dewitt. "What the fuck is wrong with you?"

"I'm just tired, that's all," he said, still sitting on the floor. "I'm tired of playing this little game. I've supported all of you, but I'm tired now. This is getting very boring."

"Motherfucka, if I was you I'd get the fuck out of here while you can," Marci spat at him. I noticed that she clutched one of my knives. It was already stained with the blood of fruit. The blade cast a sparkle from her hands.

"No, Marci, no, let's let him have his say. Talk your shit to us, Dewitt." I let go of Herm and took a step toward Dewitt.

"I didn't come here to fight," he said.

That was obvious. He'd never go anywhere where he thought there would be a fight. I'm sure he'd never been hit like that. But he was playing outside the lines, you might say. He was dealing with people who knew what it was like to settle their issues more directly. People who looked at mediation and legal procedures with more than a little trepidation. Dewitt was in trouble but I could tell he wasn't about to back down.

"Naw, Dewitt, you just keep right on. Is there anything you want to say to me?"

Dewitt pushed himself upright again. And once again he straightened his clothes as he stood up. He reminded me of Stan Laurel. He looked as lopsided as Stan would after Oliver had socked him a good one.

Then Dewitt looked at me with the weirdest expression. I felt two distinct and contradictory feelings emanating from him. The first was that he wanted to leave. That he'd had

his moment, made his great pronouncement, and was ready
to leave. But I also felt him wanting to stay. To roll up his
sleeves and joust with us. I think, to him it wasn't entirely
personal. Just that someone had to stand up to us. If it had
to be him, so be it. But us colored folks needed a reality
check and he was capable of giving it to us.

"Icky . . ." He was actually smiling.

"Go ahead, Dewitt. Why don't you just go right on and
tell me what you've got to say?"

He looked at me, and I could tell that he had made a
decision. If there had been a conflict within him about leaving or staying for the fight, it was over. He was never going
to leave this apartment. He didn't know it at the time. He
thought he was just making a brave stand. But, in fact, this
was one of the biggest decisions he'd ever make. It was a
decision which, if he'd known all the things at work both
within him and without, he would have grabbed his jacket
and gotten the hell out of there. Instead, he said, "All right,
all right . . . you want it straight?"

April interrupted him, "Dewitt, I don't know what's
going on here, but I think . . ."

But he stole the initiative away from her. "You, think?
You think? That's a laugh. You don't think. If you were
thinking, you'd think about why you're here." He waved
his hand in front of her. "I could never give money to somebody who just follows after other people. What are you
doing for yourself, April? No, don't tell me, because you
know what?"

He became more animated, almost giddy. "This is feeling quite nice, this freedom. Fuck political correctness. Fuck
it. I'm going to say what *I* think. Not what you want me to
say. And, Herm, if you want to slug me again, be my guest."

April whispered calming energy to Herm. I was sure he
wasn't about to attack Dewitt again. But I wasn't sure what

Marci or, I for that matter, was capable of. Yet, despite the danger that Dewitt was in, he seemed almost intoxicated by it. His face was so red it glowed.

"Don't get me wrong, all of you are very talented, I've told you that before. You really are. But when I really sat with the idea I had to admit that the work you are doing just doesn't take me anywhere."

I felt Marci brush by me, the knife flashing as she made her way toward Dewitt. Jenny lunged and caught her blouse by the thinnest clutch of material. I thought Marci was simply going to let Jenny pull her blouse off. But, instead, she dragged Jenny across the room.

When Dewitt saw the knife his words died. The redness in his face faded as he blanched the color of a fava bean. Any person of color knows this game of color changes in white people when they deal with us. They were like walking mood people. Red for anger, white for shock, blue for frustration.

But Marci had lost it. "Oh, I'm going to take you some-fucking-where, all right."

At first Dewitt recoiled from Marci as Dracula might from the almighty crucifix. He literally shrank back. But in a heartbeat he was back. As if he'd challenged himself to stay the course. To take this moment as Harold Bloom or, perhaps even worse, Ed Hirsch had done with his book, *Cultural Literacy*. The cultural war had its own little multiple combat theater problems. Suddenly there was combat right here in River City. Dewitt had anointed himself the local general in charge of relevancy and excellence.

He quickly regained his composure. "Marci, I knew you wouldn't disappoint me. But this is for your own good. You need to hear this." Jenny was doing her best to keep Marci away from Dewitt. And after a moment I joined her. But Marci was an incredibly strong woman and not easy to restrain. "Who do you think you are?" she screamed at the top of her voice. "Who?"

Maybe it was the knife in her hands or our angry faces clustered together, but he suddenly started gathering up his things to leave. "Well, I guess I should go . . ."

"Have you said everything you wanted to say?" I asked him.

He was breathing quite heavily. Almost heaving. I was shocked at the wide differences between his appearance from one moment to the next. There was exhaustion, anger, fear (a lot of fear), arrogance. Each moment a different burst of information.

"Well, actually, no, now that you asked." He cast cold eyes on Marci. "Where in the world did you ever learn that indiscriminate use of color has anything to do with beauty?"

I couldn't believe it. In the middle of this fiasco he was proffering an artistic criticism. But this was his weaponry.

"You weren't raised on some farm in rural Georgia. You need to give up that spooky, naive country-Christian-art stuff, sweetie. And that Afrocentric trip is very tired. Kente cloth is only so interesting. I mean, have you ever heard of joy? Why is everything you paint so goddamned depressing?" He was patting himself, ostensibly, I supposed, to ensure he had his wallet and his car keys. And then he took a step toward the hallway that led to the front door but halted. He had to pass us to get there.

Marci spat at him, "You ugly bastard."

Dewitt weaved his way to the chair where his jacket was and began putting it on. But the funniest thing happened. His arm stuck in the material. We stood stock-still, watching him as he tussled with his own coat. Like a dog chasing his tail. It was hilarious.

In the middle of this he continued talking. He turned his attention to me. "And now, Mr. Ichabod Word, novelist, storyteller." It was then I realized how angry I was. I let go of Marci's arm. If she wanted to cut his throat I wouldn't stop her.

He actually feigned a large, ridiculing yawn. "Novelist? I think not. It's a bit too long, really. You are a manifestation of the failure in this country to maintain its literary aspirations. I'm sorry, Ichabod, but your work just doesn't excite me. Nothing new there. You know what I mean. Every ten or fifteen years you folks get a chance to do your thing. Everybody opens up their checkbooks and you get all the money. But the same thing happens every time. You start attacking us. And you do it with the same old tired arguments. Racism, racism. Jesus, isn't there anything else to talk about with you folks?"

He was still wrestling with his coat, his frustration and anger rising. He was now almost drenched in sweat. I wanted him to know that I, too, had courage. And I knew he was more afraid of me than I of him. I was the black man. The demon. So I slipped through the cluster and walked right up to him. I put my arm on his shoulder. This scared him. I felt his body quaking under my touch. I even squeezed his shoulder blade just a little to let him know he was in my grasp.

"Here, Dewitt, let me help you with your coat."

He looked up at me with that sitcom face and said, "You aren't pissed?"

"Me, no, sir." I lied. "I think you're right. We needed to hear this." I turned around to my stricken multiculti comrades. "Didn't we?"

And then I was on top of him again. My eyes tearing away at his flesh. I could have killed him then. "Yes, Dewitt, we would have just kept doing the same old thing, thinking we were doing *something,* if it weren't for you. Thank God you've helped us see just how ridiculous it is.

You, meaning you, are just not going to change. It's like they say, 'You ain't tryin to hear it.' But I'll tell you what. I don't think you're going to leave just yet."

I tightened my grip as the group moved toward us. Herm's face locked in grimace. Marci with the knife. Jenny and April angered, frightened, but with us nonetheless.

I didn't know what I was doing. Or why. But I didn't want him to just rip us apart and then walk out like that. That wouldn't have been right. Would it? I mean, would you let someone come into your house and berate you and your art, not to mention your friends, and then simply put on their coat and walk out? I said to him, "No, my friend, I can tell you for a fact that you are not leaving quite yet." I didn't know then that I was right and wrong at the same time.

He looked up at me and said, "Let go of me, Icky."

And I stared down at him, holding my anger somewhere in my heart where it hurt me more than it did him. "My name's not Icky, Dewitt, it's Ichabod."

"How cliché is this? Tell me, Icky, is this the best you can do? Here I am the only white man in the room, the obvious villain. Jesus, don't you have even a trace of creativity? Surprise? Are you familiar with the idea of surprise?"

"I'm surprised you're as stupid as you are." I said what I was thinking. He was less than competently arrogant. He was frightened. A frightened defender of the cultural bastion.

April stepped into his space. "You think that you can just put our lives and our work down without any consequences?"

"Icky, I'm telling you to let me go," he said, at first ignoring April. And then he narrowed his eyes and said, "You folks are swimming in a sea of grandiosity. There ought to be a twelve-step program or some kind of treatment you could check in for. Only in Minnesota, that's what

I say. This could only happen in Minnesota, and it's an ugly, ugly picture. Will you let me go? You must not know how stupid you all look."

Marci came closer, too, saying, "You just treat us like your little pets, don't you? Slaves? We have to come through you to be validated. To get money, to eat. To be a part of history. You get the credit for discovering us. For supporting us. We pass on. We go out of style and you're looking for the next cyperpunk whiteboy bullshit to give your money to."

Even though I could feel his body convulsing he never blinked. He snapped back, "Don't you ever get tired of hiding behind your color?"

Herm screamed, "No, do you?"

And Dewitt collapsed in my arms. Somewhere in his body a vessel popped. I could feel his body cascade in on itself. I felt him slip away. Shut down. He said nothing more. At first the tribe thought he'd fainted or was faking. And then their gaze became tired. Their eyes drooped. As if they were passing into another world. Dollar signs had been replaced by words and words were now being replaced by sadness. Sadness was all around us. Even though they weren't aware he was already dead. I knew he was dead. I felt the moment when it happened. I was so shocked I couldn't move. I couldn't tell anyone. I struggled to hold his lifeless body. He was getting heavier by the second.

Jenny asked if he was all right. He didn't answer and neither did I.

I found myself talking to him. "You wonder why the cliché? And so do we. But in this story, we shall ignore the conventional wisdom. In fact, we aren't sure it's a cliché at all. In most of the situations I read about or see; in most of the history; in nearly every instance I can think of, the white man usually wins. I take some pride in the fact that we are here with you and we are still breathing."

12

it was as if another day had unfolded. As if a week had passed. Or more. The air that circulated around us was putrid. Foul smelling. Wine. Sweat. Anger. Death. He was dead. Motionless. Gone. Ghost. Out.

Marci was crying uncontrollably again. Jenny sat stoically. Herm's face was still twisted into a grimace I imagined would never release his face. He would look like that forever. I was certain. And April's delicate hand played in her blond hair. She held her saxophone like a baby with the other arm. I kept expecting her to pick it up and play "Motherless Child" or "Amazing Grace" or something like that.

Marci tried to turn back her tears and say something but I couldn't understand her. Her bottom lip was curled down, trembling, showing the soft pink underside. A sad pout. Everyone was depleted. Everyone in shock.

And me? Me. I was already thinking about the next step. About the cops and what would happen to us. Nothing, right. We hadn't done anything wrong, had we?

"We have to call the police. The hospital. Somebody."

Marci's voice was empty of emotion even as she broke through her tears to speak.

"Yeah." Herm's words had lost their smile. "We have to call somebody."

I nodded but didn't say anything. I caught April's eyes. She was afraid. So was I. But I gathered myself and asked her, "What should we do?"

She looked at me and almost smirked. As if she thought I was joking or something. No. She looked at me and asked a question with her eyes. I turned away. Tuned into Jenny. She asked the same question. Herm. He too didn't need to speak.

And then Marci, who I think was trying to say what everyone was wondering, said, "Did we do that? Were we guilty? Was it us? Were we responsible?"

"You didn't have to do it." Jenny's head was down when she said it. I stared at her. We all stared at her. Each one waiting to find out who she would look at when she raised her head up. Who was it that was guilty? Whomever she turned to would feel the collective stare that was gathering. We all wanted to know. To be able to point to someone and have that person take the growing weight from our shoulders.

I couldn't stand the suspense. "Who are you talking to, Jenny? Me? Do you think I killed him?"

"I didn't say that. I was here. I was a part of it. I wanted to hurt him. I'll admit it. But I never actually intended on *doing* it." Jenny still hadn't lifted her head. She knew, that at the moment, she held the mantle of judgment. But she quickly relinquished it by refusing to look at anyone. In fact, she put her hands over her eyes and pulled herself into an even tighter space.

"Well, what are we going to do?" Herm said.

I was there with them. I knew what had happened. I

knew that none of us had actually done anything to warrant my sense of jeopardy. But I was afraid. Dewitt was only the second person I'd seen dead. I put my head on the back of the chair. I would never know who Jenny thought killed Dewitt.

"We've got to do something." Marci was gulping air. Her tears evaporating. "We can't just sit here around a dead body without doing something. We have to do something."

April stood up. "I think we should call the police right now. What are we waiting for? I don't get it. We apply the slightest pressure on the guy and he up and drops dead. That's ridiculous. He was a grantsmaker, for God's sake. He should have been tougher than that."

I couldn't help laughing. In fact everyone started laughing. We weren't just making fun of a dead man. A "grantsmaker," as April called him. We were surprised at the frailty of his constitution. He'd never seemed frail before. We all had always been afraid of him. And then, in the one moment when we had pulled ourselves out of the muck and mire of fear and oppression; when we had fashioned some sort of concerted effort to announce our significance and our unwillingness to take abuse from him . . . that is the moment when he decided to drop dead. How fitting it was. It was, in a fashion, the truth about white mainstream power systems. You just had to stand up to them. If you did, they often fell away because they weren't very substantial in the first place. They were constructed on lies and depended on our fear of them to ensure their survival. Dewitt was born, unbeknownst to us at that moment, with a bad heart, and that, along with the confrontation, put him a heartstring away from the internal explosion that must have been enough to stop him from breathing.

Oh, if change really were that easy.

"I'm calling the cops." April had the telephone in her

hands. But I quickly made my way over to her and snatched the phone away. She looked up at me with total surprise. I suspected that no one had ever snatched anything out of her hands. I could feel how unaccustomed she was to being told what to do.

"What the hell are you doing, Icky? Give me the phone."

I backed away from her. "No. Listen. Dewitt is dead." I paused. The argument was formulating itself in my head. It was convoluted, to be sure. This entire story sprang out of this ragged moment. Perhaps out of my paranoia. Okay. I admit it. There is a kind of paranoia at work here. The others had it to a lesser degree, but they had it nonetheless. The same fear we held of white people was what over time caused our paranoia. You just start thinking you can't win. That the "man" has got everything all nailed down. If you're Hispanic or Arab or Native or black, forget it. And the question was, at least for me, how could I rid myself of this paranoia?

Something inside me pulled me in a direction. Pushed me to propose this plan which now, I must say, feels very, very shaky. But you are here. And I am here. And you are still listening. That is something.

"Wait, April. Let's talk about this a minute." I realized that I was panting, as if I'd run up three flights of steps. But this breathlessness had more to do with anticipation. You know that feeling when you think you know what you have to do and you know that whatever that is will be hard—will test you—there are spasms which emanate from deep within. So deep and intense that you lose your ability to breathe normally. The other side of that feeling is danger and collapse. The other side of that feeling is triumph. Success.

I've been dealing with this all of my life. It always comes down to what you believe about yourself. How often are you right? Can you trust yourself? I panted because no matter how arrogant or self-sure you might be about any particular point, when the stakes are high, there is no sufficient level of comfort.

"Talk about what?" Marci had stopped crying and was now sounding as if she were ready to do battle again. "What the fuck do we need to talk about now? We just need to get somebody in here to help us."

Herm just stared at me. Jenny's head was still buried in her hands.

I stood over Dewitt, "Who killed him? That's what everyone is going to want to know? Isn't it? Who?

"Okay, listen," I had chosen my path. "This is how I see it. If we call the police they'll come and arrest us. We'll tell them we didn't do anything wrong. That Dewitt just dropped dead. But when they get the entire story they're going to think we're lying. They are going to think something is fishy here. I would. Right?" I stopped and waited.

Now Jenny's face appeared. "We didn't kill Dewitt."

"I know that," I said quickly. I waited.

"But why would the cops arrest us?" she persisted. I just looked at her. I wasn't angry. Just nervous.

Herm stood up. "Don't call the police? Is that what you're suggesting?" He started pacing.

Jenny looked a little more frantic, "Why wouldn't we call the police? A man just died here. He's dead. Right here. Why wouldn't we call somebody?"

This time I decided to stay silent. It wasn't my job to convince them. They had to understand. To see the brilliance in this plan. The brilliance, I must say again, I fail to see completely at the present moment. But then. Then it truly was brilliant. A clear idea. Brave. Outlandish. Dangerous. Life-threateningly edgy.

Herm stopped walking and stared at me, "Why?"

I sensed at that moment that I had at least one ally. His voice said to me, "Give me one good reason and I'll go along." I walked over to Marci and put my hand on her shoulder. "It's going to be all right. I promise."

She looked up at me and opened her eyes to me. It was a mind full. She knew I was about to do something that I shouldn't do. I could tell that she saw it coming. I continued, I suppose in part, to satisfy her.

"What were we doing when Dewitt died? We were literally all up in his face. Herm had hit him. Marci had a knife. We were screaming. He was crying. There is no way somebody isn't going to make this out to be a murder." I paused. I gathered myself because even now, the next thing I had to say upset me. Upsets me now. "I'm not sure we didn't kill him."

Jenny locked onto me. She'd been thinking the same thing. She couldn't help but look at me. April and Marci stared also. Only Herm moved. He resumed his pacing.

I let silence become us and we scurried into the various spaces of this apartment as spirits and curled into balls with eyes and watched each other. April was the first to emerge.

"That's bullshit, Icky. Total bullshit. We had nothing to do with what happened to Dewitt."

"I think 'nothing' is a strong word, April." Jenny joined her.

Herm looked at Dewitt. "They could say we did it. They could make it look like we did it. Think about it. He was going to give one of us all that money. And then he wasn't and we got angry and killed him. That's not such a big leap." He started pacing again.

This was where I was. I'd already performed that deduction. But I held the cream. The icing, so to speak. I was the key. I was already the guilty one, wasn't I? No, not because

I was any more mean to Dewitt than anyone else. But rather because this was my house and I was black.

"If we were white," I began. "If we were white it would be a different story. But this whole thing is about race . . ."

"Stop it." April was having none of it. "Just stop it. This is not about race. This is about the fact that we didn't do anything. I didn't do anything. I know that."

Marci came to my rescue, "Of course you'd feel that way. You've never been guilty of anything greater that giving Skeeter Jones a blow job. And you probably didn't swallow, so you don't even count it."

I almost burst out laughing. Skeeter was a weather guy on one of the local channels. His name was very ironic in the middle of July when the Minnesota mosquito assault rivals any other in the country, with the possible exception of the Everglades. We all knew of April's little fling with him. She tried to keep it secret but we knew. Marci could be ruthless. She was capable of lowering the boom on anybody from six paces without the slightest hint that she was coming for you.

"Icky's right." Marci was moving toward me. "When the cops get here they're going to look around and jack us all up. This is Minneapolis, after all. I mean, yes, we be up here trying to mingle and mix and all that, but this is still one of the whitest places I've ever been. And we all know the police force is about as dangerous here as it was under Frank Rizzo in Philadelphia." She looked at me, knowing I was fully aware of the implications. No black person can think of Philadelphia and the police and not think of two things: The late Gestapo-like former mayor Frank Rizzo; and MOVE, the "radical back-to-nature" group (as it was dubbed by the media) that was shot up and bombed out in two West Philly neighborhoods. MOVE was the example of what cops do to renegade black people. A white man in

Stonehenge, Idaho, could hole up for weeks and have hundreds of feds camped out waiting for him to give up. The message was clear.

"But what are we supposed to do?" Herm was now in the kitchen calling back. I heard the pop of a can of soda. Herm was addicted to Diet Coke and I'd wondered how long it would take him to discover my stash. Especially under the kind of pressure we were dealing with. I had expected him to ask about his beloved Diet Coke much earlier. He re-entered the dining room with a wide grin on his face. It wasn't the first time I'd seen him smile, but the Diet Coke did something magical to his face. He was almost giddy. Nothing like a shot of caffeine, sweetened by aspartame, lovingly ushered in by the mysterious concoction affectionately known as cola to put a smile on a person's face.

He took a swig. It made all of us realize that we hadn't drunk or eaten anything since Dewitt had interrupted our little celebration. "What exactly can we do about it? I mean, when those motherfuckers come busting in the door, we're toast." He looked around at Jenny and April. "Well, maybe we're not all doomed. They'll kill Icky first, then me, and then, if Marci is doing anything other than laying prostrate, she's a goner. You two," he said, pointing to Jenny and April, "well, I'm not sure. But if one of those cops has been to Vietnam I wouldn't bet on Jenny making it out of here, either."

"This is ridiculous. Are you saying that even though we didn't really do anything, they're still going to act like that?" April was getting angry. Which I thought was amazing. The rest of us were afraid. She was mad.

"How long have you been hanging around black people?" I asked her.

"The thing is, Icky, that I know what you're saying could be true. I mean, I know that. I've been in enough situations where that kind of stuff has happened. But that's what I was talking about before. I don't buy into all that. And I'm not Pollyanna."

Marci wasn't about to let that pass. "Oh, no?"

"No. I'm not. I'm not naive or stupid, either. I don't know how many times I have to tell you that my commitment to people is stronger than all of yours. I know how awful racism is. You know I do. I keep presenting my credentials and you keep throwing them back in my face. But right now, that's not important, is it? I don't know what you're getting at, Icky, but I wish you would just go ahead and say what you want to say. What exactly do you want us to do?"

Marci turned away. Once again April had successfully stood up to us. "What I want is for us to make a commitment to each other. I mean, really. The first thing we've got to do is pledge our loyalty to each other. We can't let any one of us take the weight for this," I said.

Everyone stared at me. I knew they were afraid. I knew they would be just like you. Skeptical and certain that something bad was about to happen. But, like I said, this was the only way I knew that we could actually control the way things would go. Otherwise we'd be at the mercy of the police.

It made me think of an episode of the reality-based television show, *Cops*. It seemed like all the thugs they tried to arrest in this segment took off running or driving, throwing their drugs and guns away in the process. They were all black suspects and invariably when they were caught they all said they ran not because they were guilty of any crime but because they were afraid that the police would beat them. As they had another rather infamous suspect, Rodney King, who'd been mercilessly pummeled by L.A. police officers. The cops laughed when they heard the explanation.

They didn't believe them. But I did. And now I was one of them. I was acting guilty to prove my innocence.

"I'm tired of always feeling guilty," I told them. "I feel guilty so much of my life that when I hear a siren I immediately try to remember that it can't be about me. That I've actually finished brushing my teeth or buying a slice of pizza. You know?"

Herm looked at me sadly. I knew he knew what I was talking about. "You know, Icky, I can't walk into a store without people following me around. Does every native man look like a shoplifter?"

I heard him and felt the weight of his statement. It took me back to my first trip to Bemidji, when I went into a SuperAmerica store and watched a clerk follow an Indian all around the premises. He kept asking if the man needed help. I remember laughing quietly to myself. It was a significant moment in my life. It was one of the few times when I could see, from the outside, so to speak, what it looked like to be thought of as guilty simply by the force of your presence. I'd felt it myself, of course. But I couldn't remember ever watching it happen to someone else.

I know this thing has to do with love. I know that. How can I get you to expect to love me? I have a friend who talks about the "gaze" that greets us as we walk into a room. Is it friendly? Warm? Inviting? Welcoming? Is it suspicious? Angry?

"I don't want to live through what we're about to live through," I said as I walked to the bookcase. "I write murder novels so maybe I'm a little sensitive to these things. But if I were a cop coming into a situation like this, I'd be looking for a murderer among us."

"But, Icky," April interrupted. "How long will it take them to find out that whatever made Dewitt drop dead, it couldn't have been any of us? We didn't shoot him. He hasn't been stabbed or strangled. We didn't do anything."

"I hit him," Herm said.

"And we were all threatening him," I added. "Besides, I'm not really talking about reality here. I'm not talking about what we did or didn't do to Dewitt. I'm talking about what they're going to think. How we're going to be treated. I'm talking about being guilty until proven innocent. After living most of my life feeling guilty, I don't want to deal with that."

Jenny got up. "So? What? You want us to run away?"

I looked at her quite stunned. I'd never for a moment even thought about running away. It actually took my voice away. I stood straight up and looked around me. Nobody breathed. Run away. We could run away. But wasn't that what we'd been doing all along? Running. Each of us in our own way. In our own direction. We were already elusive, disconnected, movering movering. No sense of connection. No serious cultural anchor. Yes, we were people of color, but as artists we'd moved too far away from the heart of our cultural power. We existed alone, alienated, and yet we were treated as not much more than representatives of the very thing we had lost touch with—namely, home. We were each homeless. All running from the way in which America was trying to define us. Herm running from the reservation to—where? April running from her family to—where? Marci and I were both running from the same thing: the limitations of being black in America to—where? Jenny running from the horrors of her family. We were all running. But where were we going?

We made art to light our path. We painted and wrote and chipped away at stone and wood to find ourselves. Now, I wanted to stop running. I wanted to be stationary.

I found my voice. "No, Jenny, no. I don't think we

should try to run away. We wouldn't get very far, anyway. None of us knows how to do that. Besides, April's right. We didn't kill Dewitt."

"So, what are you trying to say, Icky? Damn, man. You sure can run your goddamned mouth." Marci was becoming her colored self again.

But I'd stalled as long as I could. "You have to trust me to deliver us from this building in honor. Let us invest in our own future for a change. Grant ourselves a different kind of freedom. Let's be unafraid." I paused to let the air out of the moment. I knew no one would respond yet. They still didn't really know what I was asking them to do.

"How?" Marci sighed.

It was then that I knew what I had to do. This day was constructed from that moment. "I want you to leave. Let me take care of it." Their eyes widened.

"The only thing I want," I continued, "the only thing I want is for each one of you to share something with us that is wholly condemning. Utterly shameful. Diminishing. Something which you yourself find reprehensible. A secret. Something no one or not many people know."

Herm sat down from his pacing. He looked tired. Jenny fidgeted. I could hear her leg shaking against the chair she sat in. A sure sign that she was highly agitated, or hungry, or both. "What's that about?" she said softly.

"Yeah, Icky, that sounds really kind of strange."

I didn't know if I could make them see how important this was becoming to me. It was no longer about the money. Or even Dewitt, for that matter. This was about us. About making an opening statement in the effort to make the multicultiboho vision a reality in spite of the forces out there which sought to keep us separate.

"We contribute to our own sense of being oppressed because we do not combine our outrage, our power, or our potential. I wanted that grant. I told you that. I thought I was going to get it."

"So did I," Herm said distantly.

Marci stood up. "I guess I have to admit that I thought it was me. I even thought I had a special advantage." She stopped abruptly. Of course my mind entered her thought and began trying to figure out what her "advantage" might have been.

"Well, I have to be honest," April leaned back in her place on the couch. "I never expected it. He could never have given it to me. I was just a statement he was trying to make. I was a token of Dewitt's need to express his power."

Jenny remained silent, but we all knew she was as competitive as the rest of us.

I walked over and grabbed the lifeless Dewitt under the shoulders and began pulling him away from the center of the floor. April freaked. "What are doing! What are you doing?"

"I'm moving him." He was very heavy. Herm was getting up to help when suddenly the body budged and slid easily the rest of the way into the corner. I went into the kitchen and found a couple of plastic bags.

They watched me in silence. I asked Herm to lift Dewitt's legs so I could slide one bag over his lower half and then we did the same for his upper half with the second trash bag. I then found some rope and tied the bags off. Dewitt was now a mummy. As I finished tying the rope I stood up and said, "We don't have to do this their way. We can do it our way. Or maybe this is my way. Maybe I'm the only one who is willing to put my life on the line to feel free. But this is what I want to do. I want to face the police alone. Here. On my turf, using my own strategy. And all I ask is that you support me. That you give me something that will let me know we are of one community. That we are unified in our shame. In our need for a new way of being. That we will care about the connection between us in the future. That we won't let people like Dewitt or the organizations they work for undermine us with good intentions or lots of money. We all carry our guilts and insecurities. This is what they trade on. All I want is for you to give a part of yourself to me that is precious—and ugly, a secret—and leave me here to handle this."

It was my turn to take a seat. I knew they'd have a hard time digesting everything. To tell you the truth, ever since that moment, I've grappled with the idea that I've actually lost my mind. I know you've thought it. They thought it. I've thought it.

As usual, Marci was the first to respond. "I'm not following you, Icky. What's going to happen after we leave? And, ah . . . a secret? What's with that?"

"What is more valuable, Marci? What do you have that is more valuable than a precious ugly secret? Something that no one else knows and that if they did, they'd think less of you? You don't have any money to speak of. And to be honest, I don't want money. What I want is to feel that we all can be something to each other. Bigger than family, you know? Bigger than that. It's just not true that family is the biggest thing. I don't know why we believe that. Or maybe it's that the way we think of family is wrong. But something is wrong here. Hispanics struggle. Blacks struggle. Native Americans struggle. Asian Americans struggle. Why do we struggle independently? Competitively? That's what I want to know. Maybe there is a better way. But I can't think of it right now. This is what I can do right now. If we really represented a movement the world would change tomorrow."

Jenny walked over to me and sat down. She put her arm around me and kissed my cheek. It was one of the sweetest moments in my life. "But why would you use Dewitt's death to make this statement?"

"I don't know." I thought for a moment. "But you know, it would bring meaning to his dying." Jenny gently pulled away from us and returned to the person that lived inside her. I knew she was working it out. They were all working it out. It was at this moment that I knew I loved them.

"If we leave I think we are definitely guilty of something." Herm's voice was still two dimensions away. "I mean, there's probably some kind of law which says we can't just leave here with Dewitt lying there and all."

"You won't have to worry about that," I told him. "I'll deal with that."

"But you can't keep us from going to jail for leaving here," April cut in. "Because you and I both know, Icky, that you're not going to get away from the cops. And when they get you, they'll come looking for us. And since we haven't done anything, it seems ridiculous that we'd put ourselves in that situation."

I stared at her. "Then there is no hope for us," I said. And I meant it. "There is no hope, if you can't do this for me. Forget us as a group. I'm asking you to do this for me."

Again Jenny turned to me, "But you're doing it for us."

I smiled. She got it. "Yes."

I could see that Herm and Marci were looking at each other. Just the challenge of this decision was having a very positive impact. We weren't thinking about money. We were thinking about us. And what we'd put on the line for our wholeness.

Herm turned his gaze to me and smiled. "I'm in."

"Me, too." Marci quickly followed.

Jenny removed her arm and stood up. She walked toward the kitchen. April threw her hands up. "If this is what I have to do to prove that I'm willing to struggle with you, then I'll do it."

I took a deep breath. Now I was really scared. And then Jenny appeared with a bottle of mineral water in her hands. "So it's settled. We'll tell you our fabulous, marvelous, most darkest secrets and leave you to negotiate your way out of here."

13

herm tossed his tired voice into the air. Everyone had found a space where they were comfortable. April was stretched out on the floor behind the couch where she couldn't see Dewitt's body. Even though I had carefully bagged it and moved it out of the way in the corner under the window, it whispered to us. It wasn't like a spirit or anything. It was just whispering its existence. I couldn't help but be impressed by its significance. A dead body—anything dead, human or animal—commands respect. Its existence is multileveled. It once was but now wasn't although it still existed. Only something dead could claim such a place. Anyway, it whispered. But Herm's slow speech overcame it.

"I guess I could start," he said. He was reentering the dining room from the kitchen with another Diet Coke. "I'm doing this because I think I understand what's at stake." He looked directly at me.

"And I guess I need to get this off my chest, anyway." I heard sighs escaping from each of us. One by one we exhaled. We knew this wouldn't be easy. I knew it. That's why we had to do it. These were dark thoughts. Our secrets.

I didn't know what would come out. I wasn't even sure at the outset what I would reveal about myself. But I knew it was important for us to do. Not logical. Not rational. But necessary.

"Seven years ago, I did a cross-country trip with my friend Billy. Great guy. We were in the army together. He was a little wild, you know. Angry. I used to tell him that you have to try to be healthy. Not expose yourself to the sickness that afflicts our people so often. Nearly everyone in my family was destroyed by alcohol. Same with his family. We knew that history and that it was like poison to us, but at the time it didn't matter enough. It was like liquor assumed this power over us that we couldn't fight. I don't know. Anyway, both Billy and I had had pretty hard lives.

"Anyway, we decided to go out to Seattle. Take our time, you know. I was still drinking pretty heavy back then. So we got out there and just sort of bounced around. Traveling the rez road. You know? Visiting friends and relatives out West. That's one thing about being native in this cold country. You can always find family or friends of family or just good people who'll put you up and help you until you can make it on your own. You almost never feel disconnected.

"I'm not like you, Icky. You seem not to need people around you. But I would literally die if I didn't have the kind of relationships I do. Yes, I know everybody always talks about all the women that they see me with, and I told you I don't want to keep doing that. But I will never completely be above meeting new people. Maybe flirting a little. That's just me. I don't even want to change that.

"So we were near Spokane and, well, I don't really know what came over Billy. Whenever his spirit visits me, I ask him over and over, 'why?' but he's never given me a good explanation. Anyway, we were running out of money when we stopped in this little town for a beer. We had more than one. I was drinking back then, and after we'd had about four or five apiece, we ran out of money."

Herm paused and sipped his soda. He smacked his lips and said, "Ahhh," when he finished. "As we were walking back to the car, he grabbed my arm and pulled me into this little alley. He says, 'Strong.' That's what he called me. 'Strong, we ain't gonna make it back home if we don't get some money somewhere.' And I said that I knew people near there where we could go. Maybe get work or borrow some money or something. I wasn't that worried.

"But he pulls out this gun. I swear I didn't know he had it." Herm stopped talking and swallowed hard. "He had this gun. And he said he was gonna rob this gas station up the road. It freaked me out. I had done a lot of foul shit in my time but I'd only used a gun to hunt with.

"So, I said I couldn't do it and I tried to talk him out of it. But he was bullheaded, stupid. It was like this pressure had been building in him over his entire life that made him feel like robbing that store was the most important thing. Like he had to do it. And I couldn't let him go all by himself. I couldn't do it. It's one of the downsides of being friends with a lunatic.

"He sent me in the store to buy a bag of chips and check it out. There was this old wrinkled up guy in there." I instantly felt the pain that was emanating from Herm's body. His eyes glazed. His voice trembled. We knew we were hearing something that he didn't want to remember.

"I came out and stood at the door while he went in and pulled a gun on that dude. All of a sudden I heard Billy screaming at the guy to open up the register and give him the money. The old guy must not have been willing to do it because Billy screamed it again. And then again. After the third time he said he was gonna shoot him.

"I got scared. I'll tell you now. I was scared as shit. I knew it was wrong and I also knew that we weren't the luckiest Indians in the world. So Billy is in there screaming. The old guy must just be standing there not moving or something. I finally turned back and looked in the window. And I saw the old guy coming up from the counter with this long-barreled six-shooter. Right out of the Wild West."

Tears now rimmed his eyes. "I turned and ran. I couldn't help it. I couldn't stop. I ran to the car and took off. As I started the car I heard three gun shots. I immediately turned around and drove by the station, but before I got there I saw that old man come slowly walking out the door with his gun. He seemed calm. Normal. I turned around again and took off and never looked back.

"Billy died in that store. I never even found out if I was wanted or not. It's like it never actually happened. There isn't a night that passes that I don't see that man slowly pulling that gun from under the counter. Sometimes he turns and points at me." Herm stopped abruptly. His tears blotted and evaporated. His red eyes the only real proof.

"Wow," Jenny said. "There's nothing to say after that."

"Yes, there is," April cut in. "I'm sorry, Herm. That's an awful thing to have to live with. I'm sorry that happened to you."

We all nodded numbly as Herm sipped his soda silently.

"Well, I guess I need to do this now or I won't do it at all." Jenny looked at the ceiling. "I don't think I have anything like Herm's story to tell you. And it won't take me as long to tell it. But it is something about me that nobody knows. Something that I'm completely ashamed of.

"I told you how my family was. And no matter how rebellious you are, how hard you fight against it, the influence of family is beyond calculation." Jenny brought her face level to the floor, but still stared off into space.

"I'm stalling. I don't know if I can do this." She took a deep breath. "Last year I needed some money so I started working as a phone sex girl. That's it. I spend four or five hours a day on the telephone with the weirdest men, talking nasty and listening to them jerk off."

I was stunned. Jenny?

"The bizarre thing is that I'm terrible at it. I can be so cold on the phone sometimes, but it doesn't seem to matter. They keep calling. Keep breathing heavy. No matter how I treat them. What I say. There are days when I absolutely hate myself. How it messes with my mind and consequently the poetry I'm writing. But the money is so good I can't stop.

"I guess another reason I have such a hard time talking about it, aside from the way it clashes with my upbringing, is that while I said how awful I feel about it there is a part of it that I find completely intoxicating. I love being that woman guys call to have their little sexual contact with. I'm never lonely. And I feel like I do something so important for them. Anyway, I can get completely into it and that scares me. Makes me think of all the stereotypes about the sexuality of Asian women. It makes me feel totally neutralized. Zeroed out. I disappear for weeks because I really don't exist. Just think of your favorite geisha stereotype, and you'll find me. Your favorite image of a prostitute from the Philippines or Saigon or Tokyo or Bangkok, and you've got me. That's who I am almost everyday.

"I'm deeply ashamed about that, but I keep doing it." Jenny looked through me. I'm sure my mouth was open.

"That's what this is about, Jenny. You can say it to us and it won't haunt you. It won't hurt you. We're all guilty of something," I said.

"Yeah, Jenny," April began. "I know it must be hard for

you to talk about it. But maybe it will help you make decisions in the future. Besides, I don't care. And I don't care what happened in Washington State, Herm. It doesn't change the potential of our relationships. It just doesn't.

"I wonder what you guys will think about what I did. About my story. I'll try to be quick, too. It's also not that complicated. In fact, it's one of the simplest things I've ever done. One day, three years ago, I picked up the telephone and called the Internal Revenue Service and told them that my father was cheating on his income taxes."

I heard Marci and April gasp at the same time.

"I did it. I'd been thinking about it for five years before that. Why it happened on the day it happened I don't know. The only thing I know is that I was in New Orleans, playing at this little club with a band I was touring with at the time. I finished my set. Hung out with some of the cats there and when the sun came up I got myself some coffee and beignets and made the call.

"And . . . what came out of that is that my father is currently doing time in a federal prison." She looked at Herm and smiled. "It's really not that bad of a secret. I feel bad about it, you know. But the thing is, my father deserved it. Like I told you, he started this trucking business when we lived in New York. And then he got all screwed up with organized crime. Well, when he started buying all these cars and houses and such, I got curious about it all.

"I found out that he was helping them transport cocaine and other drugs up and down the East Coast. I was dating this black guy in New Orleans at the time, and his sister had just given birth to what they call a "crack baby." Have you ever seen one?" She looked at each of us. We all shook our heads.

"Only on television," Marci said.

"Well, it's a hell of a sight, let me tell you. It just breaks your heart. I cried for that baby and I wanted to do something about it. It was really a pretty easy decision. I knew they would find stuff if they looked closely.

"The thing is, I know it didn't do anything to stop the flow of cocaine into the inner cities. But I had to make a stand for me and my family. I guess the only thing is that I never told my father that I did it. One day I'm going to have to tell him. And then it won't be a secret anymore.

"I keep wanting to write to him, but I think I need to tell him face to face, and I don't have the guts for that right now. So I just try to forget that I have a father. Forget that he's still alive." Jenny put her arm around April and pulled her tight. But April seemed nonplussed. Pensive, reflective, but not really upset.

I, on the other hand, was really feeling uneasy. Even though this was my idea, I wasn't really prepared for what was happening. I thought about going next but Marci beat me to it.

"Okay, you are going to freak out behind this. No one, absolutely no one knows this. I don't know what could happen to me if this gets out. Maybe nothing, legally, but I'd be crushed. Destroyed. It happened the last year I was in art school in Chicago. I was rooming with a classmate, Belinda Morganthal. We had an even stormier relationship than April and I do. We fought all the time. But Belinda was an amazing painter. In fact, we shared aesthetic sensibilities. We did.

"Well, after graduation, I was packing up our apartment and studio getting ready to move and I came across one of her paintings. I remember thinking at first that it was mine. But, even though it was unsigned, I realized after a minute that it was hers. It was like a montage of styles, all stitched together. Basquiat, Bearden, and Lawrence all rolled together. The image was a simple inner city street. But it was like incredibly complex. You could look at this painting for the rest of your life and see something new everyday. I never even knew what she wanted to title it. Anyway, I took it. Packed it up like it was mine.

"Before we split up, she asked me if I'd seen it, but I lied and told her no." I'd never heard this sound of Marci's voice. It lacked any sense of strength or arrogance. It lacked edge. There was no posture in it. This was what the truth did to us.

"I took it. And then, two years later when I had a studio in Boston where I was teaching, I had it framed and hung it up. Well, to make a long story short, I had a party and this guy comes up to me raving about it. He asked if it was mine and I said yes. I said it without thinking very much about it. I just said it. Come to find out this guy is a major art critic. So he decides to write this piece about me that appeared in *Contemporary Art* magazine. He raved about all my stuff, but especially that painting. He used the title I gave him, *Still Life in My Life*.

"After the article was published my career took off. I've been riding the crest of that publicity since then. It brought me here to Minnesota to teach at the Twin Cities Arts Academy. I've sold so much work in a similar vein it makes me sick. That's why I've started to only paint faces. It's as far as I can get from abstract minimal cityscapes.

"My entire career is based on a lie. I stole the one work of art I'm most known for. And if you're interested, I'm still supposed to be friends with Belinda. We talk on the telephone sometimes. But I've done everything I could to keep from seeing her since then. And even though she's an artist, and that picture has been printed in a number of publications, and, like I said, it has become my signature piece, she's never once mentioned it. It's driving me insane.

"I can't feel pleasure in anything I do. It just eats at me."

She heaved a heavy sigh. "There. I said it. I'm so glad I got a chance to say that. I don't know if this will help us as a group, but I needed this."

I'm sure we all wanted to say something to Marci that would be helpful but none of us could figure out what. Everyone looked at me, expecting, I think, that I would jump into the breach and begin my story. But at that moment, I didn't want to. I felt like asking them to exempt me, given that I would have to transform all of this into my own story. I knew then that I would have to take all of this energy and make it my own in whatever way I could.

Finally, I said, "Well, we all have something we are ashamed of. Something awful that we did. There is no way to compare these. We can't get into comparing pain. We must just accept what it is. Accept ourselves regardless. Even absolve ourselves so that we can be open to the possibilities of our collective power."

April looked at me, "Are you going to tell us?"

"Yes," I said. "This is my secret. I carry it around with me every waking moment. I can't redo it. I can't change it." I gathered myself. "I have a son. I was there when he was born. I held him in my arms. I fed him. I loved him then and I still do. But I left. Walked out of his life as if he weren't worth me. Abandoned him. And when I moved to Minneapolis no one knew, so I never had to talk about it. When people ask me if I have any children I always say no. That's what I say. I do." I felt like crying myself then. Crying for my own self.

"I have denied his existence. What kind of man does that? What kind of father? When I think about it, I usually tell myself that I was just not the type. That I was not capable of being a father. But the fact is that I think I would have made a great father. I was just too young, too impatient with my own life. I still hope that one day I can reestablish that contact." I stopped and looked at them.

"I could say a lot more because the story isn't as simple as all that. It just makes me so sad. But, okay, when we broke up my ex agreed to let me have custody of Donald. I got us a place in West Philly near where I was working at the time. Got myself a housekeeper. For about three months I was a bachelor father. And I was as happy as I'd ever been. I decided not to worry too much about being a writer and concentrate on providing a home for my son. But then, I had to go away on business and my ex-wife convinced me to let her baby-sit.

"When I got back, Donald was gone and the only thing left were finger paintings on the wall. The thing is, I never went looking for him. I just gave up. Decided to redouble my efforts at becoming a writer. Move to Minnesota. I just left and never looked back. It was too painful. Now I'm here. Trying to make a home in a place where no one knows that simple fact about my life."

"We know now," April said. "This is our beginning. It was a good idea, Icky. I'm glad we did this."

Herm walked over and wrapped his large arms around me. "We're a pretty fucked-up bunch of colored folks, aren't we?" He laughed. It was the first laughter I'd heard in quite a while.

"Yeah, Herm. I guess we are."

"But we're the multicultiboho tribe, a new group for a new time. We have to heal ourselves. Ourselves," I said.

Not long after that they all left. We all cried. We all hoped there was a reason to have hope.

ichabod had to admit that he felt light-headed. He kept trying to change positions. He'd sit at the dining room table for a while and then he'd move to the couch. For a time he even sat on the floor, amongst the broken glass and debris as he talked. His arm was on fire, and though his wound probably wasn't fatal, he had begun to think he might bleed to death if he didn't get to a doctor. The cut needed to be closed.

Lieutenant Bloom was barely conscious himself. He'd never in his life been bound and beaten and stressed the way he had this day. As Ichabod had talked, he thought mostly about his wife and how she was dealing with this crisis. He knew she was out there freaking out, trying her best to keep the captain from storming the house. And he thought about the captain and whether the chief was putting pressure on her to do something. Or if she'd already been relieved of responsibility for the situation altogether.

But throughout the entire telling of the story, Bloom had tried to keep his eyes focused on Ichabod. He'd closed them every now and then for a minute or two. Sometimes when he did that, Ichabod would kick him or shout at him to see if he were awake. But although Bloom was exhausted, he didn't feel sleepy. There was no way he could have fallen asleep as uncomfortable as he was.

Besides, hurting or not, Ichabod never stopped talking. After the scuffle they'd had, Ichabod had no energy to move around. He thought it was probably best that he not present too easy a target. He was sure there were marksmen out there. The truth was that if the police had wanted to shoot him they could have at various times throughout the day. Even sitting at the dining room table he was visible from the kitchen window. From that angle his bald head was like a balloon at a shooting gallery at the state fair.

But Capt. Iris Hirsh had decided early on that she was going to wait this situation out. She had a hunch that Ichabod would tire of this siege and eventually give himself up. And what she'd learned about the situation so far, though it was puzzling, had caused her to be optimistic.

She had deliberately withheld comment to the media as she tried to sort out the details. There were reporters all over the place trying to piece the story together. They were clamoring for information. Bloom's wife was indeed twenty feet away from their command center and in constant contact. But she'd kept all of the accomplices separated and sequestered so the press couldn't get to them.

The entire episode had confounded her. What she'd learned from all of the people who'd been at Ichabod's was that there was someone dead inside but that Ichabod had not actually murdered him. But when she asked why Ichabod had taken Lieutenant Bloom hostage if he was innocent, they all looked at her with stupid expressions on their faces.

"If he didn't kill this Dewitt McMichael, then why is he holed up there threatening my lieutenant?" she asked.

"That's what he's doing now. He's telling the cop who's

in there why," Jenny said. Of them all, Jenny understood
best what Ichabod was doing. She knew that it was a selfless
act that was designed to make them a community. She
wasn't sure it would work, but, then, nothing else had. And
it hadn't been planned. No one had expected Dewitt to die
like that. But Ichabod was trying to turn an unfortunate
situation into a positive. Accomplish two things at once. He
was committing a crime to prove his innocence. His existen-
tial and infinite innocence. And he was trying to show that
such an act had the potential of bringing people together.
"He's trying to make a statement."

"Help me out, Jennifer. What kind of statement is he
making?"

"You'll have to wait until he comes out. But I can tell
you that it has nothing to do with money."

"Money? What money?" Iris asked.

"The Shrubbery Genius Grant."

"I see," the captain said, though she didn't understand
what Jenny was talking about. "Now tell me, do you think
this Ichabod guy is dangerous? Do you think he'd actually
try to hurt my officer in there?"

Jenny had been thinking about this question before the
captain asked it. She wasn't sure. There was a part of her
that was certain that Ichabod was being symbolic. But there
was a clawing doubt in her that challenged that feeling. She
took a deep breath and said, "I think that everything will
be fine once he's told that policeman our story. That's all
he wanted to do."

Hirsh had directed the detective to lead Jenny to a safe
place out of the way. Within the hour she was joined there
by Herm, Marci, and April.

Inside the apartment, silence surrounded the two men.
Each needed his separate adventure to come to an end. Icha-

bod hadn't said a word for two or three minutes. At first Bloom didn't even realize that he'd stopped talking.

"So he just collapsed here?" he finally asked Ichabod.

Ichabod was depleted. "Yes. He just dropped dead in the middle of everything."

"So, you're telling me that you didn't kill him. That none of the other people who were here caused his death either?" When Bloom had heard the conclusion of Ichabod's tale he was skeptical, to say the least. Until Ichabod had said that Dewitt had just dropped dead he'd believed most of what he'd heard. He was sure that Ichabod had made more of Dewitt's manipulative behavior than it actually was. In fact, even from what Ichabod had told him, he didn't think that Dewitt had done anything malicious. He did however think that it was enough of a reason for a person like Ichabod to lose his grasp of reality and do something violent.

To the lieutenant, Ichabod was definitely capable of killing. And he obviously suffered from deep feelings of envy and rage. Just as he'd surmised early on, Ichabod was no different than many black men he'd met. Most of them could do with some anger counseling, he thought. It ought to be mandatory. His experience and instinct told him that in all probability Ichabod had killed Dewitt. Killers were the best liars.

"Lieutenant, I'm trying to find my own innocence here and it's not as easy as I'd thought it would be. We didn't kill him. It happened just as I said."

"And you went through all of this just to say that to me?"

"Yes."

"And you expected me to believe this story because you were willing to take me hostage and put everybody through all of this. You think that it makes your story more credible?" Bloom didn't say it, but as he thought about it, it did strike him as odd. If Ichabod was guilty, it was a particular kind of suicide.

"That's the simple version. But yes."

Bloom stared at him. The table that Ichabod was leaning on was covered with bloody towels. Ichabod's arm lay lifeless there. He looked suddenly gaunt and wrinkled, his brown skin fading to translucency.

"Suppose I don't believe you? Suppose I think you murdered that man?" the detective said, trying to keep his voice as flat as possible. He didn't know where he was going with that, but he was trying to keep his options open.

"I don't know, Lieutenant." Ichabod sat up a little straighter. "I'd hoped my abilities were up to the task. But . . ."

"Maybe it wasn't doable, Ichabod? Maybe nobody could have done it. Maybe it's just one of those unbelievable stories. You know. They happen all the time. Somebody tells you something and you say, 'no way. That couldn't have happened.' You know?"

"Are you saying you don't believe me?"

"I guess what I'm saying is that it's pretty hard to believe that you would go to this length if you hadn't done something wrong."

Ichabod threw his head back. "You've heard nothing of what I've said. Nothing."

"I heard you, Ichabod. I heard you." Bloom smiled. "Don't you find it at least a little ironic that your entire plan boiled down to getting my approval? I'm the enemy. I'm the white man."

"I never said you were the enemy. I just tried to tell you how I felt about the way things are. And I wanted you to be a white man. I want you to accept my innocence. *You.* That's why I did it."

The lieutenant lost his smile and reflected for a moment.

There was some logic in there. *If* you believed that every time you saw a black man you immediately thought he was guilty of something. "Why?"

"Why? See, I told you that you don't listen. I told you. Why? Because I have to live in this fucked-up world with you. We are here in this time together. In this country. This society. This culture. You have to learn how to see my innocence even in the midst of a situation that condemns me."

Bloom blinked once and then fixed his eyes on Ichabod, "But suppose I don't believe you?"

Ichabod turned his head and faced the bookcase. He caught sight of Bloom's gun sitting there next to Wright's *Native Son*. He had thought about this. A symbolic action without a consequence was meaningless. You can't put so many things in motion and then cheat the effects that will accumulate from all that activity. In the same way that a threat is an act of violence that remains unconsummated. He had been willing to put his very life on the line. It was still on the line. It might have been stupid, but he'd done it.

"I'll kill you," Ichabod said softly.

"You'd kill me?" Bloom *was* surprised at his answer. There was nothing symbolic about that response. "They'll blast you through the gates of hell if you do that."

"Yeah. I know."

The lieutenant retreated within. He'd miscalculated once again. There really was no easy way out of this. He was once again beginning to think that Ichabod was bent on killing him. It just made him think that Ichabod hadn't told him the truth about Dewitt's death in the first place. It made no sense.

"Okay. If that's what it takes. I'll go along."

"No, Lieutenant. I said you have to believe me. What will it take for you to believe me?"

Bloom paused. He knew this was a critical moment. He

searched himself. He was resisting the idea. He knew that. It wasn't about the story Ichabod told. It was Ichabod himself. He didn't like Ichabod. Didn't trust him. Didn't want him to be innocent. That was the truth. But he quickly reasoned that he had to move beyond that to save both of their lives.

"Have you ever been to jail, Ichabod?"

"No. Never been in any kind of trouble. Just in here." Ichabod tapped his chest. "Always felt guilty in here. And I'm tired. That's all. Something happened here that no one expected. And like the fool that I am I thought it was a chance to settle this issue once and for all."

Bloom let out a painful chuckle. "You're something else, Ichabod. I gotta say I've never known anyone like you. What if I said that I'll give you the benefit of the doubt? What if I agree to try to get them to drop all the charges that might have come out of this little trip you've taken us all on if they can't find a cause for death that doesn't involve you or your friends?"

Ichabod felt his heart flutter. "Including Herm. Remember I said that Herm hit him in the head."

"If that wasn't the cause of death . . . including that."

Ichabod swallowed hard. "So you don't think I did it?"

Bloom took a deep breath. Let the air out. If Ichabod was guilty he was a good actor, the detective thought. "I'm gonna proceed on the basis that you are innocent." Bloom suddenly let go of his ambivalence. If they were to get out of this he had to believe Ichabod. And in a way, the more he moved in that direction, the more he felt good about it. His spirits began to move again. "Okay. Yes. I believe you."

"One more thing, Lieutenant. I want you to treat me with respect when I walk out. Like I'm innocent. You know. I won't run or struggle or anything. But I've seen *Cops* and

I know how you guys always take the hostage-taker guy and slam him on the ground and all."

"That might be out of my power. After you surrender I won't have much control over how they treat you."

"Come on. If you get that woman to promise to treat me good, they'll do it. Please. It's the only other condition. I want to feel like an innocent man going to the police department to validate my innocence."

Suddenly Bill Bloom was starting to like Ichabod. His character was undaunted. "Okay. Okay. I'll get her to agree. Now, is there anything else the innocent Mr. Ichabod Word wishes before we get the hell out of here?"

Ichabod stood up and walked over to Bloom and handed him the telephone. "No, sir. Here. Tell them we're coming out." In an instant, Bloom was already talking to Captain Hirsh. "Lieutenant?"

Bloom paused in his conversation, "Just a second, Captain." And then looked up at Ichabod, "Yes?"

"I'm sorry to have put you through all of this."

Bloom nodded.

"And, ah . . . well, I know it's not going to be all that pleasant for me, but it helps to know that you believe me. I needed that. Thanks."

Bloom nodded again and went back to the captain.

Fifteen minutes later Ichabod opened the door. Hirsh held everyone back about twenty-five feet. Ichabod came out first with his hands held up high. And then, close behind him was the detective. He had both guns as he limped out.

Two officers met them five feet down the walk. Two more approached. In an instant Bloom was hustled away. And then Ichabod was jerked toward an emergency wagon. But as he moved, as Bloom faded, their eyes met. The lieutenant winked his eye. Ichabod nodded his thanks. He wasn't handcuffed but there was an officer holding each arm. If he would have stopped walking he would have moved at the same pace. In fact, his feet were barely touching the ground. They were literally carrying him.

No one said a word as he was hauled toward the wagon. But as they approached it, he saw April, tears running out of her eyes, standing by the door. He stuck his thumbs up at her. And then Herm came into view and they smiled at each other.

Marci was being held back by a policeman. She screamed at him, "Go head, brother. You did it. You did it."

"We did it, Marci. It's us now."

As they swung him around so that he could step into the back of the van, he saw Jenny. She looked sad to him. But suddenly all he could do was smile. It was just getting dark outside but to Ichabod it was sunrise. And he was slowly beginning to feel happiness. He smiled the biggest smile he could at her.

It broke her sadness, and her sweetness returned. "It's okay, Jenny. They believe me. I'm innocent. We're innocent. Just like we always knew."